*Eternal*
VOWS

# ROCHELLE ALERS

## Eternal VOWS

**HARLEQUIN**® KIMANI ARABESQUE®

Recycling programs
for this product may
not exist in your area.

ETERNAL VOWS

ISBN-13: 978-0-373-53479-1

**H** **HARLEQUIN®**

www.Harlequin.com

**Printed in U.S.A.**

## Hideaway Wedding Series

Good-natured boasting raises its multimillion-dollar head at the Cole family compound during a New Year's Eve celebration. Family patriarch Martin Cole proposes each man in attendance place a one-million-dollar wager to the winner's alma mater as an endowment in their name. The terms: predicting who among Nicholas, Jason or Ana will marry before the next New Year's Eve.

Twins Jason and Ana Cole have given no indication they are even remotely thinking of tying the knot. Both claim they are too busy signing new talent to their record label. Former naval officer Nicholas Cole-Thomas has also been dragging his feet when it comes to the opposite sex. However, within the next six months Ana, Nicholas and Jason will encounter a very special person who will not only change them, but change their lives forever.

In *Summer Vows*, when CEO of Serenity Records Ana Cole signs a recording phenom to her label, she ignites a rivalry that targets her for death. Her safety and well-being are then entrusted to family friend, U.S. Marshal Jacob Jones, and Ana is forced to step away from the spotlight and her pampered lifestyle. She unwillingly follows Jacob to his vacation home in the Florida Keys until those responsible for the hit on her life are apprehended. Once Ana gets past Jacob's rigid rules, she finds herself surrendering to the glorious sunsets and the man willing to risk everything, including his heart, to keep her safe and make her his own.

Nicholas Cole-Thomas's entry into the world of horse breeding has caused quite a stir in Virginia's horse country. Not only is he quite the eligible bachelor, but there is also a lot of gossip about his prized Arabian breeding stock. In *Eternal Vows*, Nicholas meets Peyton Blackstone, the neighboring farm's veterinarian intern. He is instantly drawn to her intelligence, but recognizes the vulnerability she attempts to mask with indifference. Nicholas offers Peyton a position to work on his farm, and when they step in as best man and maid of honor at his sister's spur-of-the-moment wedding he tries to imagine how different his life would be with a wife of his own. Just when he opens his heart to love again, someone from Peyton's past resurfaces to shatter their newfound happiness, and now Nicholas must decide whether their love is worth fighting for.

Record executive Jason Cole will admit to anyone that he has a jealous mistress: music. As the artistic director for Serenity Records Jason is laidback, easygoing and a musical genius. His brief tenure running the company is over and he's heading to his recording studio in a small remote Oregon mountain town to indulge in his obsession. But all that changes in *Secret Vows*, when Jason hears restaurant waitress Greer Evans singing backup with a local band. As they become more than friends, he is unaware of the secret she jealously guards with her life. And when he finds himself falling in love with Greer, Jason is stunned to find she is the only one who stands between him and certain death, at the same time realizing love is the most desperate risk of all.

Don't forget to read, love and live romance.

Rochelle Alers

# HIDEAWAY SERIES

Everett Kirkland - Teresa Maldorado* - Samuel Cole - Marguerite Diaz[11]

**Martin Cole - Parris Simmons[1]**
- Oscar Spencer - Regina Cole - Aaron Spencer[2]
  - Claybone, Eden

**Tyler Cole - Dana Nichols[9]** — Ariadna
- Martin, II · Astra · Samuel II

**Josephine Cole - Ivan Wilson**
- Gisela · Esther · Joseph · Felipe · Ashley

**David Cole - Serena Morris[4]**
- Gabriel Cole - Summer Montgomery[10]
  - Immanuel · Anthony · Imani
- Alexandra Cole - Merrick Grayblake[12]
  - Victoria · Cordero
  - Jason
- Ana Cole - Jacob Jones[15]

**Nancy Cole - Noah Thomas**
- Timothy Cole-Thomas - Nichola Bennett · Ynez · Grace · Malinda
  - Diego Cole-Thomas - Vivienne Neal[13] — Samuel
  - Celia Cole-Thomas - Gavin Faulkner[14] — Isabella
  - Nicholas[16]

Matthew Sterling - Eve Blackwell - Alejandro Delgado[2]
- Christopher Delgado - Emily Kirkland[7]
  - Alejandro · Esperanza · Mateo
- Sara Sterling - Salem Lassiter[6]
  - Isaiah · Eve/Nora (twins)

Joshua Kirkland* - Vanessa Blanchard[5]
- Michael Kirkland - Jolene Walker[8]
  - Teresa · Joshua-Michael · Merrick

## LEGEND

\* - Illegitimate Birth
1 - Hideaway
2 - Hidden Agenda
3 - Vows
4 - Heaven Sent
5 - Harvest Moon
6 - Just Before Dawn
7 - Private Passions
8 - No Compromise
9 - Homecoming
10 - Renegade
11 - Best Kept Secrets
12 - Stranger In My Arms
13 - Secret Agenda
14 - Breakaway
15 - Summer Vows
16 - Eternal Vows

Happy the husband of a good wife, twice-lengthened are his days; a worthy wife brings joy to her husband, peaceful and full is his life.
—*Sirach* 26:1, 2

# Prologue

Solar lighting illuminated the in-ground pool and property surrounding David and Serena Cole's sprawling Boca Raton mansion. The house was filled with four generations of Coles. The men who'd gathered in the library at the West Palm Beach family compound New Year's Day had gotten together again—this time in David's private office. The four men lit cigars and raised snifters of aged brandy, toasting their success for a covert investigation that had thwarted a hit man's attempt to kill Ana Cole.

*"¡Salud!"*

David peered at his brothers and nephew over the rim of his glass. "I know it's not in good taste to toast someone's demise, but if anyone needed to be put in the dirt then it is Basil Irving."

"I agree with David," intoned Timothy Cole-Thomas. "The bastard should've been taken out a long time ago."

Martin Cole lifted an eyebrow when he stared at his

nephew. "Damn, Timothy. That's cold. What happened to you being the gentle Cole?"

Running a hand over his cropped salt-and-pepper head, Timothy returned Martin's steady gaze. "Niceness stops whenever someone threatens *my* family."

"I have to agree with Timothy," Joshua Kirkland said quietly, his deep voice carrying easily in the soundproof room. "Irving may have met an untimely end, but there's still the matter of his younger brother who has taken over as CEO of Slow Wyne Records. I don't know how much baby boy knows about the music industry but instinct tells me he bears watching."

Timothy nodded. "You're right, Josh. That's why Diego told Simon to keep an eye on him. Ana may have evaded the trap, yet who's to say they won't shift the focus to Jason."

"My son isn't as benign as he appears," David said. "Let's just hope someone doesn't decide to challenge him." He set his glass on a side table. "Now that we've offered our insincere condolences I'd like to discuss the wedding wager. Those of us who bet on Ana marrying first are one-third closer to the grand prize."

David, his brothers Martin and Joshua and his nephew Timothy had each wagered a million dollars to establish an endowment in the name of their alma mater as to whose unmarried thirty-something children would marry before the end of the year. David had had to put up two million because he had an unmarried son and daughter.

Martin sucked in a mouthful of tobacco. "You're not going to count Ana's wedding in the wager?" he asked, blowing out a cloud of smoke.

David shook his head. "Come on, Martin. Man up and admit I'm right."

Martin squinted at his youngest brother. "You're not right, David. Ana and Jacob's marriage was a setup."

Holding his cigar between his thumb and forefinger, David blew out a series of smoke rings. "Tell him, Timothy."

A shaft of light from a floor lamp filtered over Timothy's lean dark brown face when he shifted on his chair to stare at his uncles. "Diego told me Jacob asked him to stand in as best man when he and Ana plan to renew their vows this coming New Year's Eve."

"I told you, big brother," David drawled smugly.

Martin shook his head in disbelief. "Diego sets up a bogus marriage—"

"It's not bogus, Martin," Joshua Kirkland interrupted. "Their marriage license is as legal *and* binding as any of our marriages. And it's not the first time a Cole woman has married her protector."

Timothy nodded. "My Celia married Gavin Faulkner and made me a grandpa for the second time."

Martin's expressive eyebrows lifted. "Bragging, nephew?"

"Hell, yeah, *Tío* Martín."

"Wait until you have as many grandchildren as Joshua and David before you starting boasting, *sobrino*," Martin countered.

Joshua's straight white teeth shimmered in his sun-browned face when he flashed a wide grin. "I'm about to pull ahead of David. Jolene is pregnant."

"Again?" the three chorused.

"Michael and Jolene always said they wanted six children," Joshua explained in defense of his son and daughter-in-law. "They're now planning to close on an eight-bedroom, ten-bath farmhouse set on six acres in

McLean, Virginia. Michael told me he's keeping the former owners' flock of sheep and half a dozen horses."

Bracing both feet on the terra-cotta floor, Martin rested his elbows on his knees. "Speaking of horses. There's still the question of whether Nicholas will be bitten by the love bug before the end of the year." Nicholas's obsession with horses had begun at a very early age. The first time he sat atop a pony during a friend's birthday party, he felt as if he was born to ride. Nicholas would never become a jockey because of his height and weight, but that hadn't diminished his dream to ride and breed champion horses.

"Only time will tell," Timothy said. "If he is and does marry, then I'm out of any future wedding wagers."

"Has Jason decided where he's going to set up Serenity?" Joshua asked, segueing to a topic they'd avoided discussing in the presence of their wives.

There came an uncomfortable silence before David spoke again. "He told me a real-estate agent showed him a house in Coral Gables. He also said he'll probably buy Ana's condo once she and Jacob start a family."

Joshua stubbed out his cigar in a large ceramic dish and then stood up. "I'd like to stay, but it's time I head out now. I'm planning to fly back to Santa Fe tomorrow morning."

Timothy stretched out his legs. "How are you flying back, Josh?"

"I'm going first class."

The recently retired CEO of ColeDiz International, Ltd. shook his head. "Forget the commercial carrier. I'll call Diego and arrange for you to go back on the company jet."

Joshua sat down. "Thanks. I'm getting too old to hang around airports with the huddled masses."

Timothy frowned at his uncle. "Even though your last

name is Kirkland you're still exempt from taking commercial flights." Martin had decided more than forty years before that anyone with Cole blood was forbidden to take commercial carriers following the kidnapping of his daughter. Only Judge Christopher Delgado, a federal judge who'd married Joshua's daughter, was exempt from the family edict.

"I doubt if anyone would ever link me to the rest of you guys."

"Even with the blond hair and green eyes, you're still a Cole, Josh," Martin insisted.

Joshua smiled. "I don't think you guys will ever let me forget—"

A knock on the door stopped what he'd planned to say and all conversation ended and everyone stared at the door. There was only the sound of measured breathing as David got up, unlocked and opened the door. "Where have you been?" he asked his grandnephew.

Diego Cole-Thomas hugged David, then each of the men when they rose to greet him. His deep-set dark eyes swept around the room. "I just got back from the Keys. What are you guys celebrating?"

Timothy smiled at his son. "David's crowing because he managed to get another one of his kids married—with your help of course."

Sitting on a leather club chair, Diego crossed one leg over the over. "I may have set up Ana and Jake's marriage, but remember I offered them an out. But, after seeing them together less than an hour ago I can say they'll spend the next forty or fifty years together."

Martin snorted. "Why is it that all of David's kids marry law enforcement? Gabriel married an ex-undercover

DEA agent, Alexandra hooks up with someone from the CIA, and now it's Ana with a U.S. Marshal."

David, filling a snifter with brandy, handed it to Diego. "Maybe they're turned on by guns and badges."

"Or they have a need to feel protected," Joshua added.

"Don't even go there, Josh," David retorted. "You will not attempt to psychoanalyze my kids and say I didn't protect them when they were growing up."

"I don't think that's what he meant," Martin interjected quickly. "You and Serena raised your children as if they were '70s flower children, and now that they're out in the big bad world they look for someone whose life is or was governed by a set of laws and regulations."

David relit his cigar. He pushed out his lips. "That sounds plausible."

Joshua gave him a smug grin. "Don't get me wrong, brother. I envy your kids because they live by their own set of rules. Now, we'll have to wait and see who Jason hooks up with."

Timothy gave his uncles an imperceptible nod as he raised his glass. "Here's to Jason marrying a schoolteacher."

David lifted his snifter, smiling, and the four others touched glasses, intoning, "To Jason." What he didn't say was that he doubted whether Jason would marry before Nicholas. His youngest son was still too transient and free-spirited to settle down with a woman and start a family. Jason told him as soon as the relocation for Serenity was finalized he planned to spend at least three months in Oregon where he'd set up a studio in the sprawling house he dubbed Serenity West. It was there where he wrote and edited music for the label's newly signed and veteran performers.

His brothers and nephew teased him about his children, but no one knew his sons and daughters better than he did. And, that alone would make him the final winner in the wedding wager.

# Part One
## LOVE LOST

## Chapter 1

Peyton Blackstone lay on her back, staring up at the gossamer fabric draping the four-poster bed. She'd turned off the air-conditioning the night before, leaving the windows open overnight to take advantage of the cooling temperatures.

Pinpoints of light painted the dawning sky with streaks of pink and lavender and the woodpecker living in the tree outside her bedroom window had begun tapping his beak against the bark in a rhythmic cadence that set her teeth on edge. She didn't need an alarm clock to wake her, not as long as she had her feathery neighbor.

Peyton knew she had to get up and check on a mare recovering from a localized infection of the skin before driving over to a neighboring horse farm to pick up Celia Cole-Thomas. She and Celia had an eleven o'clock appointment at a Staunton salon for a beauty makeover. Later that afternoon Celia was scheduled to exchange vows with her fiancé. The ceremony would take place in the garden at Celia's brother's horse farm. The resident minister at Blackstone Farms would officiate, while Nicholas Cole-Thomas had invited everyone living on farms within a twenty-mile radius to attend the reception.

Celia and her fiancé, Gavin Faulkner, had come to Virginia to marry and at the last possible moment decided to hold the ceremony at Cole-Thom Farms rather than at the local courthouse. Peyton, after embarrassingly revealing she liked Celia's brother, had been recruited by Celia to stand in as her maid of honor, while Gavin had asked Nicholas to be his best man. However, she knew Celia's attempt to play matchmaker was destined for failure. Whenever Nicholas visited Blackstone Farms to meet with his mentor, he would give her a barely perceptible nod, looking through her as if she didn't exist.

When she'd returned to Blackstone Farms after completing her studies for a degree in veterinary medicine, Peyton had asked her cousin about his protégé. Sheldon Blackstone was forthcoming when he told her about the swirling rumors weeks before Nicholas arrived to claim the prime land his agent had secured for him in an auction pitting him against the owner of Thornton Farms. Nicholas's representative finally quoted a price that far exceeded what Jubal Thornton was prepared or able to meet, and over four hundred acres and a dilapidated mansion were deeded to the new owner who set up Cole-Thom Farms.

Sheldon also revealed it'd taken Nicholas more than a year to restore the mansion to its original grandeur and another year to erect one- and two-bedroom prefab cottages, connecting dormitory-style buildings for resident employees, a dining hall and two state-of-the-art modern stables. Viewed as an outsider, Nicholas was touted

as brash, vain, arrogant and an upstart after he'd purchased several Arabians for breeding purposes. There
was even more chatter about him. No one had seen him
with a woman and this simply added to the mystique of
the tall, dark, handsome horse breeder.

Sitting up, Peyton swept back a lightweight blanket,
swinging her legs over the side of the bed. She combed
her fingers through the hair falling over her forehead and
around her face. Her feet touched the floor at the same
time her cell phone vibrated on the bedside table. Reaching for the phone, she stared at it. An unfamiliar number
was displayed on the screen. She punched in her pass
code, deciding to answer the call.

"Hello."

"Hey, baby. I knew you would be up. You always were
an early riser."

The voice on the other end of the connection raised
bumps on her exposed flesh. "Why the hell are you calling me?"

"Is that any way to greet your husband?"

She gritted her teeth. "Ex-husband, Reggie." Peyton
knew he hated when she called him Reggie.

His deep laugh came through the earpiece. "I'll always
think of you as my wife, Peyton."

Her hand tightened around the phone. "I don't want
you to ever call me again."

"Don't you want to hear what I have to say?"

"No! You said and did enough when we were together."
Peyton pressed her thumb to the touch screen, ending
the call.

She didn't want to believe he had the audacity to call
her when she'd told him emphatically she never wanted
to see or hear from him again. And Peyton didn't want
to believe that the man with whom she'd wanted to spend

her life turned out to be a fraud. When she filed for divorce she didn't know which of his names to use, so it'd become Reginald Matthews aka Ronald Mitchell, aka Richard Morris. The only consistent thing was his initials. She should've known there was something wrong with him because he appeared too good to be true. But at twenty-four she'd believed herself in love for the first time. However, a year later the rosy bubble didn't burst but exploded when, after he'd been arrested for solicitation, she discovered her husband had a criminal history going back to when he was a juvenile. Reginald's criminal history included misdemeanor offenses ranging from petty theft, forgery to menacing. He never served time because of his father's influence.

The elder Matthews had always bailed him out and instead of serving time in jail or prison, Reginald was mandated to community service, which he never completed. However, Reginald's luck ran out when he was arrested in Florida at the same time his parents were out of the country on vacation. Peyton had no intention of bailing him out for soliciting a prostitute, and he spent a week in jail before he was able to contact his indulgent father to put up the money. She moved out of their apartment, contacted a lawyer and filed for divorce.

Setting the phone on the bedside table, Peyton made her way into an adjoining bathroom. Flicking on a light, she stared at her reflection in the mirror, seeing a stranger staring back at her. Her dark gray eyes seemed abnormally large and haunted. A mop of sun-streaked blond hair fell around her face. The spray of freckles dotting her nose and cheeks were no longer visible. Sitting on the rails watching the horses exercise, swimming in the inground pool, and occasionally picnicking outdoors with her young cousins without a hat had darkened her normal golden-brown complexion to a rich chestnut hue.

Fortunately she'd worn the highest number SPF sunscreen to protect her skin from the damaging rays of the hot Southern sun. If her mother saw her now she would launch into a tirade about the dangers of skin cancer, and Peyton would somehow placate her saying she would check with a dermatologist if she noticed anything out of the ordinary.

She went through her morning ablution, finishing her shower and applying a liberal application of perfumed crème cologne. She slipped into a pair of jeans with a white man-tailored blouse, turning back the cuffs, and a pair of black leather flats. Reaching for a brush, she pulled it through the tawny strands, which fell to her shoulders, smooth and shimmering with pale gold highlights. It'd been more than three years since Peyton had cut her hair, and the urge to cut it again was stronger than ever.

She paused to make her bed and put her bedroom in order before she left the suite of rooms in the large two-story white house she shared with Sheldon, his wife, Renee, and their young daughter, Virginia. Although Sheldon employed a full-time housekeeper, Peyton still cleaned up after herself. She hadn't grown up with household help, so old habits were hard to break.

The sun was up when she walked to the area where a pickup truck, minivan and a SUV were garaged. Now that Sheldon had officially retired from running the farm, Peyton usually drove the red pickup with the farm's logo emblazoned on the doors. The doors to the pickup, like all of the vehicles on the farm, were never locked and keys or fobs were always left in the ignition. She kept her medical bag in a locked compartment in the truck along with a pair of knee-high rubber boots.

The farm was beginning to stir. She drove past a group of men walking in the direction of the stables. One by one the horses would be taken from their stalls, washed and groomed, while the stable hands mucked and washed down the stalls. They would be fed and watered and then turned out to pasture to graze. The Thoroughbreds training for races would be exercised before the jockeys put them through their paces. Jockeys and trainers would spend time conferring with one another as the respective trainers entered the data into laptops.

Peyton parked alongside one of the three stables, retrieved her bag and exchanged her shoes for the boots. She walked in, coming face-to-face with Ryan Blackstone, the farm's resident veterinarian.

"What are you doing up so early?" she asked Ryan. "I told you I'd make rounds this morning." He wore his ubiquitous jeans, plaid cotton shirt, battered baseball cap that had seen better days and scuffed boots. A two-day growth of whiskers shadowed his lean jaw.

The Blackstones were like the Baldwin brothers. The similarity in the actors' eye color indelibly connected them as family. Whereas the Baldwins shared the gene for ice-blue eyes, it was varying shades of gray with the Blackstones. At forty, tall and slender Dr. Ryan Blackstone was bummed because he claimed more gray hair than his father, who would celebrate his sixtieth birthday the following year.

Ryan raised his eyebrows at his young cousin. She'd enrolled in the Western College of Veterinary Medicine in Saskatchewan, Canada, earning a doctor of veterinary medicine degree. Like him she'd specialized in large animal and equine medicine. He'd found her motivated and single-minded in learning everything she could about medical care for horses. He smiled. This morning she looked ten years younger than twenty-seven with her bare face and her hair pulled into a ponytail.

He reached for her medical bag. "Don't you have a wedding to go to this afternoon?"

Smiling, Peyton nodded. "I wanted to check on Katie Dee."

"I checked her already."

"What's up, Drs. Blackstone?" quipped one of the workers as he pushed a wheelbarrow filled with hay and manure out of the stable.

Peyton rolled her eyes at him when he winked at her. A few of the single workers had started flirting with her once they'd discovered she wasn't married. What they didn't know was that she had been married, but that was something she made certain not to advertise. It was just too embarrassing.

"There is one too many Dr. Blackstones on this farm," she said under her breath.

Ryan gave her a level stare. "And there'll probably be a third when Sean goes to veterinary school."

"He's only eleven, Ryan. Are you certain he wants to follow in your footsteps?"

"I'm only repeating what he told Kelly."

Peyton fell in step with Ryan as he walked over to the pickup. "Even though I love working with you, I've been applying for positions at other farms. Unfortunately, I haven't had much luck. I had a dinner meeting with Nicholas the other night, but I didn't get the chance to ask him whether he'd let me volunteer some of my time because his sister and her fiancé had come in from North Carolina."

Opening the passenger-side door, Ryan set her bag on the seat. "Why volunteer, Peyton? You're a doctor, not an intern. Which means you should be paid for your services."

She stared at the grooms brushing a mare and her foal, and then her gaze swung back to Ryan's scowling expression. "It's not about money."

"If it's not money then what on earth could it be?"

"It's my name."

"Peyton?"

"No. Blackstone."

Ryan's frown deepened. "What's wrong with being a Blackstone?"

"Everything if I'm Dr. Blackstone, D.V.M." She sucked in a lungful of air. "Whenever someone mentions Dr. Blackstone it's never about me, Ryan. When I discovered the boil on Katie Dee's back the first thing one of the men said to me is that I should call Dr. Blackstone. They were talking about you. I may not have your experience, but dammit, I do happen to be a licensed veterinarian. Hardly anyone on this farm relates to me as a vet. You, Sheldon and Jeremy are the exceptions."

"It's going to take some time before they realize you are."

"How much time?"

"Probably a year. The more they see you caring for the horses, the more they'll come to rely on you." He dropped an arm over her shoulders. "Last night I had an in-depth discussion with Jeremy about setting up an equine hospital on the last quadrant. I could use you at the hospital because of your surgical training. No pressure," he said quickly when she lifted her eyebrows.

"No pressure but a whole boatload of guilt," Peyton teased.

Ryan winked at her. "No guilt, either." He sobered. "I want the best for you, Peyton. And if that means you working at another farm then I want you to follow your dream. The only thing I'm going to ask is if we do put up the hospital I'd like you to assist me in the O.R."

Peyton rested her head on his shoulder. "I promise. Now, are you coming to the wedding and reception?"

He dropped his arm. "I wouldn't miss it. Will you save me a dance?"

"I don't know, cousin. I'll probably be so busy dancing with all of the single men that I may not have time for an old married man like you."

"I'm not *that* old and I haven't been married *that* long."

Peyton wiggled her fingers as she climbed into the truck. "Thanks for taking over for me this morning. I'll see you later." She and Ryan alternated days checking on the horses. Not only did she want to gain greater experience caring for the farm animals, but she also wanted Ryan to spend more time with his wife and three young children. She smiled. He'd more or less given her his blessing about securing employment elsewhere. Peyton believed she would never be able to come into her own professionally if she continued to work at her family's farm.

Peyton maneuvered onto the local road leading to Cole-Thom Farms, downshifting and coming to a stop when she pulled in behind a caravan of trunks and vans inching toward the gatehouse security checkpoint. She drummed her fingers on the steering wheel in frustration as security personnel carefully checked the papers of the drivers in each van. Nicholas had pulled off a minor miracle when he contracted with an event planner to coordinate a reception for an estimated two hundred guests in less than forty-eight hours.

He had invited several neighboring farms to the soirée; the owners and their employees were already in a party mood because of the upcoming biannual open-house festivities, and the owner of Cole-Thom Farms sister's wedding was an unexpected prelude to what was touted as an inexhaustible supply of food, drink and music.

Celia and Gavin had picked up their marriage license; she and Celia had selected their gowns from a bridal boutique. Except for adjustments to the bodice, the gowns hadn't needed any major alterations. They'd also purchased wedding accessories and ordered their bouquets and the groom and best man's boutonnieres. Customarily some brides spent a year planning their wedding, while Celia's had taken a mere three days. The weather had also cooperated for the outdoor venue. There was hardly a cloud in the sky; temperatures were predicted to peak in the mid to high eighties, and nighttime temperatures in the mid-seventies.

Peyton gave her name to the guard, who flashed a warm smile. "Aren't you the lady doctor from Blackstone Farms?"

"Yes, sir."

He extended his hand. "I'm Clinton Patrick. It's nice to put a face with a name. Welcome to Cole-Thom Farms."

She shook the gnarled hand. "Thank you."

"Go straight ahead and follow the signs to the end of the allée. When you come up on the one for Cole House just make a left and you're there."

Towering trees stood along the newly paved roadway like sentinels. The smell of freshly mowed grass wafted through the truck's open windows. Peyton spied several mares and their foals frolicking in a meadow surrounded by white rails under the watchful eye of farm workers. Men and women dressed in coveralls were unloading vans with tables and chairs, while others were driving stakes into the ground for those waiting to set up tents. Printed signs were posted on trees with directions to turn right or left for parking and comfort stations.

When she'd called to ask Nicholas to meet her for dinner, she'd suggested a Staunton steakhouse. She told him to meet her at the restaurant because she didn't want him to get the impression that she was trying to come on to him. If they arrived in separate vehicles, then they would leave in separate vehicles. However, he'd insisted he would come to the farm and pick her up. Her plan to talk to him about possible employment was foiled when he called back to say he'd invited his sister and future brother-in-law to join them.

Truthfully Peyton wouldn't know how to come on to Nicholas, because he was nothing like the men she'd known. He was much too aloof, indifferent. She wasn't an ingenue when interacting with the opposite sex. By the time she'd entered high school she recognized when a boy was interested in her. The sly glances, the purposeful brush of his body against hers and those bold enough to verbalize they wanted to sleep with her.

Then, Peyton hadn't had a boyfriend in the traditional sense, but hung out with a group of brainiacs that were more interested in their grades than in hooking up. They did everything together: study, hang out at the mall, go to the movies and crowd into booths at their favorite restaurant chain. The cool kids teased them relentlessly, but Peyton and her fellow geeks closed ranks to strengthen their supportive, carefree bond. She never concerned herself about not having enough money for a movie or for their occasional Friday-night outings because every week everyone in the group would donate five dollars of their allowance to an unofficial sunshine fund. At the end of

the school year they celebrated in grand style at an upscale restaurant.

Peyton found kindred spirits in her fellow nerds.
They'd developed a friendship that went beyond high-
school graduation. As college students they continued to
communicate with one another in cyberspace and once a
year between Thanksgiving and Christmas they'd recon-
nect for a celebratory weekend in their small hometown
in upstate New York.

College was very different for her. She dated her roommate's cousin who wasn't ready or willing to come out of
the closet. Peyton wasn't ready to give up her virginity,
so going out with Collier had become a win-win situation
for both. Who she did give her virginity to wasn't worth
her taking off her clothes. However, she didn't know that
until it was too late.

She saw the sign for Cole House tacked to a tree, and
made a left turn. A trio of chimneys came into view when
she maneuvered up an incline. Peyton held her breath
when she saw the white three-story antebellum great
house at the end of a live oak allée. A full-height, columned porch wrapping around the front and sides of the
magnificent Greek Revival mansion was something she'd
only seen in books and magazines.

When she and Celia met to discuss wedding plans, the
E.R. doctor revealed that Nicholas had spent most of his
inheritance to set up his enterprise. Celia also said she
thought her younger brother frivolous, but after seeing
the farm she was forced to admit he'd proven her wrong.

Peyton parked the pickup behind Nicholas's late-
model Lincoln sedan in the circular driveway. Alight-
ing from the truck, she walked up the steps to the porch.
She lifted the massive lion's head door knocker, letting it
fall against the door painted a glossy navy blue. Seconds

later it opened and she curbed the urge to take a backward step when Nicholas loomed over her. She didn't know why, but she hadn't expected him to answer his own door.

Peyton held her breath when she stared at the white T-shirt stretched over his broad, muscled chest. Her gaze moved slowly from his throat to the faded relaxed jeans riding dangerously low on a pair of slim hips. Her gaze reversed itself when she stared boldly at his face. There was something in his large, dark eyes that wouldn't permit her to glance away. The nostrils of his delicate nose flared slightly when their eyes met and held.

"Good morning, Nicholas." Peyton didn't recognize her own voice when she stared at the stubble on his jaw. The timbre was low and breathless as if she'd run a grueling race.

Peyton failed to understand her own reaction to a man who was always seated next to her whenever Sheldon invited him for dinner. Except for a request to pass a plate or dish hardly a word was exchanged between them other than polite greetings. Their strained association had continued at the restaurant. She'd interacted with Celia and Gavin more than she had with Nicholas. However, she did get to see another side of him, a softer, relaxed part of him as he smiled at his sister's enthusiasm whenever she talked about her upcoming nuptials. He also appeared to be amused watching Celia and Gavin share surreptitious glances, endearments and an occasional caress.

She didn't know what it was about this reserved man that made her heart beat a little too quickly. It wasn't only because he was the epitome of tall, dark and handsome, but the way he looked through her rather than at her, which led her to ask herself if he found something about her that turned him off. She'd begun to ruminate on various reasons for his coldness, and the only thing she could come up with was perhaps she'd reminded him of someone in his past.

Nicholas opened the door wider. "Good morning, Peyton. Please come in." He noticed her looking at his bare feet.

"How is Celia holding up?" she asked.

"She's not."

Her head popped up. "What!"

Nicholas almost laughed aloud when he saw Peyton's shocked expression. The thick, charcoal-gray lashes shadowing her cheeks flew up. There was something so young and innocent about her that he suddenly didn't want to believe she was in her twenties. She reminded him of a high-school cheerleader with her hair pulled back in a ponytail.

"When I saw her earlier she was so nervous she refused to eat. I'd like for you to try and get her to drink something."

"Don't worry, I will."

He watched Peyton glance around the entryway. "You've never been here?"

"No."

"Would you like a quick tour?" Nicholas asked.

"Perhaps another time. Celia and I have to be at the salon by eleven. But, there is something I'd like to talk to you about that I didn't get a chance to do at the restaurant."

Nicholas studied the petite blonde woman with incredibly beautiful gray eyes and a killer, compact body. Even though Peyton Blackstone was physically the complete opposite of what he considered his *type*, he had to acknowledge she was stunning. Resting a hand at the small of her back, he led Peyton through the entryway and into the living room, seating her on a straight-back armchair, he taking a facing matching one. He'd been curious as to why Peyton wanted to meet with him.

"I'd like to apologize for the other night. Even though you'd called the meeting I still invited Celia and Gavin to join us."

Peyton waved her hand. "That's all right. If you hadn't invited them I wouldn't be your sister's maid of honor."

"It's not all right," Nicholas countered. "Not only was it rude but also selfish on my part."

"I don't want to argue about it, Nicholas. It's not that critical."

His eyes drilled into her. "Aren't you going to accept my apology?"

Peyton returned his glare with one of her own. A shiver eddied over her, bringing a chill despite the comfortable temperature in the room. If Nicholas believed he was going to intimidate her, then he was mistaken. She'd grown up with a father that made intimidation his trademark. Alphonso Blackstone was a harsh taskmaster. The men working for his construction company never slacked off in fear of losing their jobs, and his sternness was transferred to his home where her mother did everything humanly possible to keep the peace. Only Peyton was immune to his unexpected outbursts. She'd learned to tune him out whenever he complained that he had had to lay men off because business orders were down, while her mother placated him with her patent *"things will turn around soon."* Lena Blackstone was always the optimist and her husband the pessimist.

"We'll talk another time." Celia had just walked into the living room. She stood up, Nicholas rising with her. She stared at Celia, who looked as if she hadn't slept. Her eyes were puffy and lines of strain bracketed her generous mouth. Closing the space separating them, Peyton hugged Celia. "You look a hot mess," she whispered in her ear.

Celia returned the hug. "I'm an E.R. trauma doctor supposedly with nerves of steel, but I'm having a meltdown just because I'm getting married."

"What you need is some comfort food for the Southern soul," Peyton said. "We'll stop at a little takeout place and get an order of grits and eggs." She wanted to tell the prospective bride that getting married was one of the most important events in one's life, and would change Celia's and Gavin's lives forever.

Pulling back, Celia shook her head. "I don't think I'll be able to eat anything. And what do you know about soul food?"

Peyton went completely still, struggling to rein in her rising temper. "I know as much about it as you do. And please don't let the blond hair and gray eyes and the fact I come from upstate New York delude you into thinking I'm not a woman of color."

Nicholas knew it was time to intervene or Celia would start something with Peyton she had no chance of winning. "Cee Cee, you…" Peyton held up her hand stopping whatever it was he'd planned to say.

"Please stay out of this, Nicholas," she warned softly. "I can understand what your sister is going through. She's having premarital jitters, and if she doesn't get over it real quick I'm going to seduce her drop-dead-gorgeous fiancé. And you know it's been done before."

Celia's eyes grew wide. "You wouldn't?"

Peyton bit back a smile. Talking about seducing Gavin had shaken Celia from her malaise. "I damn sure will if you don't stop being a drama queen."

Squaring her shoulders, Celia straightened her spine. "Okay. I'll try and eat something."

"Once you taste Mama Lula's grits and eggs you won't be able to stop eating." Looping her arm through Celia's she forced her to put one foot in front of the other. Glancing over her shoulder, Peyton smiled at Nicholas. He returned it with a wide grin and a wink.

"Later."

Nicholas nodded. "Later," he repeated.

## Chapter 2

Peyton knew she was speeding but she wanted to get to Mama Lula's to pick up the order she'd called in, and then to the salon. If Celia had planned to marry on the weekend she doubted whether they would've been able to secure an appointment. The technicians at Unique Creations were usually booked up two to three weeks in advance.

She gave Celia a sidelong glance. She was a feminine version of her brother, reminding Peyton of a doll with her small round face, black curls grazing the nape of her neck, large dark eyes, and pert nose, curved mouth and thumbprint-dimpled brown cheeks.

"I'm sorry I came at you like a rabid dog," Peyton apologized.

Pressing the back of her head to the headrest, Celia closed her eyes. "And I'm sorry if you misunderstood me. I would never presume to identify your racial designation. I have an uncle with light green eyes whose hair was much lighter than yours. He has a grandson who looks exactly like him even though Alejandro's parents both have black hair. When Uncle Josh tans his complexion is similar to yours. And he doesn't bite his tongue when he brags about being an Afro-Cuban down to the marrow in his bones."

Peyton felt duly chastised. People who hadn't seen her parents would rudely ask *"what are you?"* And her pat comeback was "An American." "I inherited my eye color from my father and everything else from my mother. Mom is very mild-mannered and laid-back, and the only time I witnessed her going ballistic was when I came home to tell her that my second-grade teacher, who was new to the school, asked me what I was. When I'd innocently told her my name she said knew that, but wanted to know if I was white or black. My mother called a lawyer and had the teacher transferred to another school."

Celia opened her eyes. "Why should it matter what you are?"

Peyton shook her head. "I really don't know what the big deal is when it comes to a person's race. Didn't we elect a mixed-race president?"

"Word," Celia drawled. "By the way, the Coles are a patchwork quilt of different races and ethnicities."

"Do you speak Spanish?" Peyton asked.

"Yes. My father and grandmother always spoke to me and my brothers in Spanish. My father felt it was important we know more than one language. It was different with *abuela*. She didn't want us to forget our Cuban roots."

The two women talked about their medical careers, professors, fellow students, course work and internships. Their order was waiting when Peyton maneuvered up to the drive-through window at Mama Lula's. They had twenty minutes to spare, so they sat in the parking lot behind the salon eating grits, fluffy scrambled eggs and fileted whiting seasoned and fried to perfection.

Celia took a deep swallow of coffee. "Do you think we're going to be able to fit into our gowns?"

Touching the corners of her mouth with a paper napkin, Peyton nodded. "I don't see why we shouldn't. We probably won't eat anything else until later on tonight." Their gowns were scheduled to be delivered to the farm at noon.

Celia patted her flat belly. "Thank you for forcing me to eat. I really needed to put something in my stomach."

Peyton gathered the containers and coffee cups, storing them in a plastic bag. "I knew you would feel better if you ate something."

A beat passed. "Would you have really attempted to seduce Gavin?"

She looked at Nicholas's sister as if she'd suddenly taken leave of her senses. "I was just blowing smoke, Celia. I've never attempted to seduce another woman's man and I pray I don't lose my mind and actually do something that skanky."

Combing her fingers through the mass of raven curls, Celia held them off her forehead. "I don't know what's wrong with me, but I believed you. I lost one fiancé, so it's always in the back of my mind that I could lose another one."

"What happened? Talk to me while we walk."

Peyton listened, stunned when Celia disclosed the gang-related shooting rampage in the Miami hospital emergency room where her fiancé had been one of six murdered in cold blood. Two doctors died that night along with her patient and three other gang members. She and three others were wounded in a mêlée that lasted no more than thirty seconds and had turned the E.R. into a killing field.

"It's been a year, but I still have nightmares," she whispered as they entered the salon through the rear door.

Peyton wanted to know how seriously Celia had been injured and what had happened to the shooters, but it was too late to ask when they were approached by the owner of the salon. "Good morning, Mrs. Barnes. I'm Peyton Blackstone and this is Celia Thomas."

Barbara Barnes, or Babs as she was referred to by her closest friends, pressed her manicured hands together. It was impossible to pinpoint her age; the woman had been nipped and tucked to where she'd literally stopped time. She was tall and claimed a figure that would rival a woman decades younger. Her short coiffed honey-blond hair, flawless peaches-and-cream complexion and her makeup were in keeping with someone who had achieved grande dame status. It was only on a rare occasion she would be seen in the upscale unisex salon.

"Welcome, Miss Blackstone. When one of my technicians told me you needed an appointment for a bridal package I knew I had to come and personally meet you. I had Iris move several clients to another day."

Earlier that morning Peyton had complained to Ryan that being a Blackstone in horse country was more of a disadvantage than an advantage, but apparently she'd been wrong. She knew she'd been given an appointment when she told the receptionist her name; the woman called her back to inform her that someone had cancelled and they would be able to fit her and Celia in.

"Thanks so much for being so accommodating," Peyton said, smiling.

Barbara inclined her head in acknowledgment. Her

brown eyes shifted from Peyton to Celia and then back. "Who is the bride?"

Celia flashed a dimpled smile. "I am. And Peyton is my maid of honor."

"You're both lovely girls. My husband and Sheldon are very good friends. He was part owner in one of Sheldon's Thoroughbreds that made Grainger a very wealthy man. So, there isn't anything I wouldn't do for a Blackstone. I know you didn't request it, but I'm throwing in full-body massages for both of you." She winked at Celia. "A bride should be completely relaxed on her wedding day. Do you ladies have a favorite fragrance?"

Peyton exchanged a puzzled glance with Celia. "Anaïs Anaïs."

Barbara smiled. "And you, Celia?"

"Trésor."

"I asked because I know the wedding begins at four, so you'll be able to shower and apply your fragrance before we do your hair and makeup. This way when you return home you'll just have to slip into your gowns." She motioned to a young woman dressed in a flowing black smock with her name stitched on one pocket and Unique Creations on the other. "Ingrid, please take care of Ms. Blackstone and Ms. Thomas."

Peyton and Celia gave each other fist bumps, as they followed Ingrid to a dressing room where they left their street clothes in a locker and were given plush black velour robes and matching slippers. Soft, relaxing Zen-like music coming from concealed speakers competed with the hypnotic sound of flowing water in a large corner waterfall filled with stalks of bamboo. They were brought into the massage room; scented candles and diffused light threw soft shadows on the walls and ceiling. Peyton felt as if she'd entered a cave or a grotto. The masseurs stepped out while they exchanged the robes for a towel, then lay facedown on the heated massage tables.

Both women lost track of time when they were simultaneously massaged and kneaded from head to toe. The massage was followed by a facial that left their faces cool and tingling. Peyton was almost listless when she was told she had to take a shower. They headed back to the massage tables where the masseurs applied scented body creams in their favorite fragrances. Dots of perfume were applied to all the pulse points. Her entire body glistened and glowed from the ministration.

Peyton slipped back into her robe, accepted a mug of steaming herbal tea, and as soon as she finished it she was seated in a shampoo chair. She ignored the conversations going on around her, luxuriating in the feel of strong fingers massaging her scalp. Every service was performed in precision like an assembly line. The highly skilled technicians knew exactly what to do, and there was no wasted motion. Her pedicure was completed when she sat in the chair with her hair slathered in a rich avocado-based conditioner under a plastic cap. Following the conditioning treatment, her hair was blown out and styled in a loose twist behind her left ear.

Her eyes met Celia's in the mirror as they sat next to each other. Celia's raven curls were set on large rollers, and then blown straight, brushed off her face and pinned into a chignon on the nape of her long, smooth neck. Celia had decided to wear flowers in her hair instead of the traditional veil or headpiece, while Peyton had chosen pearl and crystal hairpins.

Glancing at a wall clock in the glass and mirrored salon, Peyton noted the time. It was minutes before two. All that remained was a manicure and makeup. Although the invitations read four o'clock, Celia insisted the ceremony begin no later than four-thirty.

The manicurist noticed her staring at the clock. "Don't worry, Ms. Blackstone. Someone will be applying your makeup while I do your manicure."

"What's going on?" Celia asked when Peyton maneuvered into the driveway at Nicholas's house. A woman dressed in a black pantsuit with a pair of oversize sunglasses perched on the top of her reddish-pink hair was shouting into a walkie-talkie at the top of her lungs. The color in her face went from pink to bright red in seconds. She beckoned them to get out of the truck.

Peyton came to a stop, shifting into Park. "She has to be the planner." Within seconds of getting out of the pickup two young women wearing similar pantsuits appeared as if out of nowhere.

The woman stepped forward, extending her free hand. "I'm Danielle Lawson, the event planner. We're working on a very tight time frame, which means you have to go with the bridal attendants who will help you get ready. The groom and best man are dressed, so we're only waiting for you. By the way, you look very nice." She put the walkie-talkie to her mouth. "Get someone here to move this truck to the parking area."

Celia and Peyton followed the two women around to the back of the house, entering through a rear door. A small storage room off the pantry had been converted into a makeshift dressing room. Both gowns, covered in clear plastic, hung from wall hooks and a full-length mirror was propped against one wall; the wedding flowers, boxes with shoes, lingerie and jewelry were set out on a cloth-covered table.

The bridal attendants worked quickly and efficiently

when they helped Peyton and Celia out of their clothes and into their wedding finery. Both women stared wide-eyed at themselves in the mirror as jeweled hairpins were secured in Peyton's hair, while Celia's attendant tucked tiny pink rosebuds into the ebony coil of the bride's hair.

Celia had chosen a platinum silk sheath with embroidered tulle, a sweetheart neckline, short cap sleeves, beading, sheer back and a sweep train. Peyton's gown was similar, a darker gray and designed without the train. The simplicity of the gowns, hairstyles and dramatic eye makeup was perfect for a summer afternoon wedding.

Slipping her feet into a pair of charcoal-gray silk rhinestone-studded sling-blacks, Peyton added four inches to her five-three height. Celia had decided on a pair of satin pumps with a lower heel in a becoming platinum shade. She'd admitted if she was going to be up on her feet for hours, she much preferred a two-inch heel rather than a higher one. Standing five-eight in bare feet, four inches would have put her at the six-foot mark.

"Please hold out your left hand, Miss Blackstone."

Peyton complied, her eyes widening as Celia's attendant looped a bracelet with princess-cut diamonds around her wrist, securing it with a double safety catch. Peyton looked at Celia. "We didn't order this."

Celia's dimpled smile was dazzling. "It's my gift to you for being an incredible maid of honor." She held up her hand when Peyton opened her mouth. "Please let me finish. It's the least I could do for you, because you arranged and paid for the beauty makeover. You also got your cousin to agree to let Reverend Merrill officiate. And you've also kept me sane. So please be gracious and accept it."

She wanted to be gracious, but the weight of the white metal and the size of the stones in the bracelet probably cost more than some people earned in six months. "It's exquisite, Celia. But it's too—"

"Please stop it, Peyton," Celia implored, interrupting her. "Nicholas and I grew up with trust funds, and our parents taught us it's gauche to talk about money."

Peyton's smile did not reach her eyes. She may not have been a trust-fund kid and she hadn't grown up dirt poor; however Celia's gift was not only extravagant but also unwarranted. "Thankfully I've never been accused of being gauche," she said under her breath as the attendant handed her Gavin's double milgrain platinum wedding band. She put the ring on her thumb. She reached for Celia's hand, giving it a gentle squeeze. "Gavin is very, very lucky. You are the perfect bride."

A fringe of long lashes concealed Celia's eyes. "Thank you, Peyton. And you're a beautiful maid of honor, a wonderful friend, and I hope one day we'll become more than friends." She leaned in close. "I'm willing to bet Nicholas won't be able to take his eyes off of you tonight."

Danielle walked into the room, clapping her hands. "Ladies, we're ready to begin. Maid of honor first, then the bride."

Peyton didn't want to think about Nicholas. She'd begun to believe her fascination with him was due to his mysteriousness. She'd watched him interact with other people, and not once was she able to discern from his expression what he was feeling. If he had been angry or annoyed that emotion also remained hidden behind a facade of polite indifference. She rarely saw him laugh or smile. Dinner at the restaurant had been the exception and she wondered if it had anything to do with Celia's presence. It was obvious he adored his sister.

She wanted to forget the episode in the restaurant restroom when she confessed to Celia she was in love with

Nicholas. Hours later Peyton realized she hadn't been totally truthful about her revelation. She didn't know how to explain to Celia that she'd mentally replaced Reginald with Nicholas in an attempt to emotionally exorcise a man whom she'd loved selflessly. A love he'd exploited and abused to fuel a life filled with deception.

Picking up her bouquet of pink-and-white roses, Peyton lifted the skirt of her gown with her free hand and walked out into the afternoon sunlight, following the planner down a flagstone path to an archway covered with climbing pale pink roses. The plantings were mixed, roses set among perennials that created a riot of color. Beyond the arch was a wooden fence with a doorway.

Danielle settled her sunglasses on the bridge of her nose. "I'm going to open the door, but I want you to wait until I give you the signal to go through. The maid of honor will go first, followed by the bride." A photographer stood off to the side snapping frames of pictures.

Peyton, glancing over her shoulder, gave Celia a reassuring smile. She didn't want to think about her own wedding day; she had been in love and believed when she'd married Reginald it would last forever. However, forever lasted a year and when her loving husband had called her to come and bail him out of jail her world came crashing down around her. She would've understood if he'd been arrested for DWI or DUI, but not solicitation. While she'd believed her husband was traveling on business, he'd actually been busy soliciting prostitutes.

Her musings were shattered when Danielle opened the gate, revealing a charming English garden. A videographer was on hand to tape the entire ceremony. It was the perfect setting for an afternoon wedding. Marble statues of fairies peeked through a border of ornamental grass; water spilled from the mouth of a large fish perched atop

a wide fountain and wildflowers in every variety grew
in wild abandon among with vibrant hibiscus and hanging baskets overflowing with orchids. Several low stone
benches were positioned around a large waterfall, making it the perfect spot to begin or end the day.

Peyton didn't want to look at the opposite end of the
flower-strewn path, yet she found she couldn't pull her
gaze away from the tall, ramrod-straight figure seemingly
willing her to meet his eyes. Nicholas stood next to Gavin
under a pergola intertwined with ivy and grape leaves. It
was as if he possessed special powers with an indescribable force field pulling her in his direction.

Everything around her vanished: the wedding guests
sitting on white tufted chairs waiting for the ceremony
to begin; Gavin watching and waiting for his bride; Reverend Jimmy Merrill clutching his bible to his chest and
the guitarist's lightning-quick fingers playing flamenco
on an acoustic guitar. Nothing existed except the man
with whom she felt a connection despite his overt remote-
ness. The guitarist's fingers slowed as he segued from the
staccato strumming to a hauntingly beautiful rendition
of "I'll Always Love You."

Danielle moved closer. "I'm going to start counting
and when I reach ten I want you to start walking. I want
you to take a pause a half second between each step so
everyone will get a good look at you before you reach the
pergola. Do you understand?"

"Yes ma'am." Peyton wondered if the event planner
had been a drill sergeant in a former life. She didn't ask
or make requests. She barked orders, expecting them to
be followed without question.

At Danielle's whispered signal, she began the measured walk along the path, carefully placing one foot in
front of the other. A mysterious smile parted her lips when

she recognized the shocked expressions on the faces of those who lived with her at the farm. They were used to seeing her without makeup and her hair styled in a ponytail or braid.

She gave Sheldon a perceptible nod when he winked at her. Her father's third cousin, widowed at thirty-two, had become a sought-after widower. Twenty years later he fell in love again and married Renee Wilson. He'd also become a father for the third time when Renee gave birth to a daughter.

Lowering her chin slightly, she stared at Nicholas through her lashes when she stood opposite him. The look on his face mirrored those who knew her: shock.

*Gotcha!* her silent voice shouted in triumph.

Gavin shifted until his shoulder brushed Nicholas's. "The lady vet cleans up real good," he said sotto voce.

Nicholas went completely still, as if someone had impaled him with a sharp instrument, while his breath solidified in his lungs. "No lie," he whispered back.

If it hadn't been for her hair Nicholas wouldn't have recognized the veterinarian. She may have been given a boy's name, yet there was nothing boyish about her petite, compact curvy body.

His gaze lingered on the toes of her shoes peeking out from under the hem of the gown that was a perfect match for her eyes before slowly inching up to the soft swell of breasts rising and falling above the revealing neckline. Staring at Peyton called to mind one of the dolls in Celia's doll collection: perfectly coiffed golden hair, expertly applied makeup and drop-dead-gorgeous figure clothed in an exquisite evening gown.

Nicholas had feigned a lack of interest whenever Sheldon invited him to eat with his family, where invariably he and Peyton would be seated together. He'd purposely ignored her whenever they occupied the same space because she had become a constant reminder of how much he'd missed female companionship. Peyton also reminded him of when he'd ignored his intuition and had formed a relationship with a woman who was the opposite of any with whom he'd become involved. He didn't know how, but he always felt tension radiating off Peyton, wondering why she was so uptight.

But he did get to see a very different Peyton at the restaurant. Nicholas wasn't certain whether she'd bonded with Celia because both were doctors but she laughed easily, while exhibiting a wicked sense of humor. She appeared so much younger than twenty-seven, and with her petite frame he'd tried imagining her treating an animal as large as a horse.

Twice within the space of a week she'd tried to talk to him. Well, he mused, tonight would be different. After all, he was the best man and she maid of honor and that meant they would be forced to interact with each other. His entrancement with Peyton ended when the guitarist played the opening strains of the "Wedding March." As if on cue, everyone stood up.

Nicholas had offered to walk Celia down the aisle, but she'd insisted that privilege belonged to their father. She'd also made him promise not to tell their parents she was marrying Gavin. He didn't ask why but assumed Celia had a good reason for wanting to keep her marriage a secret.

He smiled, lines fanning out around his eyes with his sister's approach. Never had she looked more serene. He'd witnessed her joy during her medical-school graduation, but this was different. Celia had been given a second chance at love. She'd been seriously wounded, while her fiancé Dr. Yale Trevor-Jones was killed instantly during the E.R. shootout. Nicholas flew from Virginia to Florida, sitting by his sister's bedside until her medical condition was upgraded to good. He'd invited her to live with him while she recuperated, but Celia, similar to their mother, did not like horses. It'd taken a year, her falling in love and her agreeing to marry Gavin Faulkner for her to visit Cole-Thom Farms for the first time.

"Sweet heaven! She…she looks amazing." Gavin's voice cracked with emotion.

"All Cole women are beautiful," Nicholas countered smugly.

Gavin chuckled. "It's like that, brother?"

Nicholas nodded. "Damn straight, brother. You'll see once you meet the family."

Gavin took Celia's right hand, tucking it into the bend of his elbow when she stood next to him. His dark eyes caressed every inch of her face. "I love you more than life itself." A murmur went up from those sitting close enough to overhear his impassioned words.

Peyton felt hot tears prick the back of her eyelids with Gavin's pronouncement, blinking wildly in an attempt to keep them from falling and ruining her makeup. It was obvious he was in love with his bride but she never would've predicated the man with the face and body of an A-list Hollywood actor would bare his soul in front of strangers. Her eyes met Nicholas's briefly before she looked away, his expression giving away nothing.

She exhaled a soft breath, concentrating on Jimmy Merrill when he motioned for everyone to sit. The tall, rawboned minister had served as an assistant pastor in a little church in Texas before coming to Blackstone Farms to work as an assistant groom. There was a school, but no church at the farm, which prompted Sheldon to approve the construction of an interdenominational church on the south end of the sprawling property.

Jimmy opened his bible. "We're gathered together here to join this man and this woman in the bonds of marriage. I will begin with a reading from the book of Numbers. 'If a man vow a vow unto the Lord, or swear an oath to bind his soul with a bond; he shall not break his word, he shall do according to all that proceedeth out of his mouth. If a woman also vow a vow unto the Lord, and bind herself by a bond, then all her vows shall stand, and every bond wherewith she hath bound her soul shall stand.'"

Peyton didn't know how, but she felt the heat of Nicholas's gaze on her face. Giving him a sidelong glance she met his curious stare. Rays of sunlight piercing the leaves of a nearby tree slanted over his face, turning him into a statue of gold. He and Gavin had elected to wear tuxedos, the tailored jacket flattering his broad shoulders. The pale pink silk tie, fashioned in a Windsor knot under the spread collar white shirt, matched the rose boutonniere. He smiled, an elusive dimple in his lean jaw deepening.

"You look lovely," he mouthed slowly enough for her to read his lips.

Smiling, Peyton inclined her head, acknowledging his unexpected compliment. She was brought back to the ceremony when Jimmy asked Nicholas for Celia's ring. Reaching into the pocket of his tuxedo, he handed Gavin the platinum band. Peyton repeated the gesture, removing the groom's band off her thumb. She held Celia's bouquet of pale pink roses tied with two yards of wide silver picot-edged ribbon.

Resting his hand over Celia's and Gavin's, Jimmy whispered a quiet prayer blessing the newlyweds' union. Smiling, a network of fine lines fanning out around his eyes, he said in a clear voice, "Gavin, you may kiss your bride."

Wrapping both arms around Celia's waist, Gavin lifted her off her feet and kissed her passionately. Celia responded by looping her arms around her husband's neck, returning the passionate kiss.

Jimmy smiled. "Ladies and gentlemen, I'd like to present Mr. and Mrs. Gavin Faulkner."

His announcement was followed by applause and shouts. Peyton handed Celia her bouquet and taking Nicholas's proffered arm, she retraced her steps down the path as the many guests showered Gavin and Celia with flower petals, rice and birdseed.

As they stepped through the garden door, they were met by the photographer. "Please wait off to the side until everyone leaves because I want to take photos of the wedding party."

Nicholas placed his arm around Peyton's waist, smiling when the bride and groom accepted best wishes from complete strangers. He shook the hands of those who congratulated him on his sister's marriage.

He knew his mother was concerned that he would never marry, yet that wasn't a concern for Nicholas. He hadn't said he would never marry. The question was when. If or when he met that special woman then he wouldn't have to be coerced to commit.

Peyton, who'd slipped her arm around Nicholas's waist inside his jacket, whispered, "It was perfect."

"Celia is more than worthy of perfection because she's gone through a lot this past year. It's the least I could do for her."

"You did real good, Nicholas."

They shared a smile. "So did you, Peyton."

The last guest had filed out of the garden, heading for

the reception area when the photographer and videog-
raphers ushered the wedding party back into the garden
for photographs that would recapture the occasion for
posterity.

## Chapter 3

"Move a little closer to the best man," the diminutive photographer instructed Peyton. "I doubt if he will bite you," he added with a Cheshire cat grin.

He'd taken frame after frame of the bride and groom posing in front of the fountain, under the pergola, the flowering archway, outside the garden gate, Gavin sitting on the stone bench with Celia, while she reclined against his shoulder. There were shots with Gavin and Nicholas, Celia and Peyton, and all four laughing, hugging and kissing. Peyton felt her knees buckle slightly when Nicholas brushed his mouth over hers. It'd only lasted seconds but for her it was long enough to savor the surprisingly gentle caress of his firm mouth.

Chuckling, Nicholas pressed his mouth to her ear. "He's right. I don't bite."

Her eyes narrowed. "That photographer is a little pervert," Peyton whispered between clenched teeth. "Didn't you see him salivating on my chest every time he tried to get me into a pose?"

Nicholas's arm tightened around her waist. He chanced a quick glance at her décolletage. The top of her tanned breasts were on sensual display each time she took a breath. "Do you want me to punch him out?"

"No! Please don't." Gavin and Celia, standing a short distance away turned and stared at Peyton with the sudden outburst. She couldn't stop the wave of heat creeping from her chest to her face. Peyton didn't know if Nicholas was serious or joking. However, she didn't want him to become the knight in shining armor stepping in to defend her and ruin his sister's special day with a physical confrontation.

Myron Essex frowned at Peyton. "Is something wrong, Ms. Blackstone?"

She lowered her gaze. "I'm sorry, Mr. Essex."

Myron threw up both hands in a gesture of exasperation. "I cannot work like this if you don't cooperate with me."

Her jaw dropped. What was he talking about? Cooperate. She'd done everything he'd wanted her to do, and still it didn't seem to be enough. "I don't know what you're talking about. I am cooperating but what is it exactly do you—"

"Enough with the melodrama, Essex," Nicholas interrupted angrily. He wasn't going to stand there and let the man insult Peyton. In fact, she had done everything he'd wanted her to do. "Let's get this done so we can go and mingle with our guests."

The harshness in his tone dared the photographer to challenge him. After all, he was paying the man top dollar for the wedding photos. He didn't know if *the little pervert,* as Peyton referred to him, liked her and had a perverse way of showing it by being overly critical; he also had tired of the endless posing that had taken up more than an hour. Peyton had been nothing short of perfection—from the way she looked to being accomplished and adept when following the photographer's directives.

Myron recoiled as if he'd been struck across the face, however he recovered quickly. "I need Ms. Blackstone to turn her left shoulder until she's half facing you. And, Mr. Thomas, I need you to place your right hand on Ms. Blackstone's left shoulder. I want both of you to look at each other. That's it," he said, his voice rising in excitement. Peering through the viewfinder of his camera, he got off five shots in rapid succession. "Nice. Now I need the entire wedding party to stand together. We'll take this one in front of the waterfall. The ladies will stand next to each other with the men flanking them."

Dappled sunlight filtered through a grove of flowering fruit trees, a slight breeze showering those in the garden with white and pink petals. Peyton raised her chin slightly as several landed on her hair and lashes; she smiled like a young child watching falling snow. Nicholas stared at her upturned face, the image caught by the camera lens. Celia resting her head on Gavin's shoulder as he lowered his head to kiss her hair was captured in the same frame.

Myron lowered his camera and puffed out his chest. Even before seeing the digital image she knew the shots were exquisite. "I'm finished for now. I'll take some more at the reception."

Reaching into the breast pocket of his jacket, Nicholas took out his cell phone and tapped several buttons. "I need you to bring the car around to drive us over to the reception area."

* * *

It was obvious Nicholas had pulled out all the stops to celebrate Celia's impromptu marriage. The invited guests, seated or standing under white tents, were drinking or talking to one another as a DJ was busy spinning tunes. Several couples were already up on the portable dance floor showing off their fancy footwork. Solar lanterns and gardenia leaves floating in water-filled crystal bowls served as centerpieces for each table.

An outdoor kitchen had been set up on the south meadow with eight chefs preparing cook-to-order meals for nearly two hundred guests. The caterer, with a staff of fifty were kept busy filling water goblets, serving alcoholic libations, taking orders and setting out plates of salad and freshly baked artisan bread.

Nicholas glanced up at the waiter who paused in front of him with a bottle of Perrier in one hand and white wine in the other. "I'll just have the water."

The white-jacketed waiter filled the goblet with sparkling water. "Would you prefer red wine?"

"No, thank you. The water is fine." He noticed Peyton giving him a questioning look. "What's wrong?"

She blinked. "Are you abstaining tonight?"

Leaning to his right, his shoulder touched hers. "I'm waiting for the champagne toast. Remember we have the open house at your farm tomorrow night and Harridans on Saturday night. You've never been to a horse farm open house?" he asked when she gave him a blank stare.

Peyton shook her head. "No. This will be my first year. I've spent the last eleven years of my life in school. And that includes college and veterinary school, including an internship and another three years of residency training. As a kid I would always spend the month of August down here, and cry my eyes out when I had to go back home."

"Had you always wanted to become a vet?" Nicholas asked.

Staring up at him through her lashes, Peyton's lips parted in a smile. "Always and forever," she crooned. "I knew I had to study very hard and that meant missing high-school dances and football games."

His gaze lingered on her mouth. "So, you were one of the smart kids." The query was a statement.

Throwing back her head, Peyton laughed softly. "I was the personification of a geek."

"No way," he countered.

"Yes way. And it paid off."

Nicholas paused. "There's nothing better than realizing your dream."

Peyton heard the wistfulness in his voice. "Have you realized yours, Nicholas?"

He cocked his head, seemingly deep in thought. "I have, but I had to take a circuitous route. Now, what is it you wanted to talk to me about?" he asked, deftly changing the topic.

Drawing in a deep breath, she told Nicholas about her attempts to secure a position as an equine veterinarian at several of the other horse farms but without success. "I'm even willing to volunteer my services."

"Isn't your farm large enough to support two resident vets?"

"You're missing the point, Nicholas. When someone mentions Blackstone Farms' vet everyone knows they're talking about Ryan. However, if I were to work for you Cole-Thom Farms would have its own Dr. Blackstone."

Nicholas draped an arm over the back of Peyton's chair. "I'd love to help you out, but I have a contract with Dr. Harry Richardson that doesn't expire until next September. And I wouldn't feel comfortable having you volunteer your services. That would be exploitation. But, if you can wait a year I'll be more than willing to consider your offer."

Peyton breathed out an inaudible sigh of relief. At least Nicholas hadn't turned her down flat like some of the other owners. She didn't want to believe it was because of professional jealousy, but competition and rivalries between horse farms was as epidemic as in other professional organized sports.

She smiled. "Thank you."

Placing his hand over hers outstretched on the tablecloth, Nicholas gently squeezed her delicate fingers. "You're welcome. Have you decided what you want to eat?" He'd noticed she hadn't checked off any of her dining selections.

Peyton eased her hand from under Nicholas's much larger one. She picked up the pencil beside her place setting. "I can't decide between the prime rib and fish selections."

Nicholas picked his own pencil. "Why don't you go for the surf and turf?"

She studied the printed menu. The caterers had listed medallion filet mignon and prime rib for beef selections and broiled salmon, Maryland-style crab cakes and pan-fried sole under fish. Chicken cordon bleu, broiled Cornish hens and herb-encrusted roast chicken were available for those who preferred poultry. While they'd posed for photos the guests were served hot and cold hors d'oeuvres along with specially mixed exotic drinks with and without alcohol. The grits, eggs and fish she'd eaten earlier that morning had managed to sustain Peyton throughout the morning and afternoon, but now she was ready to eat again.

"I think I'm going to have the prime rib and crab cakes," she said.

Nicholas checked off his choices. "I'm going totally fish tonight. Salmon and sole."

"After this weekend I know I'm going to have to either fast or detox," Peyton said. The Blackstones had decided on a cookout theme for their open-house celebration, and she hadn't heard what the Harridans were planning.

Nicholas had to agree with Peyton. Although he hadn't officially announced that Cole-Thom Farms was hosting an open house, inviting two neighboring farms to Celia's wedding reception had become a fitting substitute. He was more than aware of the lingering resentment among several of the owners with farms with racing and horse-breeding histories going back more than eighty years. He was viewed as the new kid on the block who purportedly had enough money to not take on investors.

With the exception of Sheldon Blackstone, none of them knew much about him. Once he'd taken possession of the deeded land and begun the task of restoring the house that would become his permanent home, Sheldon had come and offered to help him in every way he could to make the transition smooth and easier than it had been for him more than forty years ago.

Sheldon had become Nicholas's surrogate father, mentor and a relentless tutor when Nicholas found himself tested over and over as to different breeds and the finite mechanics that went into horse racing. Peyton claimed she studied hard to become a veterinarian and he'd studied equally hard to become a horse breeder.

Dusk had descended on the farm and light from strategically placed lampposts had come on, illuminating the landscape and turning it into an emerald forest. Strings of lights entwined in tree branches twinkled like stars in the encroaching darkness.

All of the horses were stabled before the first guests had arrived and the farm's security staff circulated inconspicuously among the assembly. Stringent precautions were taken to protect and secure millions in horseflesh whenever visitors were present. Closed-circuit TVs were viewed by the person manning the gatehouse and inconspicuously placed cameras monitored activity throughout the four-hundred-plus acres. There was another hundred acres of vacant land bordering the west end of the property Nicholas wanted to purchase not because he wanted to expand the farm but for better security. Signs were posted around the perimeter stating: *Trespassers Will Be Shot on Sight and if Still Alive, Then Prosecuted.* He'd increased security when there were rumors that someone had planned to steal a prized Arabian stallion he'd purchased for breeding.

A waitress picked up the dining requests from those at the bridal table as the maître d' urged those standing around to take their seats because the waiters would begin serving dinner. Leaning forward in his chair, Nicholas noticed that Celia was resting her head on Gavin's shoulder, and he wondered if she was overwhelmed with all of the festivities or she wasn't feeling well. It'd only been a year since she'd hovered between life and death; she'd lost nearly one-fourth her body's blood supply after being shot with a powerful handgun that could've ended her life if it'd struck a vital organ. She was luckier than many gunshot victims because she was in a hospital where immediate care was readily available.

Pushing back his chair, he stood and came around behind her. "Are you okay, Cee Cee?"

Celia gave him a slow smile. "It's all coming down on me now that I'm a married woman."

He dropped a kiss on her hair as he met Gavin's eyes. He knew his brother-in-law would take care of his sister. Nicholas had always been overly protective of his sister even though she was older. It was something that had been drilled into him as a young boy. Cole men always protect their women. He and Diego didn't have to worry about protecting Celia any longer because Gavin was more than qualified to do that.

Returning to his seat, Nicholas shared a smile with Peyton. Overhead light glinted off the diamonds in the bracelet circling her left wrist. "Nice bracelet," he said softly.

Peyton held out her hand. "It was a gift."

His eyebrows lifted. "Someone must really like you."

"You're right," she confirmed. If Celia hadn't told Nicholas she'd bought the bracelet, then neither would she. She studied his lean dark face, unaware that she'd been holding her breath. The stubble from this morning was missing and he'd had a haircut. He was so handsome that Peyton believed she'd conjured him up, and she wondered how he had managed to escape the clutches of some marriage-minded woman whose goal was to become Mrs. Nicholas Cole-Thomas.

Even if Nicholas had shown a romantic interest in her Peyton knew unequivocally she wasn't emotionally ready to become involved in a relationship. Her feelings for Nicholas vacillated like the rise and fall of the tide, and it was apparent her personal maturity hadn't kept pace with her professional maturation. And if she were to thank him for anything it would be his detachment. It saved her from making the same mistake twice.

The mood of the music changed from upbeat to instru-

mentals of classic pop songs as waiters, hoisting trays on
one shoulder began placing orders down on the many tables. Nicholas touched his glass of water to Peyton's, and
she repeated the gesture with Celia who in turned touched
her glass to Gavin's. Wine flowed liberally as the mouth-
watering aroma of food filled the air, the mood becoming more and more festive. The videographer circulated,
capturing smiles, animated gestures and the overriding
sound of laughter.

Nicholas did not want to think of his mild-mannered
father's reaction once Celia revealed she'd married a man
she'd known a month. Celia wanted to keep her marriage a secret from the family and Gavin was also keeping a secret from his wife. Secrets that could backfire
and shatter the newlywed's trust and eventually destroy
their marriage.

The volume on the music was lowered again, this time
when he stood up to toast the newlyweds. Raising a flute
filled with champagne, Nicholas smiled at Celia before
nodding to Gavin. "I'd like to wish my favorite sister—"

"I'm his *only* sister," Celia interrupted, smiling. Her
statement was followed by laughter and applause.

A single dimple creased Nicholas's left cheek. "My favorite and only sister," he corrected, bowing slightly at
the waist. "I love you and wish you more happiness than
you could've ever imagined. Gavin, I know you love my
sister and that you will *protect* her with your life. Brother.
Welcome to the family." Gavin raised his glass in acknowledgment. Cupping Peyton's elbow, he helped her
rise. "It's time for you to say something."

Peyton's heart drummed a runaway rhythm against her
ribs. She'd known Celia all of four days and she hadn't
planned on making a toast. She searched her memory for
a sonnet or bible verse pertaining to love.

There came a strange and silent hush as hundreds of eyes were fixed on her. Smiling, she lifted her flute. "I raise my glass to toast a beautiful pair on the birthday of your love affair. To Gavin and Celia. May you be lovers the rest of your lives." Shouts of congratulations and whistling followed her toast. Peyton permitted Nicholas to help her sit down, taking furtive sips of the dry wine.

"I had no idea you were a romantic," he said in her ear.

She rolled her eyes at him. "That's because you don't know me."

Nicholas leaned closer. "You're right. I don't know you." He stared at her under lowered lids. "If you plan to work for me maybe we should get to know each other."

"A lot of things could change in a year, Nicholas."

He lifted his shoulders. "True. But the fact that you're a licensed veterinarian isn't going to change."

Peyton bit her lower lip to keep from blurting out that she could possibly secure a position elsewhere. Virginia wasn't the only state with horse farms. She'd give herself another six months before sending out her resume to racetracks across the country.

The DJ's voice came through the speakers set up around the tent. "Ladies and gentlemen, I have a special request from the groom for the couple's first dance as husband and wife."

The Foreigner classic "I Want To Know What Love Is," filled the tent as Gavin led Celia out onto the dance floor. Peyton felt her eyes filling with tears when she listened to the poignant lyrics. She was saved from embarrassing herself when Nicholas gently pulled her to stand. One moment she was standing and the next she found herself in his arms, her breasts molded to his chest. The strength of his embrace, the warmth of his body and the lingering scent of his cologne swept over her, and she went completely pliant in his arms.

Peyton felt calm, astonished at the sense of serenity that made her recognize what she didn't need. She didn't need romance at this time in her life the same way she hadn't needed it when she met Reginald. Marrying him had almost derailed her studies. She'd been back in the States four months when they met at a social mixer; he appeared to be everything she wanted in a man. She was unaware he was a predator and she a consenting and willing prey.

Reginald had accused her of being a girl in a woman's body and she refused to give him the satisfaction of telling him he was right. He'd sensed her naïveté and like a piranha went in for the kill. Fortunately she'd escaped being devoured. She was left with invisible scars that had healed and were slowly fading, although there were times when Peyton wondered if her marriage to Reginald had ruined her for other men.

Peyton's reverie ended when she found herself in Gavin's arms. Tilting her head, she smiled up at the powerfully built man with large dark eyes and strong masculine features. "How does it feel to be married?"

Gavin twirled her around. "Wonderful. I'd confessed to Celia that I loved her but those words sounded so empty until I vowed to give her all that I am today and forever. And I like what you said about us being lovers for the rest of our lives. Too many times couples stop being friends and lovers once they're married. I pray that will never happen with me and Celia."

"Marriage is like a job or career. You have to work at it every day to make it better than the day before."

"Are you speaking from experience, Peyton?" Gavin asked.

Smiling, she shook her head. Her marriage had been the exception rather than the norm. "No. Those are my mother's words."

"She sounds like a wise woman."

Peyton didn't want to refute Gavin's assessment of her mother. Wherein Lena Blackstone had excelled as a mother she'd failed miserably as a wife, because she'd become a throwback to an era when women took the vow to obey their husbands literally. Lena's stance on this issue had been a source of contention between Peyton and her mother for years. It wasn't that she didn't love her father, but Alphonso Blackstone's need to dominate his wife and his employees had been the reason for her living in Virginia rather than return to her home state.

"She is a wonderful mother," she said instead.

Nicholas winked at Celia. He'd cut in on his brother-in-law because it gave him an excuse not to dwell on how good it felt to hold Peyton in his arms. And after so many hours he still hadn't recovered from her shocking transformation from the ingenue with a ponytail, jeans and flats to the startling sophisticate that left him with his mouth gaping. He also hadn't missed the lustful stares from men when she'd walked down the carpet; he also understood why the photographer had given her a hard time. Myron Essex had reverted to an adolescent boy who liked a girl but didn't know how to show it, so he either teased or harassed her.

Nicholas had left adolescence behind years ago, yet he hadn't felt the need to tease or harass her. He'd found it easier to simply ignore her, convincing himself that she wasn't there when everything about her was imprinted in his memory like a permanent tattoo. There had only been one other woman who'd affected him the way Peyton had within minutes of their meeting, and he'd known beyond the shadow of a doubt she would become his wife and the mother of their children. After an intense court-ship and a proposal of marriage, his world fell apart. Not only had the woman he'd loved selfishly walked away from him, but he was forced to walk away from a career he'd wanted for what seemed like forever.

"How can I thank you for everything you've done for me, Nicky?" Celia asked, breaking into his thoughts.

"Promise me I'll be godfather to your firstborn. Jacob Jones trumped me when Diego picked him to be Samuel's godfather."

"I promise. But I'm going to tell you right now that I'm going to ask Peyton if she'll be godmother. Aside from Hannah and a college friend, I really don't have any other close girlfriends, and even though we just met I feel Peyton's the sister I've always wanted."

Nicholas's eyebrows lifted a fraction. "She is rather remarkable."

"Oh, so you noticed?"

"What's that supposed to mean, Cee Cee?"

Celia leaned in close to her brother, her mouth pressed to his ear. "She's perfect for you. And what is the expression? If you're slow you'll blow. Every single man and probably a few married ones would like to exchange places with you tonight. She's not only smart, but also pretty. You've dealt with a few losers in the past. Especially Arden. So, please don't let Peyton get away."

Nicholas clenched his teeth, the muscles in his jaw twitching noticeably. His sister didn't know what she was talking about. "There's nothing going on between me and Peyton."

"Maybe there should be," Celia countered.

His eyes narrowed. "What's up with the matchmaking?"

Celia closed her eyes for several seconds. "This is one of the happiest days of my life and I want the same for you. You have an incredibly beautiful twelve-room house that's more of a museum than a home. You own hundreds of acres of land where you breed horses when you should be breeding babies of your own," she continued passionately. "Even if you don't hook up with Peyton I want you to promise me that you're going to stop this self-exile and start dating again. Not every woman you'll meet will be like Arden."

Nicholas spun his sister around in an intricate dance step. "I'll promise only if you quit nagging me. You're beginning to sound like our mother."

Celia sobered. "Speaking of our mother. Don't mention anything about me marrying until I get to tell her in person."

"When is that going to happen?"

"Once the trial is over I'll tell everyone." As the state's only surviving witness Celia had sought refuge in her vacation home in the Great Smoky Mountains to await the trial that would finally close the chapter on the E.R. massacre.

"You know all hell is going to break loose when you tell Dad. He's been waiting years to walk his only daughter down the aisle."

Her dimples winked at Nicholas when she smiled. "He will still have that honor when Gavin and I repeat our vows in West Palm this coming New Year's Eve. And once we make Mama a grandmother again she'll calm down."

Dipping his head, he kissed his sister's cheek. "Let's hope you're right." The dance ended and he escorted Celia back to Gavin.

Nicholas scanned the crowd looking for Peyton, find-

ing her surrounded by a group of men as if she were holding court. Some he recognized from Blackstone Farms,
but there were a few he didn't recognize. And from their
expressions they were enthralled with her. He recalled
what Celia had said about not letting her get away. He
couldn't stop her from getting away if he never had her.

And Nicholas was forced to ask himself if he did want
Peyton, and the answer was as plain as the nose on his
face. Yes, he did. What he had to figure out was for what.
Did he want friendship or a relationship that was wholly
physical in nature? He didn't want more than that, because
for him falling in love was not an option. Been there,
done that and he wasn't willing to travel that route again.

# Chapter 4

Peyton woke to the sound of the woodpecker's drumming. It was as if the bird's very life depended upon his making the infernal noise. Maybe he thought he was an alarm clock. Unfortunately she couldn't hit the snooze button and go back to sleep for another ten or fifteen minutes. She had to get up and check the horses. Pushing into a sitting position, she supported her back against a mound of pillows. She also couldn't linger in bed because she'd been recruited to serve on the open house's welcoming committee.

A soft moan slipped past her lips when she felt a twinge of tightness in her calves. It'd been after midnight when she returned to the farm and it was close to one-thirty when she finally crawled into bed after cleansing her face of makeup, taking down her hair and taking a leisurely bath to soak her aching legs and feet. Peyton had lost count of her many dance partners after the third one.

She danced with her cousins, the men from her farm and the neighboring ones. A few times she caught Nicholas staring at her with obvious disapproval, but she felt free, freer than she'd been in a very long time. Weddings fêted the joining of shared futures and she felt the bride and groom's joy as surely as it was her own.

Swinging her legs over the side of the bed she walked gingerly on bare feet to the bathroom. Forty minutes later she returned to the bedroom at the same time her cell phone stopped ringing. Please, she thought, don't let it be Reginald.

Reaching over, she picked up the phone, smiling. She'd missed one call, this one she always welcomed. Touching the screen, she listened for a break in the connection. When Lena's husky greeting came through the earpiece Peyton went still.

"Mama. What's the matter?"

"Nothing's the matter. I'm just a little hoarse this morning. I was working in the garden yesterday and the pollen got to me. Your father claims I sound sexy."

Peyton smiled. "You do."

"I just called to say hello."

Her smile faded. Her mother never called just to say hello. "What's going on, Mama?"

"Your father just stripped and varnished all of the doors and he's threatening to take the cat to a shelter if he—"

"Please don't tell me any more," Peyton interrupted. "I want you to crate Oreo and send him to me at the farm."

"You don't mean that, Peyton."

"Yes I do mean it." She enunciated each word. "Daddy's not giving that cat to a shelter because if he's not adopted then he's going to be euthanized. You have my credit-card information, so you don't have to use your own money. Ship him to the Shenandoah Valley Regional Airport. Make certain you put down my cell as the primary number on the shipping label and the farm's as the secondary number. I'll drive up and get him once he arrives."

Oreo had been a rescue cat. After she'd become involved with Reginald, Peyton gave the kitten to her mother because he was allergic to cats. Her father never liked Oreo, and was probably looking for an excuse to get rid of him.

"I really like Oreo," Lena admitted.

"But Daddy doesn't, so that means I'm taking my pet back. Please try and call me today, Mama." Peyton paused. "I just thought of something."

"What?"

"Why don't you fly down with Oreo? A change of scenery will do you good."

Silence ensued before Lena said, "It's too hot in the South this time of year, and you know I have to stay out of the sun. Maybe I'll come down in October."

Her mother had had a pre-cancerous lesion removed near her hairline four years ago, which prompted her to take extra precautions whenever she went out in the sun. It was always layers of sunscreen, long sleeves and a floppy hat during the summer months.

"Maybe isn't an answer, Mama."

"I'll promise only if you'll promise to come back here to live. You're my only baby and I miss you like crazy."

Peyton closed her eyes. *Please, not with the guilt,* she mused. "I miss you, too, Mama. I'll come up to visit, but please don't ask me to stay."

There came a beat. "When are you coming?" Lena asked.

"I'll be up for my birthday. We'll have a girls' week

when we check into a hotel, order room service and get beauty makeovers."

"That sounds wonderful. Oreo's looking at me, because he knows I feed him his breakfast around this time. Let me go, baby, so I can call and find out when I can send him back to you."

Peyton rang off. When she'd moved into a studio apartment close to Cornell University College of Veterinary Medicine in Ithaca, New York, she saw a flyer advertising pet adoptions at a local shelter. When she visited the shelter and spied the chocolate British shorthair kitten with a tiny patch of white on one paw Peyton knew they were meant for each other, and she now looked forward to reuniting with her furry baby.

She made her way down the main staircase to the first floor, stopping on the last stair when she saw Sheldon's housekeeper dusting a bleached pine table cradling a crystal vase filled with a bouquet of wildflowers.

The housekeeper was like a specter, floating silently in and out of rooms dusting and vacuuming where she'd cleaned the day before. "Good morning, Miss Garrett."

Claire Garrett turned and smiled at Peyton. The twinkle in her green eyes sparkled like polished peridots. She placed her feather duster on the table. "Good morning to you, too. I figured you wouldn't be up until later this morning."

Peyton returned the tall, heavyset woman's friendly smile. "I couldn't sleep. Not with that annoying woodpecker drumming on the tree outside my bedroom. I also need to check on the horses."

"You don't have to check on the horses, because I overheard Ryan tell Sheldon he was going to make the rounds this morning because you probably would be exhausted from the wedding." Claire smoothed back the stick-straight strands of snow-white hair she'd pinned into a neat bun. She wore her ubiquitous pale gray uniform and white rubber-soled shoes. "Now about that woodpecker. I hear that little sucker whenever I dust and vacuum your room. I wish there was some way to get him to move to another tree."

"There are a few alternatives," Peyton said. "We can use a repellent without harming him. It's known as the flasher. It is a combination of colors, fluttering and sounds that mimic the strike movements of predatory birds. I'm going to go online and order one."

"Once you get it I'll have one of the men hang it where the little annoyance can see it. By the way, you looked spectacular last night dancing with Mr. Thomas. I heard some of the young fellas talking about asking you out."

She forced a smile she didn't quite feel. She wasn't interested in going out with the young fellas. "Did you enjoy yourself last night?"

Claire nodded. "Yes. I thought it was ingenious to use a real wedding as a theme for an open house. But I'm really looking forward to ours because I love barbecues. The chefs ordered three whole hogs. They're planning to smoke one and roast the others in the ground on hot coals like they do in Hawaii." Claire excitedly outlined the entire menu for the farm's open house. She then revealed what she'd heard about the Harridans' get-together. "They've decided on a Vegas theme, complete with table and board games, slot machines and roulette wheels. When they heard we were going to have a live band and karaoke, the Harridans hired several celebrity impersonators: Cher, Elvis, Bette Midler and Lady Gaga."

"I'm really looking forward to that," Peyton admitted, stepping off the last stair.

"Bruce Thornton's housekeeper told me their open

house will be a drive-in movie. Most young folks nowadays don't know anything about drive-ins."

"There's one only a few miles from where I grew up." Claire's talkativeness shocked Peyton. Normally the woman never said more than good morning or good evening whenever they encountered each other. And it'd taken the housekeeper a long time before she'd stopped calling her Missy rather than Peyton.

"Sheldon and Renee are sleeping in late this morning."

"Where's Virginia?" Peyton asked.

"She and the other kids spent the night with Gus and Beatrice." Claire shook her head. "Those kids love hanging out at Tricia's grandpa's house. God bless Beatrice. I don't know how she's able to deal with six little children underfoot. The Lord knew not to give me any because as one of eight all I ever wanted was peace and quiet." She flushed attractively. "I know I'm running off at the mouth this morning, but I suppose I'm still wound up from last night when the DJ played all of my favorite songs from the '70s and '80s."

"He was good," Peyton confirmed.

The DJ had arranged his music by decades. He'd begun with the '50s and brought it up to date with hip-hop, techno and dance favorites. And he'd programmed his computerized playlist to play nonstop, intermingling decades so there was something for everyone. At no time was the dance floor empty.

And Peyton couldn't remember a time when she'd danced that much. She'd danced for when she'd missed her junior and high-school dances because she'd elected to stay home and study. She'd also danced for when she'd opted not to go to the club frequented by her college friends whose weekend partying began Thursday night and sometimes didn't end until Sunday morning. She smiled, because she intended to do it again later that afternoon. There was no way she would be able to make up for the sacrifices she'd made for her career choice, but Peyton intended to enjoy herself until she established herself as an independent equine veterinarian.

"I'm going over to the dining hall for breakfast. Would you like me to bring you anything back?"

Claire picked up the duster. "No, thanks, Missy. After I get through with my dusting I'll call and have someone bring me a plate. I don't need to be rattling pots and pans if Sheldon and the missus want to sleep later than usual."

Peyton groaned inwardly. The housekeeper was back to calling her Missy. "I'll see you later." She decided to walk to the dining hall instead of driving to ease her overworked leg muscles. What she wouldn't give for a massage this morning.

The instant she stepped out of the house the distinctive aroma of grilled food wafted to her nose. The tradition of hosting a yearly open house had begun to exhibit new spring foals for sale and/or breeding purposes. Then Sheldon went one step further when he served food and included music. That year he sold three retired Thoroughbreds he'd put out to stud. Several of the owners met, deciding to hold the event every two years instead of yearly, and that each farm would adopt a specific theme. The owners and their trainers now met prior to the open houses to negotiate the buying and selling of horseflesh.

It felt good to walk, something Peyton didn't do enough of and would begin now that she had a natural spa in which to exercise. Most of the farm's ten thousand acres had paved roads and footpaths. There was also the pool for swimming laps. The schoolhouse had been expanded to include a gym for the children to play and work out.

She reached the dining hall, pushing open the door.

There were six men standing around the inside. The tension in the large space was so strong it was palpable. "What's going on, Lee?" she asked one of the grooms. He'd wound an elastic hair tie around shoulder-length dreads under a baseball cap.

Turning, his eyes widened when he saw Peyton. "Oh, good morning, Doc. It looks as if there's not going to be any hot food for breakfast or lunch. The cooks claim they're too busy cooking for the open house."

Breakfasts and lunches were always set up as a buffet, while dinners were sit-down with white tablecloths, flowers, and place setting with wineglasses and water goblets. Sheldon claimed he wanted to expose the farm's children to the fine dining missing in family-style chain restaurants.

Peyton often wondered what her life would've been like if she'd been raised on the horse farm. Would she have become a veterinarian? And if not, then what? Would she, like a few of the recent high-school graduates, get into their cars and drive as far away from the only lifestyle they'd known for seventeen or eighteen years?

Before the establishment of the Blackstone Farms Day School all of the children boarded the school bus that would take them into town to the local schools and drop them off at the end of the school day. Their friends were farm children; they learned to drive tractors and other farm vehicles before reaching double digits, but there were also drawbacks to living in a self-contained community.

Many complained about the lack of privacy. There were cameras everywhere, monitoring their coming and going. For the few seeking to form relationships they found themselves hampered either by the discerning eyes of adults, but also by the discomfort of having to see an ex every day if or when a relationship ended. Some stayed after graduating and many more left the farm. Lee Washington had become one of those who'd stayed.

"What about waffles?" Peyton asked. She occasionally made her own Belgian waffles, topping them with fresh seasonal fruit.

"No waffles, no toast, no nothing," Lee spat out. He pointed to the flyer taped to the inside of the door. "There are cold cereals, yogurt, milk, juice and fresh fruit for breakfast and salad and sandwiches for lunch. They didn't do this two years ago. What the hell do they think we are? We're farm folks, not farm animals," he continued, grumbling angrily.

"It's only two meals, Lee," she said when she wanted to tell the muscular young man he could forego his usually fat- and calorie-laden breakfast and lunch for one day. She noticed most of the men fortified themselves with eggs, bacon, sausage, grits, home fries, corned beef hash and pancakes for breakfast at least five days a week. The exception was the jockeys who ordered egg whites, turkey bacon or sausage along with a lot of fruit and vegetables. Jockeys ideally weighed between 100 and 150 pounds in addition to being in excellent physical condition. Blackstone Farms' jockeys had set their own maximum benchmark at 130 pounds.

"I bet the other farms don't starve their people when they have their open houses."

Lee gave her a steely-eyed stare that almost forced her to take a step backward. But then Peyton refused to back down from the supposedly intimidating glare. "Don't even go there," she warned him in a quiet tone.

"What seems to be the problem?" asked a familiar voice. Everyone turned to find Jeremy standing in the doorway. The expression that had settled into the features of the former marine, ex-DEA special agent's face was one few saw and probably did not want to see again. Repressed rage had darkened his face and eyes. "If there are complaints about a change in today's menu, then speak up. If not, then I don't want to hear another word about it. The chef and his assistants aren't magicians, even though some of you would like them to be. It was *my* decision for them to concentrate on preparing food for tonight's open house, leaving everyone to either eat what is available or you can check with your supervisors to see if they'll permit you to leave the farm to go eat at Shorty's Diner. What's it going to be, folks?"

Lee was the first to acquiesce. "I guess I can eat cereal," he muttered.

Jeremy's expression softened considerably when he rested a hand on Peyton's shoulder. "Lee, I remember a time when you ate Cap'n Crunch cereal every morning." The other men smothered sniggles and laughter. Jeremy sobered again. He leaned close to Lee. "You grew up here and you should know better than to wear a hat indoors." It was a hard and fast rule Sheldon had learned as a boy; he'd established the regulation when he'd first set up the farm, and it was still in effect thirty years later.

The apprentice groom snatched off his cap, crushing it against his chest. "Sorry about that."

Jeremy's fingers tightened on Peyton's shoulder. "I'd like to talk you outside."

Peyton had no idea what he wanted to talk to her about, thinking perhaps Ryan had mentioned their conversation about her wanting to work for another farm. "What is it?" she asked when they stood under the sweeping branches of an ageless red maple.

"Tricia called the house and Claire told her you'd left

for the dining hall. So, I came to see if you wanted to have breakfast with us."

"I'd love to. Unlike the guys, I don't have a problem eating cold cereal."

Jeremy ran a hand over his cropped hair. "I understand the men. I outgrew cereal years ago. But when I gave Andy the head count for the number of visitors we expect to attend this afternoon he said it was going to be impossible to make breakfast and lunch for the farm folks *and* prepare for the open house. It was only after I talked it over with Ryan we decided Andy should serve a stripped-down breakfast and lunch. You'd think after all they'd eaten last night they wouldn't want to look at food this morning."

Peyton had to agree. She'd missed the cocktail hour because she'd posed for wedding pictures; however there was an inexhaustible amount of food for dinner and after dinner. She'd overheard Nicholas tell the caterer leftovers were to be donated to a local food kitchen.

"Maybe they just need something to moan and groan about," she said.

The instant the words were off the tongue Peyton thought about her conversation with Ryan, experiencing some guilt. Fortunately she didn't need to look for a position because there had been one waiting for her even before she'd received her degree. Some of her classmates had sent out résumés prior to graduation with the hope they would secure employment if only to begin repaying student loans.

Fortunately for her she hadn't been saddled with student loans. Her parents had covered the cost of her undergraduate education and as promised, Sheldon paid for veterinary school and the advanced training in the specialty of internal medicine and surgery. Living on the farm afforded her free housing and meals, and while she refused to accept a salary Jeremy had insisted on a stipend to cover what he'd considered personal incidentals.

Unlike Nicholas and Celia she didn't have a trust fund. She'd been the sole heir to her maternal grandparents' estate. It wasn't a lot of money, but more like a contingency reserve. The last time she'd withdrawn funds within the five-figure range it was to pay an attorney for her divorce. What the fast-talking legal shark didn't know was that she would've given him her last penny just to get her lying slug of a husband out of her life.

Taking her arm, Jeremy led her to the pickup similar to the one she drove. "I told Pop that he coddled the employees too much when he ran the farm. If he hadn't retired there was the possibility they could've started up a union and eventually would've gone on strike if we didn't meet their demands."

Sitting in the truck beside her cousin, Peyton gave him a sidelong glance. Although he resembled his father more than Ryan, their personalities were very different. Sheldon was the consummate father figure while Jeremy had retained all of the qualities of a no-nonsense drill sergeant.

"Don't you get tired of playing badass jarhead?" she asked.

When Jeremy smiled his features suddenly appeared boyish. "I can't when I'm dealing with nearly fifty employees. When I came back to the farm it wasn't my intention to take it over but to help Pop out. Then one day he decides he wants out, announcing to everyone he's retiring. I know meeting Renee had a lot to do with it. Running the farm had taken a lot out of him, but when Renee gave him the daughter he's always wanted he changed overnight and became a different man. Most times it's as if he could care less about the farm. Every weekend he and Renee spend time at their cabin in Minnehaha Springs. They used to take Virginia until Tricia and Kelly convinced them to leave her behind so they could have some alone time."

Peyton smiled. "I promised the girls we would camp out again. We had to cancel the last outing because it rained and we ended up in the schoolhouse instead."

Jeremy started up the truck. "I think it's safer to camp out indoors than out in the open right now. One of the men told me he saw a coyote running along the north quadrant. We've set several traps, hoping to catch it. I've also told the security people to review the closed-circuit footage every couple of hours."

"If there's one, there could be others, Jeremy. This is the time of year when coyote pups are born, and the mother and father are probably hunting prey. However, they're known to avoid humans." She'd noticed workmen erecting tents and setting up tables and chairs in the north quadrant. "Do you plan to move the tents?"

"No. We're going to set up fences along the perimeter where we'll release all of the large livestock guardian dogs. I've also arranged for the security team to patrol the area on horseback. Once we break ground to build the hospital I'm hoping they'll leave because we'll encroach on their habitat."

"So, you're really serious about building a hospital?"

He nodded. "Yes. The initial cost for construction and equipment for the operating rooms will be high, but I project we'll be able to recoup the expenditures within two to three years because we'll offer the same services to the surrounding farms as the nearest equine hospital. And with you and Ryan staffing it we'll only have to hire one or two technicians."

Peyton knew it was only fair she tell Jeremy of her

future plans. "I've asked Nicholas whether he would hire me."

Downshifting, Jeremy slowed as he maneuvered onto the road leading to his home. "What did he say?"

"He won't be able to give me an answer until next year. His contract with Dr. Richardson doesn't expire until next September. That's when he'll decide whether to renew their contract. I don't want to appear disloyal because your father did pay my veterinary school tuition."

Jeremy stopped the truck and cut off the ignition. Resting his arm over the back of Peyton's seat he gave her a long, penetrating stare. "You're not being disloyal, Peyton. Pop paid it because that's what he does. He paid for my college, Ryan's and yours because he didn't go, and not because he didn't have the grades. He enlisted in the army to spite his father who'd wanted him to take over running the farm after he graduated. Pop claimed he never wanted to have anything to do with horses, but fate proved him wrong. I don't know how much he's worth on paper, but I do know he has enough money put aside for his grandchildren's and his daughter's college educations. As for you working for Nicholas we'll revisit this conversation next year."

Peyton smiled, relieved that Jeremy hadn't tried to talk her out of leaving the farm. "Thank you."

Jeremy angled his head. "Tell me something. What's up with you and Nicholas?"

The powerful relief she'd felt subsided with his query. "What do you mean?"

"It looks as if our neighbor is quite smitten with my little cousin."

Her eyebrows shot up. "Me?"

"Duh! Who else did you think I was talking about?"

"You're wrong, Jeremy. There's nothing going on between me and Nicholas."

"Not yet," he said under his breath. "Come on, let's go inside. Tricia is waiting for us."

Nicholas slowed the car, stopping at the electronic gates emblazoned with a bold letter *B*. Leaning out the driver's side window, he stared into a camera. "Nicholas Cole-Thomas," he said when an electronic voice asked his name. Within seconds, the gates opened and closed behind him as he drove through.

"How big is this farm?" Gavin asked from the rear seat.

It was the same question Celia had asked him earlier that afternoon. "It's about ten thousand acres." He glanced up into the rearview mirror. The person in the car behind his was driving with their high beams on. Signaling, he pulled over to the right to let the car pass, and then continued along the narrow, winding road.

"How long have they been in business?" Celia questioned.

"More than thirty years. Their claim to fame is that they're the first African-American-owned horse farm to have a Derby winner."

Celia met his eyes. "I've never been to a horse race."

"That's because you don't like horses," Nicholas retorted.

"It's not that I don't like them," Celia said. "I'm afraid of them because they're so big."

"They can sense your fear, Cee Cee."

She made a clicking sound with her tongue and teeth. "There are some things I'm not ashamed to admit I'm afraid of. And a horse is one."

"What about you, brother Faulkner?" Nicholas asked. "Is there anything you're afraid of?"

"Hell, yeah. Your sister."

Folding her arms under her breasts, Celia pushed out her lower lip when her brother and husband had a good laugh at her expense. "How funny will it be, Gavin, when I cut you off cold and you'll have to resort to taking care of your own sexual needs."

"Whoa! Whoa!" Nicholas shouted. "I don't need to hear that."

Leaning forward, Gavin kissed the side of her neck. "Sorry, baby. Will you forgive me? Please, baby, please."

Shifting slightly, she stared at him over her shoulder. "I'll have to think about it."

Listening to his sister and her new husband's repartee was a reminder of the elder Cole-Thomas's banter. Timothy's refusal to argue with his wife always sent Nichola into a snit that lasted for days. Nicholas had tried to make his mother understand that after forty years of marriage her husband refused to verbally spar with a woman. Timothy would wait for her to stop talking, then smile and walk away. His decision to retreat rather than debate resulted in a peaceful, stress-free home environment.

The road diverged into four directions and Nicholas followed the sign pointing the way to the north quadrant. A towering flagpole with an American flag flying atop a black-and-red one lifted in the slight breeze. Teenage boys were doing double duty directing traffic and parking the many vehicles in an area designated for parking. He stepped out, pocketing the ticket for his car at the same time Gavin got out of the car and opened the door for Celia.

"Do you smell that?" Gavin asked.

Smiling, Nicholas slowly shook his head. *"Puerco,"* he said, answering in Spanish.

Celia sniffed the air. "You're right. It is pork."

Nicholas reached for Celia's free hand. "If you're a vegetarian or a vegan, then you've come to the wrong place tonight."

The entire Blackstone clan was on hand, greeting and welcoming everyone to the farm's open house. Nicholas stared at Peyton as she stood in the receiving line, holding one of Jeremy's triplets. She was resplendent in a one-shoulder black dress that ended inches above her knees. Four-inch black patent leather pumps added height to her diminutive frame, and also called attention to her shapely legs. She'd brushed her hair off her face and tied it with black ribbon.

He couldn't pull his gaze away from her face. The smoky-gray eye shadow made her eyes appear lighter than they actually were. The night before she'd radiated sophistication. Tonight it was unadulterated sexiness.

Reaching for her left hand, he smiled. "How nice to see you again. I hope you'll save me a dance." He dropped a kiss on the knuckle before he moved down the line, not giving her a chance to reply.

Peyton felt as if someone had just doused her with a bucket of cold water. She was shaking all over. Dressed entirely in black Nicholas appeared dark and dangerous, and the look in his equally dark eyes completely unnerved her. He had figuratively eaten her up with his hungry eyes.

Is that what others saw at the reception and she didn't or refused to see? She'd attempted to mentally dismiss Nicholas as someone with whom she did not want to become involved, but so far she was losing the battle. But, on the other hand, could she afford to throw caution to the wind and accept what was so apparent? She wasn't so detached that she was unable to recognize when a man was attracted to her. What she wanted to know was why hadn't Nicholas shown a modicum of interest before now?

Her smile was back in place when Celia leaned in; they exchanged air kisses. "Thank you for coming."

"I wouldn't have missed this. You look incredible, girl-friend."

Peyton blushed. "Thank you. So do you for a newly married woman." Celia was stunning in an off-the-shoulder red dress, stilettos and a mass of loose curls framing her face. "I'll never be able to thank you enough for asking me to be your bridal attendant." It'd given her the opportunity to talk to Nicholas about a potential position at his farm.

Celia winked at her. "Are you practicing?" She pointed to the toddler Peyton cradled to her chest.

"No," she said much too quickly. "It's going to be a while before I think of becoming a mother. This little muffin will only hang with me until the music begins. Then she's going to bed. Maybe we can get together later and talk."

"I'd like that," Celia replied. She looked around for Gavin. "I gotta go before I lose my husband and brother in this crowd." There were approximately two hundred people at her wedding, and there had to be more than twice that number at Blackstone Farms.

Celia caught up with Nicholas in the dining tent. Round tables were covered with white linen. Folding chairs, swathed in white organza, were tied with either black or red satin ribbon, representing the farm's silks. Mouth-watering smells from grilled and smoked meat wafted in the warm summer night, mingling with the scent of charcoal and seasoned wood chips. Serving pans, labeled with their contents of hot and cold dishes lined dozens of tables under two enormous food tents.

She saw roasted corn, pulled pork and roast beef,

baby back ribs, brisket, baked beans, coleslaw, potato salad, smoked and deep-fried turkey, baked ham, barbecue chicken, southern fried chicken, hush puppies, fried green tomatoes, grilled asparagus, macaroni and cheese, collard greens and sweet potato pone. And that was only in one tent. A smaller tent had been set aside for beverages, offering wine and cold beer to the adults and ice-cold lemonade to those under the age of twenty-one. The couple manning the beverage station checked anyone who appeared not to be legal drinking age.

She tapped her brother's shoulder. "Where's Gavin?"

"He went to bring the drinks. I'll get us some food, while you get a table."

Celia nodded. "I'll make certain to save a seat for Peyton."

## Chapter 5

Nightfall had descended on Blackstone Farms like a translucent navy blue veil. Those under the age of sixteen were permitted to stay and party until their midnight curfew, while four-year-old Michaela had had a meltdown when her mother attempted to disentangle her from Peyton's arms. Rather than cause a scene Peyton accompanied Tricia when she drove back to her house. She sat in the sunny-yellow bedroom with images of circus and zoo animals painted on two of the four walls, gently rocking the fretful child. Michaela's sisters, Elena and Lynette, were sleeping soundly in their beds.

Tricia Blackstone combed her fingers through her curly flyaway hairdo. "I don't know what I'm going to do with her when the new baby comes."

Peyton stopped rocking, staring at her cousin's wife. Registered nurse Tricia had grown up on the farm, falling in love with Jeremy when both were teenagers. They went their separate ways, but were reunited fourteen years later.

"You're pregnant?"

Tall, full-figured and lushly beautiful Tricia closed her eyes. "Yes."

"Have you told Jeremy?"

Tricia opened her eyes, nodding. "Yes," she repeated. "What I'd suspected was confirmed when I took a pregnancy test a couple of hours ago. And before you ask I'll tell you it wasn't planned. I told Jeremy that I'm going to make certain *this* will be our last baby."

"Congratulations."

She affected a sad smile. "Thank you. I'm telling you right now if I have another multiple birth I'm giving you one."

Throwing back her head, Peyton laughed. "What are your chances of having another multiple birth?"

"I don't want to know." Tricia stood up. "Let me take Michaela so you can get back to the party."

"I'll stay with her until she falls asleep."

"No. You didn't get all dressed up to babysit. Now go and have some fun."

Peyton kissed Michaela's forehead, then handed her off to Tricia. "Nightie, night, sleep tight, and we *don't* let the bedbugs bite," she and Michaela chorused.

Peyton returned to the merriment, wending her way along the buffet table, filling a plate with roast chicken, potato salad and a tri-color salad. Rising on tiptoe, she tried to locate the table with Celia and Nicholas but the number of people inside the tent made that impossible. Balancing the plate, she carried it and a cup of fresh-squeezed lemonade to a table with Blackstone Farms employees.

"Do you mind if I join you?"

All of the men jumped to their feet as if they'd choreographed the move. Head trainer, Kevin Manning, pulled out a chair for her. "Sure. Sit down, Doc."

"Is that all you're eating?" asked the farrier, pointing a stubby finger at her plate.

"Leave her alone, Rusty," Kevin admonished. "Doc doesn't have a bottomless pit for a belly like you." Pot-bellied Charlie Scott blushed to the roots of his receding red hairline.

Lowering her head, Peyton bit back a grin. She'd quickly learned there was a farm dining-hall hierarchy. The Blackstones always sat together as did the trainers, grooms, stable hands, carpenters, landscapers, jockeys and security staff.

Her head popped up, and she gave each man a direct stare. All of them, with the exception of Kevin, were single. "You guys look very nice tonight." Stunned silence followed her compliment. "Well, you do," she continued. They'd shaved and exchanged their jeans, T-shirts, sweatshirts and boots for dress shirts, slacks, shoes, while a few wore jackets.

Kevin swallowed a mouthful of beer. "They're all here looking for a girlfriend."

Peyton's fork halted in midair. "That shouldn't be too difficult. After all, Blackstone Farms has the reputation for having the best-looking men and women in horse country."

A thunderous Boo-Yaw, the farm's victory's cry filled the tent. Boo-Yaw had been the farm's first and only Derby winner.

Kevin nudged Peyton when the cry was repeated. "See what you started?" he teased with a wide grin when Boo-Yaws went up from the opposite end of the tent.

She bit down on a piece of moist, flavorful chicken. "I call it as I see it." Peyton had discovered many of

the single men shunned forming romantic entangle-
ments with the farm's single women, preferring instead
to date women from other farms or those they'd met in
high school.

"Yo, Peyton! Come dance with me. The band is sick!"
Lee grasped Peyton's hand, pulling her in the direction
of the dance floor. The band returned to the stage after
their break, launching into a quintessential dance tune.

It'd become a live concert with an incredible sound
system that probably could be heard for miles, flashing
lights, fog machine and eight talented musicians and male
and female lead singers. It was hard to tell them from the
actual artists when they performed Rihanna's blockbuster
hit, "We Found Love."

The energy was infectious as Peyton twirled and sang
along with the female vocalist. Somehow she lost sight
of Lee in the throng crowding onto the dance floor. A
middle-aged man with a comb-over hairdo gyrated in
front of her. Reaching for her hand, he pulled her to his
chest. Whenever he opened his mouth the smell of beer
washed over her face; it was obvious he'd had too much
to drink. The song ended and she managed to extricate
herself.

She tried holding her breath. "Thanks for the dance."
He reached for her again, and she turned, bumping into
Nicholas. "Hey, baby," she crooned. "Where were you?"
Peyton had to shout for him to hear her.

Wrapping his arms around her waist, Nicholas kissed
her hair. "I was looking for you." He nodded to the obviously disappointed man. "Thanks, man, for keeping an
eye on my wife."

"Where are you going?" she shouted when Nicholas
headed out of the tent.

"Somewhere we can talk without having to scream to hear each other."

She pulled back. "Stop, Nicholas. I have to take off my shoes. I can't walk on the grass in heels." He hunkered down, removed one shoe and then the other. Holding the pumps, he held her hand as they walked a distance away.

"Now, isn't this better?" They could still hear the music from where they stood, but at least it wasn't ear-shattering. The light from a near-full moon lit up the countryside, competing with the bright flashing lights ringing the portable stage.

Peyton stared up at the star-littered sky. "It is nice. Thanks for rescuing me."

Nicholas placed her shoes on the grass, then nuzzled her ear. "You owe me."

She smiled. "The only thing I owe you is a dance."

Nicholas chuckled. "That you do." Bowing from the waist, he held out his hand. "May I please have this dance?" Placing her hand in his outstretched one, Peyton placed her other one on his shoulder. The band had segued into a slower selection. "Where had you disappeared to?" he asked. "We were holding a seat for you at our table until we were forced to give it up to a feisty old lady who gave me the business. She was quite vocal when she said 'there are no reserved chairs here, so give it up, sonny.' Gavin tried not to laugh, but he couldn't hold it in. I walked away, leaving Celia to try and placate her."

"Did she?"

"Thankfully she did, using her best bedside manner."

"I'm sorry I didn't get a chance to eat with you guys, because I went home with Tricia." Peyton told Nicholas about Michaela throwing a hissy fit. "I'd planned to wait for her to fall asleep, but her mother took over."

"You looked very comfortable holding her."

"That's because I usually babysit my little cousins. We have playdates, tea parties, camp out and of course there's movie night. I can't tell you how many times I've watched all of the Disney classics. *Toy Story, Cars, Shrek* and *Finding Nemo* are their favorites. I've seen all of them so many times I even know the dialogue."

"Kids love repetition."

Peyton gave him a direct stare. "Do you have any children?"

Nicholas pressed his mouth to her ear. "No. Do you?"

"No."

"Do you want children?" he asked.

"I don't know." There had been a time when Peyton wanted what every normal woman wanted: a husband, the house in the country, at least two children and the requisite cat or dog.

"Why don't you know?"

"I have to try and figure myself out before I can even consider having a child."

Nicholas wound several strands of moonlit hair around his forefinger. "What's there to figure out? I have to assume you have your health, a career you're passionate about and a loving and supportive extended family."

Peyton closed her eyes. "It's rather complicated and can't be explained in ten words or less."

"I have a leather couch in my office you could use whenever you want to talk." Her husky laugh caressed Nicholas's ear. "I'm serious. I've been told that I'm a very good listener."

"How much do you charge to dispense advice?" she teased.

It was his turn to laugh. "Not much."

"How much is not much, Dr. Cole-Thomas?"

"Let me think about it. Maybe I'll offer you the family discount."

"Wouldn't I have to be family to take advantage of the discount?" she countered.

"Nah! The Thomases and Blackstones are this tight." He demonstrated by crossing his middle finger over the forefinger.

The piece ended but Nicholas continued to hold Peyton, not wanting to believe how good she felt in his arms. He still hadn't figured out what it was about her that made him want to keep her at a distance. The first time Sheldon introduced him to Peyton as Dr. Blackstone he'd found himself staring at her in disbelief.

She looked much too young to be Dr. Blackstone, irrespective of the discipline or specialty. With her fresh-scrubbed face, he'd believed she was still in high school. But it was the timbre of her voice that belied her youthful appearance. It was low, modulated and womanly. And her speech pattern was definitively not Southern. Nicholas thought he was a good judge of differentiating speech patterns because in the U.S. Naval Academy he'd interacted with cadets from all fifty states and a few from Puerto Rico and American Samoa. It wasn't until they'd sat down to dinner that he discovered she'd grown up in upstate New York in a town not far from the Canadian border.

There was only a five-year age difference between them, however, Nicholas felt much older. In his mind she was still a girl when the age on her driver's license verified she was a twenty-something woman. Only when he watched her come down the garden path as Celia's maid of honor did he see her differently. The sophisticated hairstyle, makeup and the revealing gown showing off the curves of her body stirred an emotion he'd repressed for years: desire.

His conversation with Celia at her reception came to mind. *Not every woman you'll meet will be like Arden.* Nicholas knew Celia was right. The women he'd found himself involved with were nothing like his former fiancée who'd returned his ring with a bonded courier and a terse note saying she couldn't handle his situation. And although he'd undergone months of physical rehabilitation and countless sessions with a psychiatrist he still had trust issues when it came to women.

It'd taken a while before he'd taken the psychiatrist's advice to begin dating again. In a six-month period he saw three women, but he refused to sleep with any of them. Two of the three wanted a commitment, and he was honest when he told them they'd chosen the wrong man. And never had he misled or deluded any of them into thinking there would be more than friendship.

Nicholas's hands came up and as he cradled Peyton's face, the moon, hidden behind a cloud, cast an eerie shadow over her features. It was said the moon affects people differently and in that instant he felt caught up in a spell from which there was no escape. The haunted look in her eyes was something he would remember for a long time. The confidence he'd always seen in Peyton had been replaced by a look of fear and vulnerability that caused him to wonder who'd hurt her in the past, and/or maybe continued to hurt her.

*I have to try and figure myself out before I can even consider having a child.* What, he thought, was there for Peyton to figure out? Unlike her he'd figured himself out, because he'd been taught to always have a Plan B, and even go so far as to have a Plan C. If one thing didn't work, then try again, and if necessary another.

He held her jaw firmly when she tried pulling away, lowered his head and brushed his mouth over hers in a slow, gentle caress. The more she struggled the more Nicholas deepened the kiss until she stopped, her lips parting under his. He emitted a groan of triumph when she anchored her arms under his shoulders. His hands moved from her face to her waist, effortlessly picking her up as if she were a small child.

Peyton felt as if someone was holding her underwater where she couldn't breathe or scream. Everything about Nicholas—the unleashed strength in his arms, the strong beating of his heart against her breasts, the taste and feel of his mouth on hers had pulled her into an endless abyss of craving where she'd become the slave of a controlled substance. She'd tried to fight the vaguely sensuous pull every time they'd shared the same space, knowing nothing would ever come of it. Wherein she'd found Nicholas so disturbing he'd regarded her with so much disinterest that it challenged her confidence as a woman. She'd never been self-absorbed or narcissistic, but she also knew she would never be relegated to wallflower status.

Her arms curved around his neck in an attempt to keep her balance. Peyton couldn't stop shaking despite the warmth of the summer night, her nerve endings screaming from the pulsing sensations between her thighs. A delicious shudder of wanting heated her blood until she was on fire. A prickle of awareness shook her from the sensual reverie, and she went still at the same time Nicholas did.

Her heart pounded an erratic rhythm. "Nicholas?" she whispered against his mouth.

Lowering her until her bare feet touched the grass, Nicholas smoothed back her hair. "I know, baby. I heard it, too. Someone just fired a gun." A slight frown appeared between his eyes. "Who would be shooting out here? And for what?" There was another shot, this one closer than the first one.

"There's been a coyote sighting—"

"Let's go." Bending, Nicholas picked up her shoes and forcibly pulled her across the meadow.

Peyton pulled back. "You're going to dislocate my arm!" Without missing a step, Nicholas threw her over his shoulder. The ribbon that kept her hair together slipped to the grass; her hair hung in front of her face, not permitting her to see. She pounded his broad back. The blood was quickly rushing to her head. "Put me down!"

When they were within fifty feet of one of the tents, Nicholas lowered her slowly until her feet touched the ground. Peyton's knees buckled slightly. "Did you enjoy playing Neanderthal?" Peyton whispered, pushing her hair off her face.

Nicholas towered above her like an avenging angel. He pushed his face close to hers until their noses were almost touching. "What if it was a coyote, Peyton? Did you want to pet its head and say nice doggie before it attacked you?"

She scrunched up her nose. "Very funny, Nicholas."

"It wouldn't be funny if you were bitten."

Rather than argue with him, Peyton held out her hand. "Please give me my shoes."

Nicholas ignored her demand, bending down and slipping the heels on her bare feet. Rising, he offered his hand. "Let's go, Cinderella."

"I lost my hair ribbon."

"Well, we're not going to look for it tonight."

Combing her fingers through her hair, Peyton twisted it into a coil, securing the ends and hoping it would stay in place. "How do I look?" she asked Nicholas.

He smiled. "Beautiful. Like a woman who's just been made love to."

She stared at him, complete surprise sweeping over

her features. Peyton never would've expected that type of answer from him. "Is that good or bad?"

It was Nicholas's turn to be shocked. Was she? He shook his head as if to banish the possibility that Peyton was as innocent as she appeared. There were times when she was more girl than woman, and he wondered if her admitting she'd foregone high-school dances and football games was another way of saying she'd shunned boys. Then he recalled their kiss. At first she'd resisted before she finally allowed him to show her how pleasurable kissing could be. Pressing his mouth to her ear, he breathed a kiss there. "Are you a virgin?" he whispered.

Peyton went stiff. "Are you?" she asked.

Nicholas pulled back, frowning. "No."

Hands resting at her hips, eyes flashing outrage, Peyton bared her straight white teeth. "Then you have your answer."

"But I have a reason for asking you that."

"Well, I don't want to know why you would ask me something that personal. Would you've liked it if I'd asked you if I was the first woman you'd ever kissed? I don't think so," she said, answering her own question. "Thank you for the dance *and* the kiss. BTW—I enjoyed both," she flung over her shoulder as she walked into the tent.

Crossing his arms over his chest, Nicholas watched the gentle sway of her hips. A slow smile spread across his face. So, she liked him kissing her as much as he'd enjoyed kissing her. Pushing his hands into the pockets of his slacks he recalled the softness of her lips and the feel of her firm breasts pressed to his chest. However, he'd almost ruined everything because he'd come down with a supreme case of foot-in-mouth, and he made a mental promise it would not happen again. Nicholas decided he would give Peyton time to cool off before apologizing to her. She wasn't going anywhere and neither was he. After all, they were neighbors.

He hadn't taken more than a half-dozen steps when he came face-to-face with a man he'd met at a political fund-raiser last year that had been hosted by Sheldon. Smiling, he extended his hand. "It's nice seeing you again, Judge McGhee."

Franklin McGhee took Nicholas's hand in a firm grip. "How are you, young man? Cole-Thomas, isn't it?"

Nicholas smiled. It was apparent he had an excellent memory. "Yes. I'm well, thank you."

The charismatic widowed judge had garnered more than ninety percent of the female vote in his election bid to retain his seat on the state's Supreme Court. The jurist's life story had become a blueprint for success. He was the only son of a single mother who'd worked two jobs to move her son out of public housing to a rental in a middle-income neighborhood. Franklin earned a full academic scholarship to Harvard as a political-science major. He was recruited to play on the football team, and following graduation was a third-round draft pick in the NFL as a wide receiver. He attended law school during the off season, married his college sweetheart and once he passed the bar went to work for the Southern Poverty Law Center. Franklin was a part of the team that won a landmark unprecedented 1987 anti-discrimination suit. The SPLC sued a hate group rather than individuals in the lynching death of a Mobile, Alabama, teenager.

Franklin motioned for Nicholas to step outside the tent. "Are you planning to sell off any of your stock this year? My daughter's birthday is coming up, so I thought maybe I would surprise her with a horse. She was on the equestrian team in high school and college."

Nicholas studied Franklin when he took off his wire-rimmed glasses and wiped his face with a white handker-chief. It'd been years since he'd played football, yet at the age of fifty-eight his tall lean body was as solid as it had been in his twenties. Those close to the judge still called him Big Red as evidenced by his red-bone complexion and curly red hair now liberally sprinkled with gray.

"I have a one-year-old colt you may be interested in."

"Here comes Rachel now. Please don't mention anything about the horse."

Nicholas's left eyebrow lifted a fraction with the woman's approach. Everything from her short black coiffed hair to the distinctive red soles of the designer shoes silently shouted haute couture. Franklin made the introductions, Nicholas mouthing the appropriate responses. He didn't know why, but he found himself comparing Rachel to Peyton, finding the former physically his type, but underneath her overall perfection he detected a disconcerting insipidness.

"I've been looking all over for you."

Peyton turned when she heard Ryan's voice. "What's wrong?"

His impassive expression revealed nothing. "I have something to tell you. Come with me."

She prayed it wasn't bad news. Her heart beat a staccato rhythm against her ribs when he stopped far enough away from the crowd so he wouldn't have to raise his voice.

Reaching into the pocket of his slacks, he took out his BlackBerry, handing it to Peyton. "One of my professors from Tuskegee just sent me a text. I can't accept his offer, but you can."

Peyton pulled her lower lip between her teeth. She quickly scanned the text. Taking emergency medical leave for a year. Can you cover classes: Large Animal Medicine I & II, Introduction to Veterinary Surgery, Large Animal Surgery?

"I…I don't know," she stammered.

"You have to let me know *now,* Peyton. If you're looking to advance your career, then this is an opportunity you can't afford to pass up."

"I've never considered teaching full-time." She'd always wanted to practice veterinary medicine.

"But, weren't you a graduate teaching assistant?"

Her eyelids fluttered wildly. "Yes." Not only had she been a GTA, but she'd also enjoyed it. Ryan was right. Teaching would add to her experience *and* advance her career. "When would he want me to start?"

"Monday."

"You're kidding?" Ryan shook his head. Peyton listened intently when he explained if she did accept the position she would be offered a generous salary, free faculty housing and fringe benefits to teach fall and spring courses.

"My mother is sending me my cat." She'd said the first thing that popped in her head. What was wrong with her? Why didn't she say if she accepted the teaching position she would miss everyone at the farm, especially all of the children? For a reason she couldn't fathom she was more concerned about Oreo. And Nicholas did not figure into the equation. They weren't involved with each other and it would be another year before he would be able to hire her. Timing couldn't be better.

"I'll take care of your cat."

Peyton vacillated, torn by conflicting emotions. She'd come to think of Blackstone Farms as home and now she would have to leave it. The seconds ticked, becoming a full minute as she struggled to hide her confusion.

*"Yes."* The single word spoke volumes.

She would become a nomad again, traveling southward. This time she would call Alabama home for the next year.

*Part Two*
LOVE FOUND

# Chapter 6

*One year later...*

Leaning back in the leather executive chair in his home office, Nicholas Cole-Thomas stared out the French doors. Summer had dressed Virginia's horse country in emerald lushness. The verdant landscape was reminiscent of plush green carpeting with ribbons of early morning sunlight piercing the canopy of century-old oak trees and recently planted red maple; dappled sunlight reflected off the stark white rails surrounding Cole-Thom Farms. He'd recently purchased an additional one hundred acres, expanding the farm to five hundred forty-three.

He did what he'd done every morning since purchasing the property to set up a horse farm. Nicholas rose at dawn and walked down to the stables to see the extraordinary horses before they were washed, fed and turned out to pasture to graze. He would remain long enough to talk to the stable boy and grooms, and then return to the house where his housekeeper would prepare breakfast for the resident employees living on the farm. He'd had to fire the resident cook because all of the employees were threatening to quit if they'd had to eat another pot roast or beef-stew dinner. Rather than lose his grooms, trainers, stable boy, carpenter, farrier and security personnel, Nicholas gave the man six months' salary and a letter of recommendation. He'd asked Eugenia Jamison to fill in until he hired someone to replace Cookie, breathing an audible sigh of relief when she'd agreed. That was two weeks ago. He'd placed an ad in the local newspaper, but so far no one had called to inquire about the position. The next step was contacting an employment agency.

"Someone from Blackstone Farms just delivered this."

Nicholas swiveled on the chair, staring at the tall, thin, middle-aged woman with cold blue-gray eyes and salt-and-pepper hair she styled in a long braid. She'd assumed the responsibility of keeping his household running smoothly. Even though he'd doubled her salary to cook three meals a day he knew it was just a matter of time before Eugenia would start complaining that she had too much work to do.

When he'd contacted an agency specializing in household help Eugenia had come highly recommended. In her former position she'd worked for an elected official until news surfaced that he'd been involved in a pay-for-sex scheme which eventually destroyed his political career. Upon first glance he thought she could've passed for the model in Grant Wood's *American Gothic* masterpiece because of her dour expression. It was only after she'd worked for him for several months that Eugenia felt comfortable enough to reveal that after more than thirty years in a childless marriage her ex-husband had fallen in love with a woman young enough to be their daughter. The incident had soured her on men, and it was only on a rare occasion he saw her smile.

Rising to stand, Nicholas came around the desk and took the envelope from her outstretched hand. "Thank you, Eugenia." He glanced briefly at the embossed black-and-red logo on the flap, the colors of Blackstone Farms' silks, and then his gaze returned to Eugenia. His eyebrows lifted a fraction; she hadn't moved. "Is there anything else?" he asked.

Eugenia stared at the man who'd caused a minor uproar when he'd outbid one of the wealthiest men in the region for land the latter wanted to expand his horse farm. Nicholas had not only outbid him, but had also set up a stud farm after one of his Thoroughbreds came in first in the International Gold Cup race. Racehorse owners were lining up in droves once Nicholas retired New Freedom and put him out to stud.

It appeared that whatever her boss wanted he was able to secure, and with Sheldon Blackstone as his mentor success was inevitable. She'd found her employer to be the total package: looks, intelligence and wealth. And he was the unqualified prototype for tall, dark and handsome. Nicholas stood several inches above six feet and with his deeply tanned olive complexion, cropped black hair, large dark eyes and delicate features he managed to turn the heads of women of all ages.

"The man who delivered that," she said, pointing to the envelope in Nicholas's hand, "said he was told to wait for your answer."

Reaching for a letter opener, Nicholas slid it under the flap of the envelope. He quickly scanned the engraved invitation, his gaze lingering on the name for the RSVP. She was back! Peyton had returned to Blackstone Farms. His eyes met the housekeeper's. "Tell him yes. I'll be there."

He was invited to a surprise sixtieth birthday celebration for Sheldon Blackstone. Nicholas smiled. There was no way he would miss the opportunity to honor the man who'd taught him everything he knew about the business and reunite with the woman he'd spent the past year thinking about.

The telephone rang and taking several steps Nicholas picked up the receiver when he saw the name on the caller ID. "What's up, Dad?"

"I want to bring you up to date on Ana."

Sitting on the corner of the mahogany and rosewood desk, Nicholas swung a booted foot in a back-and-forth motion. When his father had called him several months ago it was to ask whether he would let his cousin Ana stay at the farm until the people or persons who'd attempted to kill her were apprehended. He hadn't hesitated when he told his father that he would be more than happy to have her live with him, but things changed when his older brother asked a friend who just happened to be a U.S. marshal to step in as her protector.

"*Abuela* called me the other day and told me Ana intends to stay married."

"Damn," Timothy drawled. "I told Mama not to say anything until I called you."

Nicholas snorted. "No one tells Nancy Cole-Thomas what she should or should not do. You must know that by now." His grandmother was not only opinionated, but also dictatorial, possessing an air of entitlement that was palpable. Her mother had raised Nancy and her siblings as if they were Cuban royalty, which led her daughters in particular to believe they were better born and bred than the others in their social circle.

Timothy's soft laugh came through the earpiece. "I was hoping that she would change."

"Keep hoping," Nicholas countered. "I'm surprised to hear that Ana didn't want to annul her marriage to Jacob Jones."

"Ana and Jacob both admit they're in love with each other and have decided to make a go of their marriage."

"A marriage set up by my brother."

Timothy laughed again. "Diego must have known his friend would make a good match for Ana, or he never would've concocted something so archaic. You have to remember that arranged marriages are still the norm in certain cultures."

Nicholas stared at the pattern in the rug covering the floor. The colors of light and dark green and chocolate-brown were repeated with the furnishings and accessories in the masculine home/office: an overhead Tiffany-style hanging fixture, matching floor lamps, a bottle-green leather seating grouping, mahogany tables and chairs and a collection of Chinese-inspired jade vases and figurines lining the fireplace mantelpiece. An antique corner table held family photographs, dating back nearly ninety years when his great-grandfather Samuel Cole married Marguerite Joséfina Isabel Diaz in Havana, Cuba.

Nicholas smiled. "Jacob must have the patience of Job to put up with Ana. I love her dearly, but she *can* test the patience of a saint."

"I saw them briefly before they took off for the Keys, and I must say she's different."

"Different how, Dad?" Nicholas asked.

"She's calmer, almost serene. I don't know if the realization that someone was trying to kill her was the reason, but personally I believe falling in love has changed her. She was even talking about starting a family."

"Damn," Nicholas said, repeating what his father had said when he told him that his grandmother had filled him in on what was happening in Florida. "She *has* changed."

"Marriage will do that to you."

"I wouldn't know anything about that, Dad, because that's something not in my future at this time in my life."

"Are you saying you don't plan to get married?" Timothy asked.

"No. I didn't say that. It's just that I'm not ready to settle down."

"You'll be thirty-four in a couple of months and—"

"I know how old I'll be," Nicholas said, interrupting his father, "but reaching a certain age doesn't require getting married."

"Well, it was different with me, son. When I met your mother I knew she was the one I wanted to spend the rest of my life with."

"That's because you'd met the right woman. So far I haven't met *that* woman."

"That's only because you hang out with those damned horses. If some woman had four legs, a tail and whinnied instead of talked you'd pay her some attention."

Nicholas clamped his teeth together. "Did you call me to give me a family update, or did you call to harass me, Dad? Diego and Celia are married, and that's two out of your three children. And you're a grandfather with a grandson *and* a granddaughter. What else are you missing?"

"It's not me as much as it is your mother, Nicholas. She worries about you."

"Tell her there's nothing to worry about. I'm healthy, solvent and happy as a pig in slop because I'm doing exactly what I want. Convince her to come and visit and that way she can see for herself that I'm okay."

"You tell her when you call her."

Nicolas knew that wasn't going to happen. He'd lost count of the number of times he'd invited her to come and visit with him, but she'd refused because like Celia she was afraid of horses. There came a beat. "What's up with you and Mom?"

"Nothing's wrong. You know how your mother is."

"No, I don't," Nicholas retorted. "You tell me, Dad."

There was another prolonged pause from Timothy. "She had a dust-up with your grandmother again about her cooking skills. When my mother added that she never learned to speak Spanish because she was intellectually challenged it was like two colliding locomotives carrying explosive materials."

"You and Mom have been married more than forty years, and nothing has changed. What's it going to take to end this senseless feud between her and your mother?"

"I don't know, Nicky. I wish I had the answer."

Nicholas knew his father was upset because he'd called him Nicky. It was on a rare occasion that Timothy shortened his children's names. Whereas he called his sister Cee Cee and she in turn called him Nicky, it was always Diego for their older brother.

"Does Ana plan on having something where the entire family can meet Jacob?" he asked, deftly steering the topic of conversation away from his mother and grandmother.

"David said they plan to have a formal New Year's Eve ceremony."

"That's one wedding I don't plan to miss." The last Cole family wedding was held at Cole-Thom Farms when Celia married Gavin Faulkner. He remembered the maid of honor…

Peyton had asked Nicholas whether he would employ

her as an assistant vet to gain experience, because she hadn't wanted to use the Blackstone name to advance her career. Nicholas had asked her to wait until the contract he'd signed with another veterinarian expired. That would happen in another month.

"Are you seeing anyone special?" Timothy asked, breaking into his thoughts.

"No, Dad," he answered truthfully.

There was a woman he'd met at the Blackstone open house and saw several months after Peyton moved to Alabama, but decided to end it because spending time with Rachel was like watching paint dry. She was pretty, feminine, but inexorably dull. There was nothing about her that elicited a modicum of excitement. It was when she'd broached the subject of marriage and children that he told her it was better they stop seeing each other because he was unable to give her what she wanted. His inability to commit had served him well, while hopefully softening his rejection.

"Maybe I should've asked whether you're dating anyone."

"No again, Dad. I was seeing someone, but it didn't work out."

"What was wrong with her, Nicholas?"

There came another pause. "She's dull as hell."

Timothy laughed. "That will do it every time."

Nicholas smiled even though his father couldn't see it. Timothy had admitted to him that he'd married Nichola Bennett because she was feisty and outspoken. What Timothy hadn't realized was that his wife's personality was similar to his mother's, which was why the two women constantly bumped heads.

"If I'm going to get *that* involved with a woman, then she has to be more than just a warm body."

"Good for you, son. Your mother wants you to settle down, but she knows if she mentions it to you it's going to start an undeclared war where I'll end up as collateral damage when I tell her to mind her business."

"I just tell her I don't want to talk about it."

"That works for you because you don't have to sleep next to her every night."

"Do you mind if I suggest something, Dad?" Nicholas asked.

"Sure."

"Take a couple of months off and go somewhere exotic for a second honeymoon. You're retired and so is Mom, so there's nothing keeping you guys in the States. Go to Italy, the Greek Isles and stop over in Paris. Stay in the best hotels and let her shop until she drops. I'm willing to bet when you get back she'll be a different person. She'll forget that she still has an unmarried son and an overly critical mother-in-law. You can also use the time to teach her a little Spanish. And I've heard they offer cooking courses in Italy. I'm certain she would like to take part in those especially if they're taught by celebrity chefs."

"That's an incredible idea! We can close up the house and travel for months. And if your mother takes a particular liking to any city, then I'll think about buying vacation property there."

"There you go, Dad. That sounds like a plan."

"Thank you, Nicholas. I'm glad I called you."

Nicholas smiled again. "So am I. Don't forget to call me before you leave."

*"Tan pronto como yo completo nuestro itinerario de viaje que permitiré usted sabe,"* Timothy said in Spanish.

*"Bueno y gracias,"* he replied in the same language. His father had promised to call as soon as he completed his travel itinerary. Nicholas knew he would feel less anx-

ious if he knew where and when his parents were going abroad.

Whenever he spoke Spanish to the stable boy and the grooms it wasn't as if they didn't understand English, because they were bilingual. It was to keep himself fluent with the language he'd been forced to speak whenever he went to visit his great-grandmother. Marguerite-Joséfina, or M.J. as she'd asked to be called, was fluent in English and Spanish, but it was toward the end of her life that she refused to speak English.

He ended the call, feeling somewhat smug that he'd convinced his father to take his mother abroad. Timothy had retired at sixty and spent most of his free time golfing and sailing, while Nichola kept herself busy volunteering for her favorite charities.

Nicholas's gaze shifted to the invitation on his desk. Sheldon's surprise celebration was two weeks away; that meant he didn't have too much time to come up with an appropriate gift for his mentor. He hadn't known why he'd felt drawn to Sheldon until he realized there was something about him that reminded Nicholas of his father. The two men were close in age and were retired businessmen. Even their personalities were similar: soft-spoken, yet no-nonsense.

Reaching for his cell, he tapped Contacts, scrolling through the names under the letter *B*. There were listings for more than half a dozen Blackstones. He tapped Peyton's name, then waited for a break in the connection.

Peyton Blackstone patted the pillow for her cell when she felt it vibrating. Her right hand closed around the phone as she opened one eye. Punching in her password, she stared at the name of the caller, her heart stopping momentarily before starting up again.

"This is Peyton." Her voice came out in a breathless whisper.

"Is this not a good time?" he asked.

There was a pause before she spoke again. "Nicholas?"

"Yes. I can always call back."

She sat up, supporting her back against the pillows, while combing her fingers through the hair falling over her forehead. "No, please don't. I'm sorry, but I'm a little disoriented this morning. I was up all night with a mare that had a difficult foaling. What's up?" she asked around a yawn.

"First of all. Welcome home. And secondly, someone from your farm delivered an invitation to Sheldon's birthday party and—"

"Are you coming?" Peyton interrupted.

"Yes."

Her smile was dazzling. "That's good!"

It was beyond good. Knowing Nicholas planned to attend her cousin's surprise birthday celebration was wonderful—for her. It'd been a while since she'd spent more than thirty minutes with Nicholas. The last time had been at the church in West Palm Beach, Florida, where she and Nicholas became godfather and mother for Celia and Gavin's daughter, Isabel.

That weekend was one she'd wanted to erase from her memory. Anything that could've gone wrong did. She'd driven from Tuskegee to the Montgomery Regional Airport to board a flight to West Palm Beach, Florida, but after a three-hour delay the flight was cancelled because of a mechanical problem, and the next flight wasn't scheduled to leave until the following afternoon; her only alternative was to drive.

More than nine hundred miles and fifteen hours later Peyton pulled into a hotel where she called Celia to let her know she was in Florida, but wouldn't be able to meet her family for Sunday brunch; she called the front desk to schedule a wakeup call, then fell into a deep dreamless sleep. She made it to the church on time, holding Isabel while she and Nicholas repeated their responses making them godparents, then she was back in her car to make the drive back to Tuskegee.

"Peyton, are you still there?"

Nicholas's voice pulled her from her musings. "Yes."

"I'm calling you so I can get an idea of what to give Sheldon. I know he probably has everything he could ever need or want, but I still want to get him something. It's not every day everyone can celebrate the big six-oh."

"You're right about that. Renee, Kelly, Tricia and I are on the planning committee and we hold all of our meetings off the farm. We're having another session tomorrow, and Renee will probably be able to tell me what Sheldon would like that he doesn't have."

"I don't want to buy something someone may be considering," Nicholas said.

"Renee told me she's buying him a new set of golf clubs. Jeremy and Tricia are having a saddle custom-made for him, and Ryan and Kelly are giving him fishing equipment. Between his wife, sons and daughters-in-law that doesn't leave too many choices for the rest of us."

"What about the other folks at the farm?" Nicholas asked her.

"I've overheard some of the men talking about buying him a bottle of one-hundred-year-old scotch, while the women will probably opt for gift cards."

"What about you?"

"Sheldon has a collection of aged scotch, bourbon and whiskey, so I've been on the internet trying to find antiques shops in the area that carry crystal decanters."

"I think I can help you out with that."

"How?" Peyton asked.

"My aunt is an interior designer and she deals directly with antiques dealers. I'm certain she'll be able to find what you'd like."

"Can she find something within a week? If not, then I'll have to look for something else."

"I'm sure she can. I'll call her, then call you back. Parris will scan them, download them to me and I'll forward them to you."

"Don't forward it. Call me and I'll come over to your place to look at them. So far we've managed to keep Sheldon in the dark, but I don't know for how long."

"Isn't there an expression that says the only way two people can keep a secret is if one of them died?"

Peyton laughed softly. "You're right about that. Don't forget to call me," she reminded him.

"I won't. By the way, are you still interested in becoming Cole-Thom's resident vet?"

"Of course." It was the reason why she'd returned to Virginia rather than stay on at Tuskegee. The head of the veterinary school was so impressed with her that he'd arranged for a permanent faculty position.

"Even though Dr. Richardson's contract expires at the end of September I'd like to bring you onboard a little earlier so you can familiarize yourself with the employees and the stock. What day are you free for an orientation?"

"I'm off Tuesday and Wednesday." They were the only days, barring emergencies, she had to herself.

"Tuesday is good for me," Nicholas confirmed. "How's ten o'clock?"

"Ten works for me."

"Are you certain it won't cause a problem with Jeremy if you work for me?"

Peyton shook her head, and then realized Nicholas couldn't see her. "Jeremy and I talked about this before I left for Alabama. Remember, Ryan is the resident veterinarian and I'm his assistant. Blackstone Farms doesn't need two resident vets."

"I'll hire you as long as I don't get flack from Jeremy."

"Trust me, Nicholas. You won't."

"If that's the case, then we'll discuss salary, benefits, housing and perks."

"Can you give me a hint as to what perks you're offering?" she asked. His deep laugh caressed her ear.

"Not yet, because I still have to think of a few."

It was Peyton's turn to laugh. "Are you going to make me an offer I can't refuse?"

"That's my plan. I'll call you as soon as I hear from my aunt."

"Thank you, Nicholas."

"You're welcome, Peyton."

Peyton hung up, adjusted the pillows under her shoulders and closed her eyes. To say she was exhausted was an understatement. She'd monitored the pregnant mare on a daily basis once the foal dropped, settling lower in the dam's belly, predicting it would be another week before foaling. However, it was nearly two weeks before she and Ryan realized that it would become a difficult birth. They'd taken turns sitting up around the clock with Golly Miss Molly. It was after eleven when Peyton told Ryan to go home; she'd planned to assist in the foaling if there were complications; it wasn't until four o'clock that morning when the mare gave birth to a coal-black colt that was the mirror image of his sire, Shah Jahan. If the colt was anything like his father, then there was no doubt he would also become a winning Thoroughbred.

After making certain the colt was breathing, standing on its own, and nursing within the first hour of life and that the dam had bonded with her foal Peyton finally left the stable to return to her room, showered and fell across the bed. Although exhausted, sleep was slow in coming. She was still operating on pure adrenaline after witnessing the foaling. It was something she didn't ever want to get used to.

Rising on an elbow, she peered at the clock on the bedside table. It was after nine-thirty. Normally she was out of bed before seven, but today was the exception. She didn't want to think of the turn her life would've taken if she hadn't gone online at sixteen to research the Blackstone name. Much to her surprise there were Blackstones in Virginia, Tennessee and Ohio. Census records indicated some Blackstones who owned slaves and others that were free people of color. Her father was a descendant of former slaves. Once she'd ascertained that she and the Virginia Blackstones were distant cousins, Sheldon invited her to spend the summer at the farm. It took less than a month for Peyton to change her career choice from nursing to veterinary medicine. And it was during that summer that she'd come to regard Sheldon as her surrogate father and Ryan and Jeremy as her older brothers.

Although she enjoyed working alongside Ryan, Peyton didn't want to spend the next thirty years as an assistant veterinarian. All thoughts of her past faded as she fell asleep; however, the image of Nicholas's face drifted in and out of her dreams.

## Chapter 7

Peyton downshifted as she maneuvered up to the gate-house to Cole-Thom Farms. It had taken less than four hours for Nicholas to contact her with news that his aunt had found a dealer with a collection of fully leaded crystal decanters. She'd been in the stable with Ryan, Golly Miss Molly and her foal when she'd received a text from Nicholas about the decanters.

Leaning out the window, she removed her sunglasses and smiled at the man in the booth as he slid back the window in the air-cooled structure. He reminded her of an aging hippie with his long gray hair and full beard.

"Good afternoon, Mr. Patrick."

Clinton Patrick squinted over the top of a pair of half glasses at the woman behind the wheel in the red pickup truck. "Dr. Blackstone?"

Peyton took off the wide straw hat with the turned-up brim, placing it on the passenger seat. This year she'd begun wearing hats to protect her face from the damaging rays of the intense summer sun. "Yes, it's me."

"Long time no see, Doc."

"It has been a while," she agreed.

"The boss told me to expect you." Clinton punched a button on the console and the electronic gates opened. "Try not to be a stranger," he said as she shifted into gear.

Peyton wanted to tell him she would no longer be a stranger once she became the farm's veterinarian. Although all of the owners took the necessary steps to protect millions of dollars in horseflesh, many took additional measures with state-of-the art electronics and armed security personnel. Nicholas's property was smaller than the others in the region, but the net worth of his stud farm far exceeded several farms in business for generations. Not only did he breed Thoroughbreds and Arabians, but he'd also purchased Lipizzaners and quarter horses.

The trio of chimneys atop the three-story antebellum great house at the end of the live allée came into view as she maneuvered up the incline. A full-height, columned porch wrapping around the front and sides of the spectacular Greek Revival mansion always made Peyton feel as if she'd stepped back in time, because the interiors were as stunning as the expertly manicured, landscaped exterior overflowing with Japanese- and English-styled gardens.

The front door opened, Nicholas walked out onto the porch, and leaned against a column. Her gaze swept over his crisp white shirt with turned-back cuffs, relaxed jeans and boots. She tried to ignore the flutters in the pit of her stomach, while she didn't want to believe she was lusting after another woman's man.

Although she'd been at Tuskegee teaching, Peyton hadn't been that far removed from what had been going on in Virginia's horse country. She and Tricia exchanged emails several times a week, Tricia keeping her posted on her pregnancy and what she called inane chatter. Her cousin's wife had also mailed her copies of the local weekly and Peyton felt her heart sink when seeing photographs of Nicholas with Rachel McGhee and occasionally Judge McGhee. The photographer had snapped a picture of the smiling trio at a fund-raiser. All the gossip about him not being seen with a woman had been debunked because it appeared as if he and Rachel were definitely a couple.

She waved to him through the open window. "Where should I park?"

Pushing off the column, Nicholas walked down the porch and came over to the pickup. His eyes met a pair in smoky-gray in a face tanned a golden-brown by the summer sun. Her complexion was reminiscent of a lush, over-ripe peach. The Peyton he recognized was back. When she'd walked into the church for Isabel's baptism Nicholas hadn't been able to believe she was the same woman with whom he'd been transfixed since seeing her for the first time in her cousin's dining room. Four months ago she'd appeared emaciated. Her eyes were sunken and ringed with dark circles as if she hadn't slept in weeks.

"Leave your truck here. Someone will pull it around the back." He opened the driver's side door, assisting her as she stepped out. "Good afternoon, Professor Blackstone."

Peyton stared up at Nicholas through a fringe of long charcoal-gray lashes. "Good afternoon, Nicholas," she said, smiling. "I'm hardly a professor. Adjunct lecturer would be a more appropriate title."

"Professor, adjunct is nothing more than semantics. You still taught college courses."

He cupped her elbow. "I've missed you."

She lowered her eyes. "I've missed you, too."

Nicholas found himself captivated by the demure gesture. His hand slipped to the small of her back. "Come inside out of the heat." He led her into the house and down a narrow hallway off the expansive entryway. "When did you get back?"

"A couple of weeks ago."

"Didn't the semester end in May?" He'd asked because it was now mid-August.

"Yes, but I drove up to see my parents. I'd only planned to stay a month, but one month became two, and it would've been three if Kelly hadn't called me about Sheldon's birthday. I did call Celia before classes ended and told her I was coming to visit with her before driving to New York to see my parents, but I came down with a cold and I didn't want to get Isabel sick. Spending three months with my folks was therapeutic. The first week I slept around the clock because I hadn't realized how sleep deprived I was, and eating three meals a day helped me regain the weight I'd lost because my mother is a phenomenal cook."

"You were *very* thin the last time I saw you. Were you sick then?"

Peyton glanced down at the floor. "No. I...I was just a little run-down."

Nicholas wanted to believe Peyton when she said she'd been run-down, but it was her hesitation that gave him pause, and because she refused look at him. What, he mused, was she attempting to conceal?

"Cee Cee's coming up for the Labor Day weekend. She's not certain whether Gavin will be able to get off to come with her."

"I haven't spoken to her in a while, but has she said anything to you about going back to work?" Peyton asked.

Nicholas shook his head. "Not yet. I know she mentioned going back when Isabel's six months old but Gavin talked her into waiting a year and going back as an on-call E.R. doctor every other weekend."

"Who's going to watch Isabella when Celia's working?" Peyton asked.

"Gavin will probably watch her whenever he's not working weekends. Otherwise Celia has a neighbor with two young children who's willing to babysit my niece."

Peyton quickened her pace to keep up with Nicholas's longer legs. She was practically running. "Please slow down. Thanks," she said, smiling when he complied. "When I saw the televised footage of Gavin at a news conference covering the capture of one of America's most wanted, I couldn't believe he was an undercover FBI special agent."

Nicholas laughed softly. "He'd fooled a lot of people, including his wife. Cee Cee had no idea that the man she'd hired to be her personal bodyguard was a federal police officer."

"I can't believe he married her while hiding his profession." Peyton knew she sounded accusatory because of her own experience. Reginald had successfully lived a double life until he missed his safety net.

"He couldn't because he was working undercover," Nicholas said in defense of his brother-in-law. He'd discovered who Gavin was, while his sister had been kept in the dark until after her husband completed his assignment. Nicholas's curiosity had gotten the better of him when he called a family member who worked for the CIA to run a background check on Gavin. When Merrick informed him that information on Gavin Faulkner was classified he knew Gavin was probably a special agent for the ATF, DEA or FBI. Once he mentioned the different agencies

Merrick affected a cough when he said FBI. His cousin's husband had answered his question without verbally breaching Gavin's confidentiality.

"Celia mailed me a picture of Isabella, and I can't believe how much she looks like her mother."

Nicholas stopped outside the door to his office. "The Diaz genes are quite evident in every generation."

Peyton gave him a questioning look. "Diaz? Don't you mean Cole?"

He shook his head. "It's Diaz. Every generation someone inherits my great-grandmother's dimples and black hair. It's probably the same with the Blackstones and their gray eyes."

She laughed. "You're right. Every one of Sheldon's children and grandchildren have varying shades of gray eyes, including Jeremy's son." Tricia had given birth to a boy, much to the new mother's relief. After triplets she was fearful of having another multiple birth.

Nicholas stepped aside to let Peyton walk into the office, then followed her, closing the door behind them. He didn't give her time to react when he rested his hands on her shoulders. He took a step, molding his chest to her back. "I didn't just miss you, Peyton. I was also worried about you."

Peyton closed her eyes. The press of Nicholas's body, the scent of his cologne and his deep drawling voice ignited a longing she'd managed to repress for a year. It was only when she went to bed that the images of their brief encounters flooded her brain, keeping her from a restful night's sleep. Her dreams were filled with them dancing, posing for wedding photos and the soul-searching kiss they'd shared in the moonlit meadow.

"What were you worried about?"

His hands slipped down her arms to her waist. "When

you walked into the church for the baptism you appeared more dead than alive. You looked so fragile I thought you were going to drop my niece. You were there, and then you were gone. And when I asked Celia if she'd seen you she told me you had to get back to Tuskegee for a Monday-afternoon class."

"I did have to get back." She turned to face Nicholas. "That was the weekend from hell." Peyton watched Nicholas's expression change before her eyes like a snake shedding its skin when she related the circumstances of her marathon drive from Alabama to Florida, and the return drive.

His eyes burned into her. "Why didn't you call and tell me you couldn't get a flight?"

She returned his steady stare. "There was nothing you could've done, Nicholas."

The lines of tension bracketing his mouth disappeared when he smiled. "That's where you're wrong. My brother would've sent the company jet to pick you up and take you back."

"That's extreme and excessive when you consider the short distance and the cost of jet fuel."

Cradling her face, Nicholas kissed Peyton's forehead. "Wrong again. The pilot's flight plan included picking up family members in New Mexico, Mississippi, Massachusetts, Virginia and Brazil. I'm certain a stop in Alabama wouldn't have put him off course."

A flush darkened her skin further. "I didn't know," she whispered.

His smile grew wider. "Now you know. If there's ever anything you need, and I do mean *anything,* just ask."

Wrapping her arms around his waist, Peyton rested her head on Nicholas's shoulder. "So you're going to become my personal genie. All I have to do is rub you and you'll grant my wish." She rubbed his back over the crisp white shirt.

"Yes."

"How many wishes do I get?"

"As many as you want. I'm the genie that keeps on giving," he teased. He hadn't lied to Peyton. It'd taken a year for him to come to the realization that not only had he missed her, but it was her unabashed innocence that elicited a need to protect her.

"Will the genie want something in return?"

Dipping his head, Nicholas buried his face in her hair. It smelled of rain and wildflowers. It was apparent Peyton had changed—inwardly and outwardly. She was more confident, assertive; she also projected a maturity that hadn't been there a year ago.

"What makes you think I want *something?* Hasn't anyone helped you without asking for something in return?"

"Sure. Sheldon."

"He's family, Peyton. He doesn't count."

Easing back, she stepped away, putting distance between them. "Then I don't know. That's something I'll have to think about."

"Come sit down and look at what my aunt sent me," Nicholas said, deftly steering the conversation to a neutral topic. There was something about this new Peyton that had him feeling a bit out of control, and he'd almost always prided himself on being in control.

Waiting until she was seated in the chair at the computer workstation, he picked up a chair at a small round table in the corner of the office where he occasionally ate breakfast or lunch and sat next to Peyton. Striking a key, the images for eight decanters appeared on the monitor. They were different shapes, one with a handle, a few enameled or engraved, and several made of cut leaded crystal.

A soft gasp escaped her parted lips. "Wow! They are exquisite!"

Leaning closer, Nicholas inhaled the subtle scent of her perfume. The fragrance was as mysterious as its wearer. What, he mused, was there about her that drew him to her like an invisible wire, pulling him closer and closer when he should run in the opposite direction?

She turned her head, their gazes meeting and fusing. Damn! She'd caught him staring at her instead of the computer screen. A beat passed before she glanced away.

"Which one do you want?" he asked.

Peyton focused her attention on the images. "I like all of them."

"Then buy all of them."

Peyton rolled her eyes at him. "Very funny."

Nicholas smiled. "One has to stand out more than the others, and don't worry about the price."

She gave him a long, penetrating stare. "Why not?"

"The price that's listed won't be what you'll have to pay. Now select one."

"Well, if I have to pick one then it would be the ship's decanter." It was fully leaded crystal with a faceted diamond pattern. It was also the most expensive piece.

"Good choice. I'll call my aunt and let her know. I'll be certain to tell her to give you the family discount."

Her features became more animated. "I remember you offering me the family discount before."

"And the offer still stands—because once you're hired you'll officially become a part of the farm family."

Peyton studied the decanter rather than look at Nicholas. If Cole-Thom was an extended family, then it could be said that Blackstone Farms was a small village. Over the years Sheldon had added an onsite church and school in addition to the dining hall and cottages for resident employees. There were a few single men that lived in a dormitory-styled building. During her absence Jeremy had authorized the construction of a fully functioning equine hospital on several acres of vacant land. Having an onsite hospital eliminated transporting the animals to the nearest hospital miles away and the cost of medical treatment.

Not much had changed for Peyton since her return. She still lived in the west wing of the main house, while Sheldon, Renee and their daughter occupied the east wing. Although Sheldon's house was much too large for three people, she couldn't help but feel like an interloper. If she'd been able to secure a position with one of the neighboring farms she would've rented an apartment in Staunton. That was what she'd planned to do once Nicholas hired her, but living and working at Cole-Thom was a requisite for employment.

"Will I be able to utilize the family discount again when I order a birthday gift for my mother?"

An elusive dimple winked in Nicholas's left cheek when he flashed a wide grin, and for several seconds Peyton found it difficult to draw a normal breath. She didn't find Nicholas as good-looking as he was sensual. Everything about him aroused her senses. It was his balanced features and tall, slender body; the haunting scent of his masculine cologne; his soft drawling speech pattern; the uncoiled strength in his arms when they'd danced together at his sister's wedding; and the taste of his champagne-scented breath when he'd brushed a kiss over her mouth to thank her for helping to make Celia's wedding day a special one. She didn't want to think about the kiss in the moonlight, because it was a constant reminder of her sterile love life.

"Not to worry, Peyton. The discount is for perpetuity."

Peyton returned his grin with a dazzling one of her own. Pushing back the chair, she stood, Nicholas rising with her. "That's good to know. Once you let me know the price of the decanter I'll write a check. But, you'll have to let me know who to make it payable to."

Nicholas nodded. "You've solved your dilemma of what to give Sheldon and now I have to think of something to give him."

"May I make a suggestion?" she asked.

His expressive eyebrows lifted a fraction. "Of course."

She pulled her lip between her teeth, wondering how he would react to her suggestion. Either Nicholas would like it, or he would think she'd completely lost her mind. "Give him a foal. Preferably a colt he could use for future breeding." Peyton was nonplussed when he stared at her. His expression was a mask of stone until a hint of a smile tilted the corners of his mouth. Without warning, she found herself in Nicholas's arms, he lifting her off her feet. Instinctually her arms went around his neck when he pressed his forehead to hers. "So, you like my suggestion?"

"Yes. And I'm going to leave it up to you to select the colt."

It was as if someone had flicked on a light switch in a pitch-black room. Nicholas suddenly became aware of where he was and who Peyton was. The room was filled with an emotionally charged silence that was deafening. They were cloistered in his office; she in his embrace, their mouths a breath apart. His gaze lingered on the soft curve of her lower lip. The longer he held her, the more overwhelming the feelings he didn't want to feel escalated. Slowly, deliberately he lowered her until her feet touched the floor.

Peyton blinked as if coming out of a trance. It had taken all of her willpower not to press her mouth to Nicholas's. Never had the urge for her to kiss a man been that strong. Not even with Reginald. The cell phone in the pocket of her jeans vibrated. Each time her phone rang her heart literally jumped into her mouth before she stole a peek at the display. Peyton decided to wait until she was back in the truck before answering the call. She took a backward step, putting space between them.

"I'll look over your stock when I come Tuesday. I'm going to have to get back to check on the foal."

"Colt or mare?"

"Colt. His sire is Shah Jahan, and his dam is Golly Miss Molly."

Nicholas whistled softly. "Talk about extraordinary bloodlines."

Peyton nodded. "He's Shah's mirror image, right down to the marking on his forehead. Now, if he can run as fast as his mother and father, then Blackstone Farms will definitely have another champion Thoroughbred."

Crossing his arms over his chest, Nicholas angled his head. "You race them and I breed them."

"That's what I call a win-win combination. Maybe one day Blackstone Farms will race a horse raised on Cole-Thom Farms," she said, smiling.

"Now you sound like Sheldon."

"That's because I'm a Blackstone."

He wondered why she made it sound as if she were a member of a royal family. But if the truth were told the Virginia Blackstones had become horse-racing royalty. They still were far behind legendary Calumet Farm that had produced eight Kentucky Derby winners, more than any other operation in U.S. racing history, but they were gaining quickly in many of the other major races throughout the country.

"Have you named the little fella?" he asked.

A smile spread across Peyton's face like rays of sunshine. "I was given the honor of naming him."

"What did you come up with?"

"Outlaw."

"Outlaw?" Nicholas repeated.

Her smile faded. "Yes."

"What made you come up with that name?"

Peyton smiled again, bringing Nicholas's raven gaze to linger on her mouth. "I predict he's going steal the purse in every race in which he's entered. I could've named him Thug Life, but I don't think that would've gone over too well with my cousins."

Chuckling under his breath, Nicholas lowered his arms and cupped her elbows, leading her over to the French doors. The scent of colorful hibiscus wafted into the room when he opened the doors. "Naming him Thug Life probably would've made him a suspect for doping."

She frowned. "Doping horses is illegal, and I refuse to break the law."

They stepped out into the bright late-afternoon sunlight. Peyton did not want to talk about the practice of doping horses before or after races. It went against everything she'd been taught.

"That's one of the reasons why I got out of horse racing," Nicholas said, reaching for her hand and tucking it into the bend of his elbow. "When I first set up the farm I'd discovered several of my horses tested positive for dermorphin. And because of this they weren't allowed to race."

Peyton gave him a sidelong glance as they walked

around to the back of the house where someone had parked her truck. She was more than aware of the properties of dermorphin. The performance-enhancing drug made from frog secretion was purported to be forty times more powerful than morphine.

"Did you find out who did the doping?"

"No. That's why I fired everyone except the grooms and stable boys. Sheldon was generous enough to let me use some of his people until I was able to hire new staff."

"Before you finalize my hire, I'd like to go over which drugs, if any, I'll use to medicate your horses."

Nicholas stopped at the red pickup with the Blackstone Farms logo emblazoned on the doors. Releasing Peyton's hand, he opened the driver's side door. "I'm a neophyte in the horse racing, breeding and stud business, so you can say I'm still a work in progress. I know nothing about veterinary medicine. That's why I contracted with Dr. Richardson to take care of my horses. In another month you'll become responsible for the physical and medical care of everything on this property with four legs." He leaned closer. "I want you to know one important fact. Cole-Thom Farms is my wife and the stallions and mares my children. And I intend to pay you very well to take good care of them, and that includes keeping them in peak physical condition. I've invested blood, sweat, tears and a lot of money to make this farm viable, and one thing I don't intend to do is fail. Three of the four horses that tested positive broke down and had to be euthanized. I swore an oath that would never happen again. And if I have to fire everyone, including the veterinarian, then I'll do it again."

Tilting her head, Peyton met his unwavering gaze. "Why are you telling me this when I told you I don't believe in doping horses?"

"I just want to let you know where I'm coming from and that I don't like losing. Not only did I lose three splendid animals, but I also couldn't collect on the insurance policy because a drug was cited as the cause of death."

She knew trainers injected horses with powerful pain-killers; veterinarians reported the overuse of pain medicine not only masked injuries, but put both horse and rider at risk. State racing commissions had become more vigilant after a rash of fatal breakdowns at many racetracks. Officials were examining past performance charts of horses for telltale signs of injury. Pulling up or being transported off the track were certain signs of injuries.

Peyton's cell vibrated again. "I really have to go." She smiled. "Thanks for everything." Nicholas stepped back and she got up into the pickup and closed the door. "I'll talk to you later."

Pushing the start-engine button, she shifted into gear, driving slowly along the gravel path leading back to the farm's entrance. Glancing up in the rearview mirror, she watched Nicholas's image grow smaller and smaller. Words she'd wanted to fling at him tasted like bile in her mouth. Peyton knew if she didn't need the experience to work as a vet on a horse farm she would've told Mr. High and Mighty Nicholas Cole-Thomas just what he could do with his inflated ego.

She'd studied hard, while she'd sacrificed a lot for her career. And for him to imply that she would even consider doping a horse was preposterous. *Cole-Thom Farms is my wife and the stallions and mares my children.* His statement stayed with Peyton as she drove through the gates, leaving the property of one of the most arrogant and insufferable men she'd ever met. Well, it was definitely his business if Nicholas preferred horses to having children of his own. And if the land he'd won in a hotly contested auction was his wife, then she hoped it afforded him with a sense of gratification and well-being.

When they'd danced together at his sister's reception she'd found him likeable and charming. She didn't want to read more into their sharing a kiss during the Blackstone open house. Nicholas was in a festive mood and so was she, while the setting was perfect for romance. She'd hope it would signal the beginning of a friendship where they would spend more time together but the offer to teach took precedence, changing her and her outlook on her future.

# *Chapter 8*

Slowing and pulling off the road, Peyton shifted into Park and retrieved her cell from her pocket. A smile parted Peyton's lips. It wasn't Reginald. Two years after their divorce was finalized her ex had begun calling. He called her every morning at six. After a month the calls decreased to one or two a week. Then they'd stopped and she believed he'd finally given up. Then the calls began again, this time on New Year's Day and with a number she didn't recognize. Each subsequent call was from a different number. It reached a point where she was afraid to answer her phone. He was no longer calling her at six in the morning but at any time of the day.

She felt she was losing control of her life when she developed a fear of answering her phone. Peyton was tempted to change her cell-phone number, then decided not to answer any number she didn't recognize. Two weeks ago he'd called again, and she was thoroughly nauseated by his heavy breathing. Before hanging up she'd threatened that if he didn't stop calling her she was going to report him to the police.

This caller was someone she hadn't heard from in months. Punching a button, she said cheerfully, "Hey, stranger," when she heard the familiar voice.

"Hey, yourself. What are you up to? Don't answer that, Peyton. It's probably horse manure."

"Wrong, Caroline. The stalls are usually mucked out by the time I check on my patients," she teased. "I tried calling your cell a couple of weeks ago, but it just went to voice mail."

"I'm now living in D.C. with my brother and his family. That's only temporary because I found a place in Foggy Bottom. But, I can't move in until the Labor Day weekend."

Peyton's brow creased in confusion. The last time she'd spoken to her former college roommate she was living in the Pacific Northwest. "What's going on with you and Eric?" There was only the sound of breathing coming through the earpiece. "Caroline? Are you still there?"

"I'm here, Peyton. There's no me and Eric. We broke up last year. He waited until New Year's Eve to tell me he wanted a divorce. And before the ink was dry on the divorce papers he got married again. The new Mrs. Eric Meyer definitely meets with his parents' approval."

Peyton didn't want to believe she'd spoken to her friend a number of times over the past six or seven months, and not once had Caroline given any indication her marriage was in trouble. Eric was the only child of a couple whose family had made a fortune in the logging industry. Caroline had been there for Peyton when her short-lived marriage ended and she knew this was the time for her to support Caroline.

"Are you working?" she asked.

"I'm freelancing for several magazines. I write articles about things that interest me, then send them in. So far, I've managed to sell two."

"What are you doing for money?"

"Eric may have blindsided me, but yours truly made him pay. I only agreed to a no-contest quickie divorce if he made it worth my while. After asking around I found a pit bull for an attorney and she managed to get me a seven-figure settlement. And I heard just before I left Portland that Eric was about to become a father. I never told you this, but I…I can't have children."

Peyton's jaw dropped. She'd believed there wasn't anything she and Caroline hadn't shared with each other. "A lot of women can't have children."

There came another swollen silence. "It's a long story, Peyton."

"Please talk to me."

"This is something I can't talk about on the phone."

Peyton knew her friend was in pain and needed someone to lean on, otherwise she wouldn't have called her. "Now that you don't have a nine-to-five, you should come and hang out with me for a couple of weeks."

"I can only spare a week."

"Then come for a week."

Caroline's sigh came through the earpiece. "I was hoping you would say that. I was going to ask you to come to D.C., but it's better that I come and see you. Let me tie up a few things here, pack a bag and I'll see you Sunday."

"I can't wait. By the way, we're giving my cousin a surprise sixtieth birthday celebration in two weeks. I'm on the planning committee, so you can't mention anything about it around Sheldon."

"Are your parents coming?"

"No. Dad's busy putting up several barns before the cold weather sets in."

"What about your mother? I haven't seen her in ages," Caroline said.

Peyton didn't want to go into the dynamics behind her parents' relationship. If her father was working on a construction project he expected his wife to be there whenever he called or returned home unexpectedly. Lena who'd always been a stay-at-home mother had perfected the art of canning fruits and vegetables; she sold her exotic concoctions at farm stands and fairs not only in their small upstate New York town near Plattsburgh but also in neighboring Vermont.

"I've been trying to get my mom to come and stay with me for a few weeks, but she claims this is canning season for seasonal berries." Then it would be corn, squash and other autumnal produce, Peyton mused. Lena refused to stop whatever she was doing to kick back and relax. It was as if canning had become her therapy.

"Tell her I asked about her whenever you speak to her again," Caroline said. "I'm going to hang up and get my things together. I'll call you early tomorrow to let you know when I expect to arrive."

"Does your car have navigation?"

"Yes, it does."

"Blackstone Farms doesn't have a street address, so once you enter the town limits for Staunton, you'll see signs directing you to the various farms."

"I'm really looking forward to seeing you and those beautiful animals you're always talking about."

"And I can't wait to see you again," Peyton countered.

She ended the call, placing the phone on the seat with her hat, and continued home. *Home*. The four-letter word resonated with Peyton; she'd lived so many places over the past ten years she felt like a gypsy. She'd slept in the very feminine-decorated bedroom in her parents' home for seventeen years. Then it was her college dorm room for the next four years. This was followed with six years in an apartment in Saskatchewan, Canada, when she'd enrolled in the Western College of Veterinary Medicine. She'd come back to the States not to New York, but to Massachusetts, much to the disappointment of her parents—her father in particular—to enroll in advanced surgical courses at Tufts University of Veterinary Medicine. Now at twenty-eight she was prepared to move again. This time it would be to a neighboring farm, and Peyton who'd likened herself to a nomad hoped it would be her last move for a while.

She'd once considered opening her own practice, but her interest in equine medicine and large exotic animals was better suited to a horse farm or zoo. Her father had tried to persuade her to move back home when he'd offered to give her the money she'd need to set up a veterinary clinic. She'd softened her rejection, saying she wanted to see if she could make it on her own. Meanwhile, Peyton had no intention of becoming beholden to her father. It would be history repeating itself.

Alphonso Blackstone had offered to marry Lena, who was the minister's daughter, when she'd found herself pregnant with another man's baby, but the selfless act proved futile when his bride miscarried in her first trimester. Her mother had admitted to Peyton that she hadn't been in love with Alphonso when she married him, but only agreed to marry him to protect her family's name. It had to be a perverted sense of gratitude that she'd permitted her husband to dictate every phase of her life. Peyton loved her mother and her father yet refused to allow a man to control her life. Alphonso was kind, gentle and loving yet was prone to mood swings. When she'd suggested he see a doctor because of his erratic behavior he vehemently denied there was anything wrong with him.

She parked the pickup near the garages, leaving the vehicle unlocked and the keys in the ignition.

Instead of heading for the main house, Peyton made her way to Jeremy's office. She tapped on the door, then stuck her head through the opening. "Do you have a few minutes?" she asked.

Jeremy, the younger of Sheldon's two sons, had taken over running the farm since his father's retirement. He'd relocated the farm's official business office from Sheldon's home to the expanded space at the rear of his house. A Stanford University business degree graduate, Jeremy had enlisted in the marines, and once he'd fulfilled his military obligation joined the Drug Enforcement Administration as a special agent. As a member of a Black Ops team he nearly lost his life when an undercover mission went awry. He was discharged from a military hospital, resigned his position with the DEA and came back home to stay.

Flecks of gray shimmered in his cropped black hair; the summer sun had darkened his face to a rich, deep nut-brown. Jeremy had inherited his father's gray eyes, but they were darker, smokier. He smiled, beckoning her closer. "Sure. Come on in."

Peyton walked in and sat down next to the workstation. She didn't feel as close to Jeremy as she did with Ryan. Maybe it had something to do with her spending more time with Ryan. Not only did Jeremy look like Sheldon, but their personalities were similar. She attributed that to their military backgrounds. He wasn't as approachable as his older brother and the trait served him well when his overall responsibility involved the supervision of more than forty-eight employees, protecting a half billion dollars in horseflesh and the upkeep of two thousand acres of land within miles of the lush Shenandoah Valley.

"Next month I'll be working for Cole-Thom Farms. I've accepted the position to become their resident vet," she said in a quiet voice.

A frown furrowed Jeremy's smooth forehead. "You're going to live there." The question was a statement.

She nodded again. "Yes. That's what Nicholas wants."

Leaning back in the chair and crossing his arms over his chest, Jeremy cocked his head. "You know I don't want to lose you, but neither will I do anything to stop you from advancing your career. Ryan says you're good, so I hope Nicholas will realize what he's getting."

"I think he does."

Jeremy glared at her under lowered brows. "Well if he doesn't, then I'll make certain to let him know. I'm going to miss seeing you and I'm also going to leave it up to you to tell the girls you're going away."

Peyton exhaled slowly. She knew Jeremy couldn't stop her from accepting another position but she knew he wasn't thrilled she'd decided to leave the farm for the second time within a year. "I'll be sure to let them know I'm not going that far and I'll still be available for our play dates. After all, I did promise them we're going to camp out one of these nights."

Camping out was turning one of the meeting rooms in the school into a makeshift cabin. Instead of sleeping bags they slept on air mattresses, roasted marshmallows in the fireplace for s'mores, while watching their favorite movies on the flat screen.

She'd become the unofficial babysitter for Jeremy's, Ryan's and Sheldon's children. Sean, Ryan's son from his first marriage, was rapidly approaching twelve and preferred staying with boys within his own age group rather than hang out with his sister and girl cousins.

Rising to his feet, Jeremy came around the desk and gently eased Peyton off the chair. "I meant it when I said I'm going to miss you."

Anchoring her arms under his shoulders, she rested her head on her cousin's chest. Jeremy had teased her when she came to the farm for the first time, declaring she couldn't be a Blackstone because not only wasn't she tall, but Blackstones weren't traditionally blond. When she showed him a photograph of her parents he promptly backtracked, apologized and declared she didn't need a DNA test to prove they were related. Alphonso and Sheldon, third cousins, looked enough alike to have been brothers. Both were tall, with light brown complexions and light gray eyes. It was Lena who'd passed her petite body and ash-blond hair along to her daughter.

Sheldon and Alphonso bonded immediately, both recounting stories they'd heard about their relatives. Peyton had sat, transfixed, when they spoke of people and events going back more than a century, a bit shocked and disappointed that her father had kept this information from her. It was then she realized she hadn't known her father as well as she should have. It'd always been her mother's people with whom she'd had a relationship.

"Why do you make it sound as if I'm moving to Russia? I'm going to be less than a mile away."

Jeremy smiled. "I know I sound a little selfish, but I'm thinking about my girls. They really love you, Peyton."

Pulling back, she stared up at him. "And I adore them."

The now five-year-old identical triplets were bright, inquisitive and loved teasing one another. Tricia, who'd recently given birth to a son, looked forward to enrolling them in pre-K in the coming weeks, declaring they needed the structure day care didn't provide for their precociousness. Elena, Michaela and Lynette would now interact with other young children at the farm day school. This year Sean would attend classes off the property with all of the middle and high school students.

Jeremy kissed her cheek. "I heard that some of the single girls and guys are going to a club in town. Why don't you go with them?"

It was Friday night—date night at the farm, and many of the younger residents usually got together and drove into town to go clubbing. Peyton had gone once since her return, becoming the designated driver when a few had had too much to drink.

"I'd love to, but I'm afraid I'd end up as a party pooper. I'm still exhausted from staying up all night with Golly Miss Molly."

"The colt's magnificent."

She smiled. "Outlaw has all the makings of a champion."

"If he has his father's heart, then we can look forward to racing him in the Derby in another three years."

Shah Jahan's chance for a Derby run was forfeited when he came up lame after winning a qualifying race and Ryan, fearing further injury, decided to withdraw his name. The Thoroughbred was retired, having won every race he'd entered, and was put out to stud. Everyone on the farm was disappointed because Shah had been favored to win the Triple Crown.

"Have you thought of breeding him with a few of Nicholas's mares?"

Jeremy released Peyton. "I leave all that breeding business to you and Ryan. If Renee hadn't computerized the farm's books years ago, I'd really have a problem keeping everything straight."

The farm was truly family-owned and operated. Kelly was the school's head teacher and Tricia its nurse. Tricia's grandfather's wife was responsible for the farm's infirmary and Renee worked with Jeremy as his office manager. Peyton would become the first Blackstone to work off the farm.

She smothered a groan when suddenly a wave of fatigue swept over her. She knew she had to go to bed or fall on her face. "I'm going to turn in now. I'll see you tomorrow at breakfast."

"Aren't you going to dinner?"

"Not tonight. If I'm hungry I'll raid the refrigerator." Renee always made certain to keep the refrigerator well-stocked, because there were nights when she preferred cooking for her family rather than eating in the dining hall. "By the way, I have a friend from college coming to stay with me for a week."

"No problem, Peyton. Give me her name and I'll pass it along to the security people." No one other than permanent residents was permitted access to the property unless they went through security.

Peyton wrote Caroline's name on a pad, then left the way she'd come, walking out the back door. Late-afternoon shadows covered the landscape as the sound of chattering birds hopping from branch to branch competed with the loud buzzing of cicadas. She made her way to Sheldon's home, opening a side entrance to the staircase leading to her wing of the house. Peyton made a mental note to pack up her clothes and personal items. She wanted to be ready whenever Nicholas decided he wanted her to begin working.

Her steps were slow, heavy when she climbed the staircase to her suite of rooms that were as spacious as an apartment. The only thing missing was a kitchen. It had a bedroom with a sitting room and dressing area, a full bath and a living/dining area. She made her way to the bathroom, undressed, leaving her clothes in a wicker hamper; she walked into the shower stall, adjusting the water temperature, and stood there as lukewarm water flowed over her hair and body. It was a full two minutes before she reached for a bath sponge and a bottle of scented body wash, and then went through the ritual of washing and rinsing her body. Removing the elastic band at the end of her braid, she combed her fingers through the tangled strands. Turning her face up to the spray of water from the oversized showerhead, Peyton closed her eyes, luxuriating in the feeling of being rejuvenated. She turned off the water, wrapped her hair in one towel and her body in another. Walking on bare feet, she entered her bedroom and fell across the neatly made bed.

Warm air flowed through the screened-in windows, but she was too relaxed to get up and close them and turn on the air conditioner. It was convenient that each wing in the house was regulated by a separate heating and cooling system; she'd grown up in upstate New York and attending college in Canada had prepared her for extremely cold temperatures. Whereas many of the folks on the farm wore heavy coats whenever the mercury came close to freezing Peyton usually didn't follow suit until it was well below freezing. She loved snow and most winter sports. She also enjoyed swimming in the farm's in-ground pool. That was something else she'd miss when living at Cole-Thom. All thoughts as to her future faded when she sank into the comforting arms of Morpheus.

The next day, Nicholas stood at the French doors, smiling at the antics of several puppies frolicking in the flower bed. He was certain they'd escaped the watchful eye of their vigilant mother. The mixed-breed bitch had wandered onto the farm several months back, limping and obviously pregnant. Dr. Richardson examined her, reporting she was less than a year old. He'd placed her broken hind leg in a cast, and instead of turning her over to an animal shelter, Nicholas decided to keep her around. Horses were sociable animals and when stabled needed to interact with other animals. Some horse farms had goats, others chickens and many more dogs.

The stable personnel named her Ginger because of her reddish coat, and when she went into labor they took turns monitoring what had become a difficult birth. It took hours before she was able to whelp three tiny puppies. The cast hampered Ginger's locomotion, so whenever the puppies wandered away from the stables it would take her some time to come to fetch her rumbustious pups.

The phone on his desk rang, shattering his entrancement with the animals. He recognized the ringtone. The property had three numbers: a general number for the farm; the second was the direct line to the stables; and the third was Nicholas's private line. Walking over he glanced at the caller ID. There wasn't a name, but he did recognize the Miami area code if not the number. He picked up the receiver before the third ring. "Cole-Thom Farms."

"Umm—I'm looking for a Mr. Thomas."

The male voice was unfamiliar. "This is Mr. Thomas."

"I'm calling because of an ad in the newspaper. It says you need a cook."

Nicholas pumped his fist. It was the first and only call about the position. "I do need a cook. Have much experience have you had?"

"Over thirty years. My folks owned a small restaurant in Miami, and when they retired I took it over."

Nicholas sat on a corner of his desk. "Who's running it now?"

"No one. It burned down. I caught static from the insurance company, because they claimed I hadn't upgraded the electricity, so rather than deal with a long fight with them I just walked away."

"What type of food did you serve?"

"Everything. Southern, Caribbean, Italian, Cajun and most of the stuff you'll find in chain restaurants."

Nicholas smiled. "The position calls for you to live on a horse farm."

"That's not a problem. I'm not married."

He wanted to tell the man even if he was married he still would be eligible for the position. More than half the men on the farm were married. A few even had small children. He'd set up housing accommodations for those with families while the single men lived in two connecting buildings with dormitory-style room suites. The cottages were prefab units with furnishings from Ikea. If hired, the cook would have his own apartment adjoining the mess hall.

"When are you available for an interview?" Nicholas asked.

"I'm available now. I've been staying with a cousin in Waynesboro."

Nicholas took a quick glance at his watch. "Can you get here by eleven?"

"No problem."

It took less than three minutes for him to gather pertinent information on the man who'd identified himself as Jackson Hubbard, former owner of Mama's Down Home Cooking in Miami, Florida. By the time Mr. Hubbard arrived Nicholas would know if the farm would have a new resident chef, but only after he called the agency responsible for conducting background checks on anyone without security clearance. He couldn't risk having someone living at the farm with outstanding warrants or a laundry list of felonies.

He'd just hung up with the agency when the telephone rang again. "Cole-Thom Farms," he said in his usual greeting when *Private* appeared on the display.

"Mr. Thomas?"

"Yes, it is."

"I'm Mrs. Bronwyn's social secretary. She asked me to call everyone on her guest list to confirm their attendance for tonight's fund-raiser. You'd indicated you were coming with a guest. Is that correct?"

Nicholas smothered a curse under his breath. How had he forgotten about the fund-raiser? When he'd responded to the invitation months ago he was still seeing Rachel. Asking her to accompany him was something he didn't want to revisit.

"Yes, that is correct." What else could he say? Now he was faced with a quandary. Who could he ask to go with him?

"Thank you, Mr. Thomas. I'll let Mrs. Bronwyn know she should expect you."

Nicholas ended the call, and then ran his hands over his face. He needed a date. And like yesterday. The event was a sit-down affair. If it had been any other event he would've forwarded a generous check with a note of apology, but the charity was one he was particularly close to. It was to renovate the homes of returning veterans to accommodate their physical disabilities. Not only was he an official donor, but he also made it a point to attend the Bronwyns' biannual fund-raiser. There were quite a few servicemen and veterans in the region that had returned from their deployment and were amputees or were confined to wheelchairs.

His gaze shifted to one of the photographs taken at Celia's wedding with him, his sister, brother-in-law and Peyton. He had his arm around Peyton's waist and they were smiling at each other as if sharing a secret or private joke.

Nicholas was more than aware that Peyton was an attractive woman, but it was her natural beauty that had been captured by the photographer's lens. She was ravishing in a shimmering gray silk gown with her hair styled in a loose twist behind her left ear and festooned with pearl and crystal-encrusted pins.

Celia and Gavin had shocked him when they'd announced they were going to marry after what could only be called a whirlwind courtship.

Nicholas had taken an immediate liking to Gavin. The lawman was exactly who his headstrong sister needed to soften her a bit. If he'd taken an instant liking to Gavin, then it was the same with Celia and Peyton. So much so that Celia had asked Peyton to stand in as her maid of honor.

He didn't remember much about that day except that he'd paid an event planner an obscene amount of money to pull everything together in forty-eight hours. He'd invited two neighboring farms as the kickoff to the following weekend's horse country open-house festivities.

He did remember dancing with Celia and Peyton, and probably every woman present that night. He'd danced more than he had in years, drunk more than he had in a very long time and laughed a lot more than he could remember laughing. The wedding had become his calling card and acceptance into the elusive circle of horse-racing society. However, Nicholas wasn't ready to delude himself into believing everyone accepted him. Even now, overt resentment still lingered. It'd begun with him outbidding the owner of Thornton Farms for the parcel of land he'd wanted to expand his property.

Nicholas had been called brash, an upstart when one of his Thoroughbreds came in first in the International Gold Cup race. Instead of continuing to race the colt, he retired New Freedom and put him out to stud. The resentment exacerbated even after he'd exhausted most of his personal wealth to purchase four pure-breed Arabians, several Lipizzaner and quarter horses. Instead of racing he'd become a breeder, and the payoff surpassed anything he could've imagined.

Nicholas pulled his gaze away from the photographs, knowing what he was about to do would no doubt impact his relationship with his incoming resident veterinarian. Reaching for his cell, he scrolled through the directory for Peyton's number. He was taken aback when she answered. Why hadn't he paid attention to her dulcet voice before? It was soft, melodious and husky enough to be identified as sexy.

"How are you?" he asked.

"I'm well. How are you?" she asked.

Nicholas knew he had to get right to the point. "I have a dilemma." He told Peyton about confirming his attendance at the fund-raiser, but had neglected to ask someone to attend with him. "I know this is very short notice, but will you go with me? If you need something to wear or you want to get your hair done, I'll pay for it."

His request was met with silence. A long, suffering silence that had him clenching his jaw in frustration. It wasn't as if he could open a little black book and select a name from the women in his past. And if the truth were known there weren't that many women in his past. He'd had a couple of what he'd called flings—one or two dates before calling it quits. Nicholas had also had a couple of relationships lasting more than two years. Then, there was the one in which he knew he'd wanted it to be his last, but fate had not only decided his career choice but also his love life. A head-on collision with an unlicensed driver ended his naval career and any hopes of marriage to the one woman with whom he'd wanted to share his future.

"I don't need you to pay for a dress or for my hair. If I go with you, then you'll owe me, Nicholas."

"I owe you," he repeated.

"Oh, yes, you do," she crooned. "If I need an escort, then I'll expect you to return the favor."

He smiled. "That definitely won't be a problem."

"What type of affair is it?" Peyton asked. "And what time are you picking me up?"

"It's semiformal. Pre-dinner cocktails begin at five. A sit-down dinner at six, with dancing to follow."

"What time are you picking me up, Nicholas?" Peyton repeated.

"Four-thirty."

"Goodbye, Nicholas."

He held the small phone to his ear for several seconds. She'd hung up on him. Nicholas didn't want to analyze her reaction because he had a date.

## Chapter 9

Peyton slipped her cell phone into the back pocket of her jeans. Her eyes met Ryan's when he closed his medical bag, stood up and stared at her. "Is there something wrong, Dr. Blackstone?"

A hint of a smile tilted the corners of his mouth. "Not at all, Dr. Blackstone," he teased.

At forty years of age, Ryan was in the prime of his life. His first wife had divorced him, leaving Ryan to raise his son. Everything changed when Kelly Andrews was hired to run the Blackstone Farms Day School and Ryan fell in love with his four-year-old son's teacher. He and Kelly married and they'd increased their family with a daughter and then another son.

Ryan had no interest in running the farm, so that responsibility fell to Jeremy once their father announced his retirement. Once thing Peyton had noticed about Ryan was that he was grayer than his father who was twenty years his senior.

Peyton closed her own bag. Like doctors making rounds at hospitals, she and Ryan did the same with the horses that were diagnosed with injuries. "Why the Cheshire-cat grin?"

"You're dating your boss even before you begin working for him?"

She rolled her eyes. "It's not a really a date. He's going to a fund-raiser and he needs a dining partner for the event." She moved closer. "What's the matter, Ryan? I thought you liked Nicholas." The light coming through the stable's skylights reflected off his cropped salt-and-pepper head.

"I do. I guess I never thought the two of you would actually hook up."

"We're not hooking up, Ryan. I'm just doing him a favor."

Ryan gently tugged her braid. "Good for you. Now, don't you think you should go and do whatever you ladies do to look gorgeous for your man?"

"He's not *my man.*"

Ryan walked out of the stable. "He will be tonight," he said over his shoulder.

"No he won't," she whispered, staring at his retreating back.

If Ryan hadn't been there Peyton would've asked Nicholas about Rachel. Why wasn't he taking her to the fund-raiser? It was a question she would ask when she saw him again.

Peyton stood on the porch, watching the shiny black Lincoln MKZ's approach. She descended the stairs at the same time Nicholas opened the door and stepped out of the late-model sedan. It was all she could do not to laugh aloud when his jaw dropped. There was no doubt he was reacting to her dress. The only time he'd seen her without her ubiquitous jeans, shirt and boots was at Celia's wedding and the Blackstone open house.

Most women her age had wardrobes that included clothes for work, casual slacks, jeans, shirts, T-shirts and chic dresses and stilettoes. With Peyton it had been either jeans or dressy until she had to augment her wardrobe with several suits, blazers and tailored blouses and slacks when she taught at Tuskegee. The toffee-colored off-the-shoulder silk chiffon sheath dress with a narrow velvet black belt, hugged every curve of her petite body, ending at the knees. The color complemented her tanned skin and sun-bleached hair. A pair of black patent-leather four-inch pumps pulled her winning look together.

Fortunately now she didn't have to leave the farm for a beauty makeover. The head trainer's granddaughter had graduated beauty school and the newly licensed technician didn't have to go very far for clients. Everyone on the farm went to her for haircuts, manicures and pedicures, facials and makeup application. Carrie-Ann Manning had washed and set Peyton's hair on large rollers and styled it in a loose chignon on the nape of her neck. She'd applied brown eyeliner and taupe shadow on her eyelids that made her eyes appear larger, more radiant.

Nicholas moved closer, pressing a kiss to her forehead. "You look incredible." Not only did she look incredible, but she also smelled delicious.

Closing her eyes, Peyton inhaled the masculine cologne that was an aphrodisiac. The scent was as sexy as its wearer. Placing her palm on his chest, she felt the strong, steady beat of his heart over the fabric of his crisp white shirt. Her eyes shifted from his neatly barbered hair to his smooth and shaven jaw.

"Thank you. I'd like to ask you one question before we leave."

Nicholas stared at her under lowered lids. "What is it?"

Her eyes met his. "Why did you ask me to come with you tonight? I thought you were dating Rachel McGhee."

Resting a hand at the small of Peyton's back, Nicholas led her to the passenger side of the car. "Rachel and I are no longer seeing each other."

"When did you break up?"

He stopped. "What's up with the interrogation, Peyton?"

She pressed her lips together. "I'm asking because I don't want a problem with some crazed ex-girlfriend who believes I'm after her man."

Nicholas reached up and held her shoulders. "Is that what happened to you?"

Peyton knew she'd revealed too much when she'd mentioned an ex-girlfriend. "No," she half lied smoothly. With Reginald it hadn't been ex-girlfriends but the man himself. He'd continued to harass her.

"Do I have to concern myself with a crazed ex-boyfriend?" Nicholas asked. There was no expression on his face.

Peyton gave him an easy smile. "Never."

He returned her smile, bringing her gaze to linger on the single dimple. "Now that we've settled our exes, are you ready to leave?"

"Yes."

Bending gracefully, she slid onto the leather seat, staring up at Nicholas before he closed the door. The interior of the car smelled of leather and cologne. Peyton secured her seat belt when he got in behind the wheel. She didn't know why, but it was if she were seeing him for the first time—all of him. She noticed the texture of the coarse hair against his scalp, the rich olive undertones in his sun-browned face, the delicateness of his features—features well suited for a woman and the breadth of his broad shoulders under the custom-made shirt with monogrammed initials on the French cuff. His hands were slender, long-fingered and beautifully formed.

There was only the slip-slap sound of the tires as Nicholas maneuvered along the wide roadway, leading away from Sheldon's house. Reaching into her small evening purse, Peyton pressed a button on the remote device, activating the electronic gates protecting the farm's entrance. They swung open, and she waved to the armed man sitting in the gatehouse, who returned her wave.

Accelerating, Nicholas drove along a county road, passing a number of smaller farms. By the time he crossed the property line for Bronwyn Farms he saw a line of idling cars as dark-suited men checked each vehicle.

One man, carrying a bullhorn, walked ahead of the others. "Ladies and gentlemen, please have your invitations out where I can check them. If you don't have an invitation, then you will not be admitted."

Nicholas turned to Peyton. "Please open the glove box and hand me the invitation."

She complied, and then settled back to watch the slowly passing landscape as the car inched toward the entrance. She stared at the marker documenting T.J. Bronwyn had established Bronwyn Farms in 1922 as a horse breeding and Thoroughbred racing stable. The farm's celebrated racing history included the Hamiltonian, Preakness Stakes and the Belmont Stakes.

By the time they'd passed the security checkpoint, red-jacketed valets were handing out tickets and parking cars. Nicholas got out, reaching for the jacket to his suit. He slipped his arms into the sleeves and came around to assist Peyton. Her heels put her head level with his nose. He was six-two and probably a foot taller than she was. Again he realized Peyton went against his type. His preference for tall women was something that Cole men repeated with every generation. This is not to say there weren't petite women in the family, but they were the exception rather than the norm.

Reaching for Peyton's hand, he held it protectively as they climbed the many steps leading to the restored antebellum mansion. Light blazed from every window in the historic structure. Smiling, he handed the engraved invitation to a woman sitting behind the reception table. She checked off his name on a printout and handed him a place card with his name written in flowing calligraphy.

"Mr. Thomas, I need the name of your guest."

"Dr. Peyton Blackstone," he said, gently squeezing Peyton's fingers.

The receptionist wrote Peyton's name on a place card in the same flowing script. "You and Dr. Blackstone are assigned to table eight." She handed him the cards. "Thank you for supporting a very worthy cause."

Nicholas nodded as he and Peyton walked into the great room where waiters were passing out hot and cold hors d'oeuvres along with flutes of champagne. Prerecorded music provided the backdrop to the soft babble of voices as guests greeted one another with handshakes and kisses.

Veterans dressed in the uniforms of their respective branch of service, leaned on crutches, canes or sat in wheelchairs. Nicholas thought of his own Navy uniforms in garment bags hanging in the back of a closet. After he'd accepted the doctor's ruling that his military career was over his first impulse was to throw away the uniforms. But at the last possible moment he changed his mind once he realized how much he'd sacrificed to become a naval officer.

He spied the very person he'd hoped *not* to see. Rachel stood next to her father, her attention diverted elsewhere. All she had to do was turn to her left and she would see him. Nicholas wasn't concerned about Rachel making a scene, because for her, image was everything. And there was always her father's image. The popular widower state Supreme Court judge was highly regarded not only on but also off the bench.

Reaching for a flute, he handed it to Peyton, and then took one for himself. He touched his flute to hers, his gaze lingering on her sexy mouth. Light from the many chandeliers reflected off the gold in her coiffed hair. "Here's to a worthy cause and a very special evening."

"To a worthy cause," she repeated. Peyton took a sip, then handed him her flute. "I'll be right back."

Nicholas watched Peyton as she approached a soldier in desert fatigues supporting himself with a cane in his left hand, while attempting to balance a plate with the right. She took the plate, holding it while he picked up the fork and fed himself with his free hand. Nicholas didn't know if Peyton knew the man, but there was something about the selfless act he found endearing.

"Are you here by yourself?"

Nicholas drained his flute, and then turned to look at Rachel. There had never been a time when she didn't appear as if she hadn't stepped off the pages of a glossy magazine. Everything about her was perfect, always too perfect. Her short chemically straightened hair was always coiffed, makeup perfect and her clothes the pinnacle of fashion. Rachel was a walking billboard for the one-of-a-kind garments she sold in her upscale boutique. A full-length yellow satin, one-shouldered gown flattered her slender figure and flawless mahogany complexion.

"No."

"Well?" Rachel asked. "Where is she?"

Nicholas gestured to where Peyton stood with a marine. "She's helping out one of the servicemen."

Rachel narrowed her eyes. "Where on earth did you find *that?*"

A shiver of annoyance swept over him with the sarcastic taunt. Rachel had shown Nicholas a side of herself he'd never seen before. It wasn't jealousy, but spitefulness. And it'd been more than two months since they'd stopped seeing each other. "I hope things are well with you." Turning on his heels, Nicholas walked away, struggling not to lose his temper. He set Peyton's flute on the tray of a passing waiter.

Peyton met his eyes as he closed the distance between them. They were bright with excitement. "Nicholas, I want you to meet Jesse Baxter. He grew up on Blackstone Farms, and has only been back a few months. Jesse, this is Nicholas Cole-Thomas."

Leaning heavily on his cane, Jesse shook Nicholas's hand. "My pleasure, sir."

Nicholas shook the proffered hand. A Purple Heart, Silver and Bronze Star were pinned to the Marine Corps uniform blouse. He estimated Jesse to be between thirty and thirty-five. His military-style sandy-brown hair showed flecks of gray, and the lines around his hazel eyes were probably more from squinting in the sun rather than age.

"I'm honored to meet you, Sergeant Baxter."

A flush crept up Jesse's neck and face, obviously embarrassed. "Thank you, sir. I've heard a lot about your Arabians."

Nicholas smiled. His herd of purebred Arabians had

garnered a great deal of attention in the region. "Anytime you want to come and see them, just let me know."

"Thank you, sir," Jesse repeated. A wide smile split his face. "Excuse me, sir. But my folks just got here."

Peyton nodded to Jesse. "I'll see you later."

Nicholas watched him limp away. "How seriously was he wounded?" he asked Peyton.

"His leg was shattered by bomb fragments when a suicide bomber blew himself up days before he was scheduled to leave Afghanistan."

"Did he lose the limb?"

Smiling, Peyton shook her head. "Luckily for him he didn't. The doctors inserted rods and plates to support his leg and ankle. He'll probably always need to use a cane, but that's insignificant when the alternative was becoming an amputee. He's staying at the farm until he can find work. His parents moved to a retirement community in Florida, so he can't live with them."

"If he needs a job, then I'll hire him."

Peyton stared at Nicholas as if he'd suddenly grown a third eye. "Doing what?"

A mysterious smile parted his lips. "That's something I'll have to discuss with Jesse. Everyone's always talking about hiring veterans, so I'm going to step up and do the right thing."

He could use someone like Jesse because if he'd risen to the rank of sergeant in the corps, then he had to have acquired excellent leadership qualities. Nicholas's eyes caught and held Peyton's when she gave him a penetrating stare. "What else do you want to know?" he asked softly.

An attractive flush darkened her cheeks as Peyton dropped her gaze. There was so much she wanted to know about the man who was going to become her employer. "Am I that transparent, or do you have the ability to read minds?"

"Neither," he admitted. "It's just that whenever you appear to be thinking about something you squint."

"I never realized that," she countered.

"That's because you can't see yourself like I do."

"Do we ever see ourselves as we should?" Peyton asked.

"I do," Nicholas stated emphatically. "I know exactly who I am and what I'm willing to do or not do. Now what is it you want to know about me?"

"Do you miss—" Peyton's query died on her tongue when she met the malevolent glare thrown at her by the very woman she'd asked Nicholas about. Rachel was as turned out as a high-fashion model, but the scowl sweeping over her features distorted her beautiful face.

Nicholas turned to see what had distracted Peyton. Putting an arm around her waist, he pulled her closer to his side. Pressing his mouth to her hair, he whispered, "Don't let her get to you."

"I've never fought over a man, Nicholas, and I don't intend to start now. If she decides to cause a scene, then I expect you to handle it. After all, she was *your* boo."

He frowned. "She was never, as you put it, my boo and there definitely won't be a scene. Rachel's too vain for that."

"Even vain people get stupid at times."

"It's not going to happen," Nicholas whispered.

"Just make certain it doesn't," Peyton whispered back.

As an only child she'd been forced to stand up for herself. And she hadn't had to deal with bullying or intimidation from other kids because she'd always been the one to establish the ground rules for friendship or a relationship.

Her outspokenness had come from either her mother's unwillingness or inability to speak up for herself.

"Oh, Nicholas. There you are," called out a middle-aged woman wearing a silk suit in a becoming lilac shade. "They told me at the reception desk you'd arrived."

Nicholas dipped his head and kissed Judith Bronwyn's cheek. "This is one soirée I wouldn't miss." Reaching for Peyton's hand, he eased her to his length. "Judith, I don't know if you've met Peyton Blackstone. Peyton, this is Mrs. Judith Bronwyn, founder and chairperson of the Wounded Warriors foundation."

Judith angled her head, smiling. "There's been a lot of talk about you tonight, Miss Blackstone. A number of the single men have asked about you and I can see why. You're a stunning young woman."

"Did you tell them she's not available?" Nicholas stated emphatically.

Peyton looked at Nicholas, then Mrs. Bronwyn, seeing shock freeze the other woman's features before her lips parted when she expelled an audible gasp. It was obvious Mrs. Bronwyn, like most people in their social circle, had believed Nicholas and Rachel were still a couple.

Judith recovered quickly. She placed a hand over the diamond-and-amethyst necklace resting on her generous bosom. "No, I didn't. But, I'll be sure to let them know she's taken."

Nicholas affected a cold smile that didn't reach his raven-black eyes. "Thank you. It looks as if you have a wonderful turnout," he said smoothly as if the topic of Peyton and the men who'd expressed an interest in her had never come up.

"The committee wanted to hold it at the Adamson House, but they were booked solid for the summer, and we didn't want to host it any later in the year because then we're into the holiday shopping season. So, I agreed to let them hold it here. And instead of our usual one hundred-fifty invitees we had to limit it to eighty. And that number includes our military guests and their family members." She took a quick glance at her watch, prisms of light from an overhead chandelier reflecting off her diamond wedding band. "I'm sorry to dash off, but I have to check with the planner to see how the caterer is doing."

Waiting until their hostess was out of earshot, Peyton rounded on Nicholas. "I don't need you to speak on my availability status," she said between clenched teeth. He smiled the slow sensual smile she usually found so engaging. But right about now she wanted to drive the heel of her stiletto into his instep, causing him untold excruciating pain.

"I only spoke the truth. You're not available *tonight*."

Peyton leaned into him. "That's not what you said, Nicholas. You led Mrs. Bronwyn to believe I'm off the market for any man that may show the slightest interest in me."

"Are you looking for a man?"

"No!" The admission was out before she could censor herself.

Nicholas's hand moved up to the nape of her neck. "If that's the case, then why are you in such a snit?"

She pushed out her lower lip. "I'm not in a snit."

He stared at her mouth. "You shouldn't do that, Peyton."

She blinked. "Do what?"

"Pout. You look as if you're waiting to be kissed."

Peyton bit down on her lower lip so hard it throbbed like a pulse. A rush of heat flooded her face when Nicholas threw back his head and laughed. "What's so damned funny?" she said under her breath.

Pulling her close, Nicholas rested his chin on the top of her head. "You. I was only teasing you."

"I don't like to be teased," Peyton mumbled. Her arms went around his waist inside his jacket. Despite her annoyance she sank into his warmth. His tailored clothing artfully concealed a lean, hard body.

He kissed her forehead. "I'm sorry, baby."

Tilting her head, she tried reading his expression. "Are you really sorry?"

"Very sorry," he said before brushing his mouth over hers. "I'm going to get something from the bar that's a little stronger than champagne. What would you like?"

Peyton's eyebrows flickered. She didn't know if Nicholas kissed her because it was something he'd wanted to do; or had it been to thwart the advances of other men, while sending Rachel a message that he'd moved on. Although she'd never been one for public displays of affection it wasn't what she thought of as a kiss. It had been the same when he'd touched his mouth to hers at Celia and Gavin's wedding. Their sharing a kiss at the open house was something she could not forget.

"I'll have whatever it is you're drinking."

Nicholas took her hand, steering her in the direction of the bar. "Are you sure you'll be able to handle it?"

"Would you ask me that if I were a dude?"

"Point taken, beautiful."

*Please don't tell me he's a sexist!* The realization came at Peyton with the velocity of a fastball. Rather than admit he was wrong Nicholas had taken the high road with an ambiguous response. "Yes or no, Nicholas."

"No, I wouldn't."

She gave him her most beguiling smile. "Thank you for your honesty."

The great room was beginning to fill up with invitees,

and Nicholas had to wend his way around small groups eating, drinking, talking and laughing with abandon. The crowd at the bar was two-deep and when he was finally able to get the attention of a bartender he ordered two tequila shots. Reaching into the pocket of his suit trousers, he placed a bill on the mahogany bar after the man set down two glasses with a clear liquid, another glass with lemon wedges and a small saltshaker.

The bartender nodded and smiled in appreciation. "Thank you, sir."

Nicholas handed Peyton the saltshaker and the glass with the lemons, then picked up the glasses of tequila. They found an empty table in a corner. He set down the drinks and pulled out a chair for her. Under another set of circumstances he would've downed the drink at the bar, but he wasn't certain how Peyton would react after drinking straight tequila.

He touched his glass to hers. *"¡Salud!"*

She smiled, nodded and then moistened her hand between her thumb and forefinger and shook salt on it. She licked the salt, downed the shot and followed the burning in her chest by sucking on the lemon. Peyton was hard pressed not to laugh at the stunned expression on Nicholas's handsome face. "Are you going to drink yours? If not, then I'll drink it."

Nicholas repeated the action. The tequila and the acid from the lemon set the back of his throat afire. He resisted the urge to blow out a breath. What he did do was grimace as his eyes filled with moisture. The tequila had to be 100% blue agave.

"Damn!" The word had slipped out of its own accord.

Covering her face with her hands, Peyton smothered the giggles bubbling up and threatening to escape. The tequila was stronger than anything she'd ever drunk, but there was no way she was going to reveal that to Nicholas. She'd become an expert in hiding her inner emotions.

That was only after she'd embarrassed herself when she couldn't stop retching. She'd been the only one in her class to react violently to the stench of decomposition from the bloated carcass of dead cow. The smell had lingered with her even after she'd showered and washed her hair over and over. Unfortunately she'd been the only female in the class, which had exacerbated her embarrassment.

Reaching out, she rested her hand over Nicholas's. "Are you all right?"

He puffed out his cheeks. "I'll let you know once the burning stops." Peyton removed her hand and stood up. Nicholas rose to his feet. "Where are you going?"

"I'm going to get us something to eat."

He sat back down, crossing one leg over the opposite knee, while watching Peyton as she approached a member of the waitstaff. His gaze lingered on her legs in the heels. The shoes flattered her shapely calves and slender ankles. He smiled. Now he knew why men wanted to meet her. Judith Bronwyn was right. Peyton Blackstone was stunning! Not only was she smart, but also sexy and feisty.

His forehead furrowed in concern, wondering how his male employees would react once they discovered their resident veterinarian was an attractive young woman. There was one thing Nicholas knew he would never tolerate and that was sexual harassment whether from male or female. He stood up when she returned with forks, napkins and chopsticks.

"I ordered sushi, miniature crab cakes and calamari."

Nicholas seated her, and then pulled his chair closer. "You're definitely a keeper."

Peyton smiled. "Are you saying I'm hired?"

"Of course you're hired. You're definitely a keeper when it comes to dating."

"The date isn't over and you're ready to commit to another one?"

Nicholas nodded. He didn't know why but at that moment he felt as if he and Peyton were the only two people in the expansive space. Everything around them appeared to have disappeared—no people, music or incessant chatter. What, he mused, was there about her that made him feel so calm, at peace?

"Weren't you the one that said I will have to reciprocate whenever you need an escort?"

Her lids lowered. "Yes, and that may be sooner rather than later."

"Well, whenever you need me I'll make certain to be available."

The waiter arrived with their order, shattering the sensual spell Peyton had created by their sharing the same space.

## Chapter 10

With the cocktail hour winding down the assembly was ushered into the mansion's ballroom. There were ten round tables with seating for eight, set with china, silver and crystal, on red, white or blue tablecloths. Peyton was pleasantly surprised when she discovered Jesse and his parents were seated at the table to which she and Nicholas had been assigned. Another soldier with his parents also joined them. She chatted comfortably with Jesse's mother and the others at the table, while Nicholas spoke quietly with Jesse.

He'd talked about hiring her and Jesse. Peyton had heard talk that Nicholas was a member of one of the wealthiest African-American families in the country. She'd gone online to research his family, but found very little personal information on him or ColeDiz International, Ltd., the privately held family owned conglomerate. Celia had mentioned that Nicholas had planned on a career in the navy, but was forced to retire because of an accident. Physically he appeared to be healthy, so she wondered how serious could it have been for him to give up his military career.

Conversations faded when Judith Bronwyn tapped a handheld microphone. All eyes were trained on the woman whose unwavering support of servicemen and veterans had begun when her grandson, who'd survived burns over fifty per cent of his body returned home only to die by his own hand. She'd set up the not-for-profit foundation to meet the needs of returning servicemen who'd served in the Middle East.

The foundation contracted with licensed therapists to address the issues of dealing with depression and PTSD. Several contractors donated their time and materials to renovate homes to make them wheelchair accessible and the latest focus was job training leading to employment for returning men and women.

Judith flashed a wide grin. "I would like to thank everyone for coming out tonight. I'd like to get my speech out of the way so everyone can eat in peace. Our foundation would not be possible without your financial support. And events like this would not be possible without the people who volunteer their time and energy to support our servicemen and wounded warriors.

"I've heard some grumbling when we raised the price of the tickets for our biannual fund-raiser. Come now, my friends and neighbors. Nearly everyone here owns at least one horse, and you are more than aware of the cost of feeding a horse for a month. My comeback is if you can feed a horse then you can feed a veteran." Thunderous applause followed her pronouncement. "One of the reasons we decided to hold this event every two years is to give you enough time to save your *spare change*." She paused when there was a chorus of laughter and moans. "Our focus for the next two years will be to hire a vet. I don't have to tell you that no one is better disciplined or has a better work ethic than a serviceman or woman. I see my husband giving me the signal to end this, so again I thank you for your ongoing generosity. Eat, drink up, dance and please get home safely."

Waiters stood at each table, filling water goblets and wineglasses. Salad, entrées of filet mignon, broiled Cornish hens, plank-grilled salmon and lobster tails were prepared to perfection and accompanied by steamed seasonal vegetables.

Peyton leaned into Nicholas. "Is there something wrong with your wine?" She'd purposefully lowered her voice.

He gave her a lingering stare. "What are you trying to do? Become the designated driver?"

Her eyebrows shot up as she affected a look of unadulterated innocence. "Of course not, Nicholas. I just thought you'd be used to doing tequila shots."

"And why would you think that?" he asked.

"What's the expression? Drink like a sailor."

Nicholas shook his head as he tried not to smile. His lips parted, displaying straight, white teeth. "I didn't know you were a comedian as well as a vet."

Her smile matched his. "The expression had to come from somewhere." She jumped slightly when he placed his hand on her knee.

"That's nothing more than a stereotype. By the way, where did you learn to do shots?"

"Sheldon taught me."

"You're kidding?"

Pressing her shoulder to his, Peyton told him that it had become a Blackstone tradition to gather in Sheldon's living room and toast a special occasion with a shot of premium bourbon. "Thankfully there aren't too many special occasions because I'd probably lose a few brain cells."

"Most families have their traditions. The Coles always get together the week between Christmas and New Year's at the family compound in West Palm Beach. Many family weddings are held the last day of the year."

"That's a wonderful tradition. How long has it been going on?" Peyton asked.

"It's close to ninety years. It began when my great-grandfather married my great-grandmother in Havana, Cuba."

"Was she Cuban?" Nicholas nodded as Peyton studied his face, feature by feature. "Do you speak Spanish?"

"Yes."

"I took it in high school and college, but I'm still not fluent."

"That's because you have to speak the language to become fluent," Nicholas said.

"How do you stay fluent?" Peyton asked.

"I speak it with a stable boy and a couple of the grooms. Would you like me to practice with you?"

Peyton's face lit up like a child on Christmas morning. "Yes."

"We'll begin with *estoy contento usted decidio venir conmigo esta noche*."

"That I understand."

Nicholas winked at her. "What did I say?"

"You're happy I came with you tonight."

He narrowed his eyes at her. "Are you certain you're not fluent?"

"I said I'm not fluent, not that I don't understand the language."

Nicholas wanted to tell Peyton that she was steps ahead

of his mother. Not only didn't Nichola understand or speak the language, but she had declared that she had no interest in learning. He knew it was more to irritate her mother-in-law than anything else.

"If that's the case, then it should be easy to learn to speak it. The trick is to think in the language. Forget about what you've learned about conjugating verbs, because that will trip you up."

"How did you learn?" she asked.

"Whenever we went to visit my grandmother she would speak only Spanish to me and my brother and sister. The minute I knew I was going to see *abuela* something in my head switched over to Spanish." Nicholas rubbed her back in a comforting gesture. "Don't worry. You'll do okay."

Peyton knew becoming bilingual was a plus *if* she decided to open a private practice. She liked being around horses, but she also wanted to treat exotic and domesticated pets. The difference from becoming a DVM and a MD was the many different species. She liked and needed variety.

Dinner concluded with dessert and cordials. Again Peyton and Nicholas declined the liqueur, opting instead for coffee as a DJ began spinning tunes in the great room. Pushing back his chair, Nicholas came to his feet. He assisted Peyton, then cradling her hand in the bend of his elbow he led her from the ballroom, following the others who were there gliding across the floor to the music.

Pulling her to his chest, he swung her around and around in an intricate dance step. "Let me know if you have a curfew?"

Throwing back her head and baring her throat she laughed softly. "It's been a long time since I've had a curfew."

His expressive eyebrows lifted. "And even longer for me."

Peyton closed her eyes, smiling dreamily. "I've really enjoyed myself tonight."

Nicholas felt the same; he'd actually enjoyed spending time with her. Peyton was easy to talk to, and more importantly she didn't bore him. In fact she was full of surprises. He never would've expected her to down a shot of tequila.

"The night is still young," he crooned. The fund-raiser was scheduled to end at ten; if it'd been held at the Adamson House it wouldn't have concluded until midnight. Ten o'clock was much too early to go home, especially on a Saturday night.

Peyton peered up at him through her lashes. "What do you have in mind?"

"I want to meet Outlaw."

She stopped in midstep. "Tonight?"

"Yes, tonight."

A beat passed. "Okay," she agreed.

Nicholas cupped her elbow. "We'll stop at my place because I need to change."

"I'll also have to change," Peyton said. "I don't want to ruin my shoes."

She'd found a kindred spirit in Ryan's wife; she and Kelly loved nothing better than shoe shopping. As a former New York City schoolteacher, Kelly had been the epitome of a Big Apple diva. She'd exchanged her tailored suits, pencil skirts and stilettos for flats, slacks, twin sets, jeans and blouses. But that hadn't kept Kelly from purchasing a new pair of shoes whenever there was a pre-party race or charity event.

Peyton was her partner in crime when she always found a pair she just had to have or couldn't resist. The shoes in her collection varied by fabric, heel height, color, sling back or pump. It was the same with dresses. At no time would she ever proclaim she had nothing to wear.

"Let's go, Nicholas. I can't wait to introduce you to my baby."

Forty-five minutes later, Peyton punched in the code on the door of the stable housing Golly Miss Molly and her foal. She opened the door, walked in and motion lights lit up the stable. A collie-terrier trotted over, sniffing her hand. She reached down and scratched him behind the ears before he returned to his favorite spot near the door.

"Come on in," she whispered to Nicholas. "Miss Molly is at the far end."

Nicholas followed Peyton past stalls of horses with personalized nameplates indicating sex, date of birth, sire and dam. Fresh air filled the ultra-modern structure through ridge roof ventilators and louvered fitments in the gable ends. The stalls were large enough to accommodate a horse that preferred lying down or stretching out to sleep. He'd become accustomed to the smell of hay and manure.

When he'd driven back to his house Peyton had waited on the veranda although he'd invited her in while he changed his clothes, and when they'd arrived at Blackstone Farms he'd waited on Sheldon's front porch, something he'd done many times when conferring with his mentor.

His gaze shifted from the horses to the sway of Peyton's hips in a pair of fitted jeans. Whether wearing a body-hugging dress or jeans, she was blatantly sensual and probably didn't know just how sexy she was.

He stopped at a stall, studying the gray standing at

least sixteen hands high. "I didn't know Blackstone had a Gelderland."

Peyton stopped, turned and retraced her steps. "We use Fritz as a carriage horse for hayrides." She stroked the horse's nose when he nudged her with his head. "I know what you're looking for, big boy, but I don't have any carrots with me."

Nicholas patted Fritz's neck. "He's beautiful."

"That he is. I'm surprised you recognize his breed."

Crossing his arms over a black waffle-weave cotton shirt, Nicholas cocked his head at an angle. "I knew if I was going to get involved in horse breeding, then I had to know the different breeds."

Peyton assumed a similar pose. "What do you know about the Gelderland?"

"Is this a test, Dr. Blackstone?" he asked.

Her teeth flashed whitely in the diffused light. "Yes, it is."

Lowering his arms, he stood a step. They were close enough for Nicholas to feel the whisper of Peyton's breath on his throat. "What do I get if I pass?"

"A gold star. Kelly has some in the schoolhouse."

Nicholas shook his head. "Nah. Stars are for little kids."

"And you're a big kid?" Her voice had dropped an octave.

He loomed over her. "A real big, big kid."

She leaned into him, then at the last possible moment pulled back. "All I'm offering tonight is a gold star."

Clasping his hands behind his back, Nicholas paced back and forth. The first suggestion Sheldon had given him was to learn everything he could about the different breeds of horses. He read countless books, went to horse shows, and auctions and racetracks. He ate, slept and breathed everything equine.

"The Gelderland is usually fifteen and a half to sixteen hands. He has a long and very strong neck." He stopped pacing, staring at Peyton staring back at him. "They have powerful shoulders, a wide, strong back that runs deep through the heart. Should I continue?" She nodded. "Their heads are ram-shaped with rather long ears."

"Where did they originate from?"

"Holland. But Gelderlands ceased to be bred officially in the late '60s."

"Very good," she crooned. "We have a Gelderland mare in one of the other stables. When she comes into heat we plan to breed her with Fritz. Ryan would like to have more carriage horses on the farm."

"She is also gray?"

"No. She's chestnut."

"When can I get my gold star?"

Peyton stared numbly at him. She never would've imagined him sulking. "I'll bring it to you Tuesday."

Nicholas sobered quickly. On Tuesday everything would change between them. He would interview Peyton, give her a tour of his farm, followed by an orientation. Their relationship would change from neighbors to employer and employee.

Lifting one hand, he trailed his fingers along the curve of her jaw. "You can bring the gold star, but come Tuesday I probably won't be able to do this." Nicholas kissed the end of her nose. "And this." He trailed a series of light kisses along her jaw, over the diamond stud in her ear. "And especially this." He kissed her soft mouth, increasing the pressure until her lips parted.

Peyton anchored an arm under Nicholas's shoulder to maintain her balance. Pleasure shot through her like electricity, short-circuiting her senses. Her breath coming in short audible gasps left her light-headed, weak and confused. It took Herculean strength, but she managed to extricate herself before she begged him to make love to her.

Nicholas's head came up when he heard the distinctive sound of someone cocking a firearm. Moving quickly, he shielded Peyton with his body. He didn't want to believe he was staring into the bore of a double-barrel shotgun. "Don't shoot!"

Peering around Nicholas's shoulder, Peyton didn't want to believe the scenario playing out in front of her eyes. "What do you think you're doing, Mr. Ritchie?" she screamed at the man who'd entered the stable without making a sound. "Put that gun away!"

The security guard aimed the barrel of the rifle toward the floor. "I'm…I'm sorry, Miss Blackstone. I didn't know you were in here. I saw the light and I…I thought someone broke in."

Her heart was beating so fast Peyton was certain it could be seen through her T-shirt. "I was just showing Mr. Thomas the horses."

Nicholas glared at the elderly man. "You should know better than to sneak up on someone with a gun. Especially if it's cocked."

Billy Ritchie's head bobbed up and down. "I'm sorry," he apologized for the second time. "It won't happen again." He backed out of the stable, closing the door as quietly as he'd entered.

Peyton let out an audible sigh. She was still trembling. "I never heard him come in."

Pulling her to his chest, Nicholas pressed his mouth to her hair. "I didn't hear him either, but I did recognize the pump of the shotgun."

She closed her eyes. "All he had to do was check the

closed-circuit monitors. And if you try and open the door without disarming the system the alarm can be heard for miles."

Nicholas went completely still. "There're cameras in here?"

Peyton nodded. "There're cameras set up around the perimeter of the property and in all of the stables. They're hard to detect because the technician concealed them in each of the stalls."

"So, someone looking at the footage would see us together?"

Despite the seriousness of the situation, she managed to laugh. "They would, but we weren't doing anything R- or even X-rated. Most of the extracurricular action on this farm takes place in one of the barn's haylofts. Just for fun Jeremy installed a bell that chimes whenever the door is opened to warn those literally rolling around in the hay that they're about to be busted."

It was Nicholas's turn to laugh. "That's enough to give someone heart failure."

"It's mostly teenagers that get caught in the act. And there's usually hell to pay if the girl's father doesn't want her with the boy."

Cradling her face in his hands, he kissed the bridge of her nose. "What's going to happen when your cousins discover I kissed you in the stables?"

Grasping his wrists, she pulled his hands away from her face. "I'm too old for my cousins to be concerned about who I kiss."

Peyton didn't want to talk about her and Nicholas, because there would be no Peyton and Nicholas. She didn't mind going out with him but that's where their relationship would begin and end. He'd stated emphatically that the farm was his wife and the horses his children, which meant he wasn't looking for a wife, while she certainly wasn't looking for a husband. Been there, done that. She'd met men and women who were serial daters; however, it was a trend that never fitted comfortably into her lifestyle. It was probably why she'd married Reginald.

Turning on her heels, she made her way to Golly Miss Molly's stall, unlocking the door using the kick bolt. "Here's the new mama and her baby." Outlaw stood up, nuzzling his mother's belly.

Nicholas stroked the dam's neck. "*¡Qué belleza! Felicitaciones, mamá.* And look at you, little fella," he whispered in English when the foal flicked its ears. "Are you going to be a champion like your daddy?" He stroked the dam's nose, and then closed the self-locking door. "They are beautiful," he said reverently. "You did a good job helping to bring this little guy into the world."

"Thank you," she said as if she were the proud mother.

They left the stable, Peyton punching in the code and arming the security system. The light from a full moon silvering the landscape overshadowed the glow from strategically placed solar streetlights lining the paved roads and footpaths. The short walk to where Nicholas had left his car was accomplished in complete silence.

At that moment Peyton wanted to be alone so she could sort out her jumbled thoughts. She liked Nicholas yet it wasn't the same emotion she'd experienced a year ago when she'd fantasized being in love with him. The realization that he may have been involved with a woman had become a definite wakeup call. And she didn't need to lie on a therapist's couch to know she'd been vulnerable, that she had been looking for someone other than her relatives to lean on, confide in and to protect her.

She hadn't returned home after completing her education, preferring instead to live at the farm. Peyton rationalized she wanted to avoid taking sides in her parents' marriage. Their constant bickering had taken a toll on her emotional well-being and the first summer she spent at Blackstone Farms had given her a glimpse into a family dynamic totally different from everything she'd known. She knew even if she had moved back to Plattsburgh nothing would change unless her mother admitted she was in a toxic relationship.

Her initial attraction to Nicholas was instantaneous. She'd been like an adolescent girl with a crush on the popular high-school jock or the latest teen pop idol. In her head Nicholas had become a replacement for Reginald, a man she'd married and believed would share her life and dreams.

A year later she knew she'd made the right decision not to return home. Living and working on the farm was therapeutic, helping her to achieve a measure of emotional balance, maturity and focus.

A sweep of headlights came into view, and Nicholas gently nudged her off the roadway as the driver slowed, then came to a complete stop. She recognized the driver as Billy Ritchie. "Good night, Mr. Ritchie."

He tugged on the worn bill of his baseball cap. "You have a good night, Miss Blackstone. You, too, Mr. Thomas. And sorry about the gun."

"Are you going to tell Jeremy?" Nicholas asked Peyton once the guard drove off.

"No. He made a mistake."

"A mistake that could've gotten you or me killed."

She walked over to his car, and he fell in step with her. "He would've shot you first."

"That's not funny, Peyton."

"I didn't intend for it to be funny, Nicholas. Mr. Ritchie made a mistake and I doubt if he'll do it again."

"He's too old to be carrying a gun," Nicholas mumbled.

Peyton looked at Nicholas as if she'd never seen him before. "That's age discrimination."

He stood three steps, then turned and walked back to her. "No, it's not. It's practicality. The man has to be over eighty, and if you didn't notice his hands were trembling. Unsteady hands and slow reaction time is like throwing a live grenade after removing the firing pin."

"What do you expect Jeremy to do? Fire him?"

Nicholas shook his head. "No. He just shouldn't be out on patrols with a firearm. He's better suited sitting in the gatehouse or monitoring the closed-circuit station. You can tell me it's none of my business, but if he worked for me I wouldn't allow him to carry a firearm."

"If you say his hands were shaking, then I'll have to let Jeremy know about it." Peyton pulled her lower lip between her teeth. "I just hate snitching."

Putting an arm around her waist, Nicholas dropped a kiss on Peyton's hair. "The code on the street is snitches get stitches. That doesn't apply here or to us. Each farm is an extended family. Our code is that we protect one another."

Opening the door, he waited for her to get into the sedan. Minutes later he sat watching as Peyton opened the door to the side entrance to the two-story house and disappeared inside. Nicholas sat, staring out the windshield, his mind filled with images of the hours he'd spent with her. He'd felt an intrinsic urge to protect her, stepping into the line of fire when Mr. Ritchie could've possibly discharged the shotgun. He didn't want to think of the consequences if that had happened.

Executing a U-turn, he drove back to the main road, exiting the security checkpoint. He recalled what he'd said to Peyton before kissing her. Once she became an employee of Cole-Thom Farms he would consider her off-limits to anything sexual in nature. They would continue to interact socially, but Nicholas knew it could never go beyond friendship.

This had been drummed into his head since he was old enough to understand the dynamics between male and female. His great-grandfather had cheated on his wife with a female employee of his company. The liaison resulted in an illegitimate child that to this day remained the Coles' dirty little secret. It'd taken years for Nicholas's grandmother, aunts and uncles to claim Joshua Kirkland as their brother. The wound had healed but the invisible scars were a blatant reminder that every action has consequences. He didn't want to become physically involved with Peyton, and face the fallout from a breakup. It would be similar to a divorced couple living in the same house.

He shook his head. He'd invested too much time and money in the farm to jeopardize losing her professional services.

## Chapter 11

Peyton waved her arms when she spied Caroline Gordon's brand-new BMW coupe's approach. She got into the car, leaning over and kissing her friend's cheek. "Follow the road to the back of the house. You can park alongside the garages."

She had to admit Caroline looked well. It'd been years since they last saw each other but whenever they reunited it was like time had stood still. She wasn't classically pretty but she also wasn't a plain Jane. Subtly applied makeup and a fashionable hairstyle was enough for her to turn a few heads. Caroline who'd always struggled with her weight looked toned and healthy. There were occasions when she would gain ten to fifteen pounds in the span of a month when she was stressed out. Standing only five-three in her bare feet the weight gain was more noticeable than if she'd been taller. Her chin-length chestnut-brown hair was cut into a flattering style with

an off-centered part framing her round face. The journalist's round light brown eyes and the profusion of freckles
across a pert nose made her appear much younger than
twenty-eight. The two women thought it hilarious they
were still being carded at clubs and restaurants whenever
they ordered alcohol.

Caroline downshifted, maneuvering into the area and
parking next to a pickup. "I can't believe the size of this
place. Once I left the gatehouse I kept driving and driving, wondering when I was going to see the main house."

"The farm is ten thousand acres."

"You know I stink when it comes to mathematical
conversions. What would it be in miles?" Caroline asked.

Peyton smiled. "It's a little over fifteen square miles."

"That's larger than some towns."

"I always think of Blackstone Farms as a village."

Caroline gave her a skeptical glance. "It's more than
a village," she countered.

Opening the door, Peyton got out, reaching for one of
the two bags stored behind the seats. "You'll just have
enough time to unpack because we sit down to eat at
three."

Caroline picked up the remaining bag. "I tried to get
here sooner, but there was an accident on Interstate 81
and it was more than an hour before I was able to get off
and take another route. The GPS must have recalculated
the route four times before I finally got to Staunton."

Carrying the bags, the two women went into the house
and up the staircase to the west wing. Peyton opened the
door to a suite across the hall from hers. "This is where
you'll stay."

Caroline glanced around the space. "Wow, Peyton.
This is a far cry from our dorm room."

"It's a far cry from every dorm I've ever had," she concurred. She set the bag down next to a drop-leaf table. "I'm across the hall. After dinner I'll take you on a tour of the farm."

"Do I have to get dressed up for dinner?"

Peyton shook her head. The first thing she'd learned when introduced to her roommate was that Caroline hated dressing up. Jeans, sweats and oversized T-shirts were de rigueur for the then-aspiring journalist. It was probably one of the many faults her former in-laws found in her. Caroline always believed in keeping it real, and this is why people she'd interviewed felt so comfortable around her.

"We usually don't dress up unless there's a race. Sometimes we hold a pre-race party which is less formal than an after-party if we have a winner. Jeans are the norm around here."

"You're singing my song," Caroline said, smiling. She sobered. "I just thought of something."

Peyton stared at her friend. Whenever Caroline mentioned thinking she knew it had something to do with her coming up with an idea for an article. "What?"

"What if I write a piece about horse farms. I don't have to mention Blackstone Farms by name, not unless I was given permission. Aside from the racing community, regular folks only take notice of horse racing when it comes time for the Triple Crown."

"What would the piece cover?"

Caroline's eyes were shimmering with excitement. "Everything from purchasing land, laying out the farm to the buying and selling of horses. I'd like to interview everyone from the owners to trainers, jockeys and everyone who lives or works on the farm."

"It sounds very ambitious."

"How many people are that familiar with the inner workings of a horse farm?" Caroline asked.

Peyton lifted her shoulders. "Probably not too many. I believe they would be more curious about the practice of doping. Unfortunately the practice isn't just relegated to human athletes."

Combing her hands through her straight, blunt-cut hair, Caroline smiled. "You're right. Is it as pervasive in horse racing as it is in professional sports?"

"It probably is, but because the athlete is an animal most people don't think of it as cheating."

"Maybe I'll write the article on doping but only if you help me with the medical terminology."

Peyton crossed her arms under her breasts. "I'll help only if you promise anonymity. I don't want my name to appear anywhere in the article."

"I give you my word that your name will not be anywhere in the article. I won't even mention Blackstone Farms. That way none of the information will be traced back to you."

"Will you let me read what you've written before you submit it?"

Caroline nodded, smiling. "Of course." She glanced at her watch. "I better shower and change my clothes."

"We normally eat in the dining hall on Sunday, but today we're going to eat here. You'll get to meet Sheldon, the man who set up the farm, his wife, Renee, and their daughter, Virginia, who's quite the chatterbox. So, don't be surprised if she asks you a lot of questions. Sheldon says she's a Chatty Cathy doll, while Renee says she's a wannabe Barbara Walters."

Caroline laughed. "She sounds adorable."

"I may sound biased but all of my cousins are adorable." The statement was out before Peyton could censor herself when she remembered Caroline saying she couldn't have children. "I'm sorry, I forgot you can't have—"

"Don't you dare apologize," Caroline snapped angrily. "I refuse to become a participant in my own pity party."

Peyton closed the distance between them and threw her arms around her friend's neck. "I swore off pity parties when I got rid of that bum."

Pulling back, Caroline stared at Peyton. Her former college roommate and maid of honor looked beautiful. Her sun-bleached hair was the perfect foil for her golden-brown complexion. "Do you still hear from the bum?"

Peyton closed her eyes. "I'll tell you about him later." She dropped her arms. "I have to shower and change, too. I left a supply of beauty and personal products in the table in the bathroom. If you need anything you'll know where to find me."

At exactly three o'clock, Peyton and Caroline walked down the staircase to the first floor. Raised voices and laughter drifted from the direction of the living room. Peyton recognized Jeremy's voice and Tricia's laughter. She entered the living room, her heart skipping a beat before it returned to its normal rhythm. All of the men stood up. It was the first time since her return that Sheldon had invited Nicholas to eat at the farm. Her gaze met and fused with his. A hint of a smile tilted the corners of his mouth as he gave her a barely perceptible nod. He was dressed like the other men in jeans, shirt open at the throat and boots.

"Here she is," Sheldon announced.

Everyone turned to stare at Peyton. She hadn't introduced Caroline to anyone so she assumed he wasn't referring to her friend. Ryan rushed into the room, visibly out of breath.

"Am I too late?"

Now Peyton was really confused. "What's going on?" she asked when Kelly and Ryan walked in without their children.

Tall, powerfully built Sheldon strode forward, arms outstretched. "We're here to congratulate you on becoming Cole-Thom Farm's veterinarian."

She struggled to breathe when Sheldon tightened his hold on her body. It was apparent he was mistaken. Nicholas still had to interview her before he approved her hire. Going on tiptoe, she pressed her mouth to his ear. "Aren't you being a little premature? Nicholas hasn't hired me yet."

Sheldon released her, his silvery gaze going from Peyton to Nicholas. "Is she or is she not your resident vet?"

Nicholas's impassive expression did not change with Sheldon's clipped tone. "Of course she is. There are a few things Peyton and I need to discuss. However, she is the resident vet for Cole-Thom, effective immediately."

Sheldon stared at Peyton. "If the boss says you're hired, then that makes it official." Dipping his head, he kissed her cheek. "I'm so proud of you."

"Thank you," she whispered. Peyton found herself surrounded by her family as they hugged and kissed her.

"You're expected to say something," Ryan called out.

Peyton felt a flush suffuse her face. "First of all I'd like to introduce my college roommate. This is Caroline Gordon. Caroline, these wonderful people are my family, and you already know my new boss," she said, giving him a sugary smile. One by one she made the introductions: Jeremy, Tricia, Kelly and then Nicholas.

Caroline wiggled her fingers. "Hello, Peyton's wonderful family and new boss."

Everyone laughed, as Sheldon offered Caroline his hand. "Welcome. Is this your first time visiting a horse farm?"

"Yes, sir."

He frowned at her under lowered lids. "It's Sheldon. We're all family here. Right, Nicholas?"

The lone dimple deepened in Nicholas's left cheek when he smiled. "You're right."

Renee walked into the room, wiping her hands on a towel. A smile softened her lush mouth, deepening the dimples in her nut-brown cheeks. The men stood up again. She approached Caroline. "I'm Renee. Welcome to Blackstone Farms. Did everyone introduce themselves?"

Caroline nodded. "Yes."

Pressing her palms together, Renee nodded to her husband. "Sheldon, will you please bring out the turkey? Caroline, I hope you're not a vegan or vegetarian because the Blackstones are certifiable carnivores."

Shaking her head and blowing out her cheeks, Caroline drawled, "Do you remember the Wimpy character from the Popeye cartoon? Well, I'm the second coming of Wimpy."

"I hear you," drawled Ryan. "You have to let Peyton take you to Shorty's Diner. They've earned the reputation of making some of the best burgers in the state. I'd eat them every night if I could."

Kelly, sitting on the love seat, looped her arm through her husband's. Light from a chandelier glinted off the gold in her large expressive eyes. Even after giving birth to two children her body was still incredibly slender. Tricia had teased her sister-in-law saying she had a rubber band body. It snapped back as soon as she pushed out her babies. Meanwhile Tricia struggled to lose her pregnancy weight. She announced she would begin dieting once she stopped breast-feeding Carter.

"Now, you know at your age you have to watch your cholesterol," Kelly warned Ryan.

The veterinarian shot her a lethal glare. "What you trying to say, woman?"

Kelly sucked her teeth loudly. "You're forty, mister. And that means you have to start monitoring your health."

Turning his head to hide a grin, Ryan looked at Nicholas. "See what you'll have to go through once you're married?"

Nicholas crossed one leg over the opposite knee. "I think it would be nice to have someone love me like that." Kelly rose slightly to give Tricia a high-five handshake, while Jeremy and Ryan glared at Nicholas.

"Yo, man, Nick. I thought you had my back," Ryan argued.

Nicholas bit back a smile. "I got your back, but your wife is right. You can't eat red meat every night."

Ryan glanced over at Jeremy. "Aren't you going to help me out here, brother?"

Jeremy shook his head. "Now you can't expect me to agree with you when Tricia is a nurse. She watches what I eat like a hawk."

"That's because I want you to live a long time to help me raise your babies," Tricia countered.

Jeremy ran a hand over his cropped hair. "They're either my babies or our children. It's never Tricia's babies."

"By the way, where are the children?" Peyton asked.

"They're with my grandfather and Beatrice," Tricia replied.

Peyton nudged Caroline. "You'll probably get to meet them tomorrow."

* * *

Nicholas stared at Peyton from under lowered lids. There was something about her that mesmerized him. She'd braided her longer hair in a single plait, securing the ends with a red elastic tie that matched the silk blouse she'd paired with body-hugging skinny jeans. His gaze moved lower to her narrow feet in a pair of strappy red sandals. He smiled. The polish on her groomed feet was bloodred. Very sexy, he mused.

When Sheldon called inviting him to dinner, Nicholas had been forthcoming when he told him that he was hiring Peyton. It didn't matter that he hadn't interviewed her. It was her poise and maturity that had sealed the deal. He'd watched her at the fund-raiser and the gentleness with which she stroked the mare and her foal. Both animals were so still, only their nostrils flaring slightly when she whispered something he wasn't able to hear. He'd heard of horse whisperers but had yet to meet one. Nicholas knew she would be perfect for one of his highstrung Arabian stallions.

The expression on her face when Sheldon congratulated her on her new position was one he would never forget. It was one of shock and awe. She had to know he would hire her or she wouldn't have returned to Virginia. Ryan had let it slip that the trustees at Tuskegee had offered her a permanent teaching position but she'd turned it down. In a moment of crazed arrogance Nicholas wanted to believe she'd rejected the opportunity to teach at a prestigious veterinary college because she preferred working at Cole-Thom but then realized he was wrong.

It would've been different if they'd continued to communicate during her absence. The last time he saw her, other than at his niece's baptism, was at her family open house. He'd looked for her at the Harridan open house and when she didn't show up Nicholas assumed she was still angry because he'd questioned her virginity. It was a week later when Sheldon called to confer with him about mating one of his stallions with a mare that he asked about Peyton.

The news that she would be away for a year made it impossible for Nicholas to draw a normal breath. Then he chided himself for not acting on his feelings sooner. Each and every time he sat at Sheldon's table he'd totally ignored her. Although she looked nothing like Arden his initial reaction to her was the same, and never could he have imagined how his relationship with Arden would end.

He'd gone through four rigorous years of study at the U.S. Naval Academy and was assigned submarine duty, yet becoming involved with a little slip of a woman had him running in the opposite direction. He'd healed from all of his physical scars while the emotional scars lingered for far too long.

*You've dealt with a few losers in the past. Especially Arden. So, please don't let Peyton get away.* He didn't know why he could remember Celia's warning as if she'd uttered it seconds before. Earlier that morning he called his brother for advice. It'd been years since he and Diego talked about the women in their lives and Nicholas told Diego everything about Peyton. When he expressed his reluctance to become involved with her because of the unwritten rule that Cole men don't get involved with their female employees his brother suggested he hire Peyton as a contract worker. Diego also teased him, saying there were special occasions when rules don't apply, especially when it involved matters of the heart. Diego had married his personal assistant, and now he and Vivienne were the proud parents of a son whom they named for the architect of the family owned conglomerate.

Nicholas knew he wasn't in love with Peyton, but his feelings for her went deeper than mere friendship. Hiring her was easy. The hard part was convincing her he wasn't as indifferent to her as he appeared.

Sunday dinner took on a festive tone when those sitting at the table in the formal dining room lifted wineglasses to toast Peyton's latest successful endeavor. She smiled at Nicholas over the rim of her glass when he winked at her. Renee had rearranged the seating where he sat opposite her instead of next to her.

Caroline was included in the conversations when she revealed her journalism background. "I worked as a crime beat and investigative reporter for a Portland daily." She fielded questions about some of the cases she'd covered, many of them connected with drugs and prostitution.

Peyton closed her eyes when Caroline mentioned prostitution. She still found it hard to wrap her head around the realization that Reginald had been arrested for solicitation. She doubted whether it had been his first time and shuddered to think of the times when he'd come home to sleep with her after engaging in sex with a woman who'd had an infinite number of sexual partners.

She exhaled an inaudible sigh when the topic of conversation segued to movies and then food.

Ryan patted his father's shoulder. "Pop, I think you should enroll in culinary school. You've outdone yourself with the turkey."

"It is delicious," Jeremy concurred.

Sheldon inclined his head. "Thank you, but cooking is a hobby for me." He'd made the turkey, while Renee had prepared the side dishes: potato salad, smothered red cabbage and homemade yeast rolls.

Nicholas smiled at Sheldon. "If I'd known you like

cooking that much I would've asked you to fill in for Cookie while I looked for a new cook."

"What was wrong with your old cook?" Peyton asked Nicholas.

"He was stuck in one gear. It was either pot roast or beef stew."

Sheldon shook his head. "He definitely wouldn't have had continued employment at this farm if that's all he could put on the table."

Nicholas nodded. "That's why I had to let him go. It'd reached the point where the employees signed a petition stating either he had to go or they were quitting."

"Damn!" Ryan and Sheldon chorused.

"Have you replaced him?" Jeremy asked.

Everyone listened intently when Nicholas told them about his new cook who was expected to begin midweek. "When he came for an interview I had him prepare a sample meal."

Renee leaned forward. "How was it?"

A flash of humor crossed Nicholas's face. "I'm inviting everyone sitting at this table to come to the farm next Sunday to find out. Please bring the kids."

Slumping back in his chair, Sheldon stared at his protégé. "Something tells me we're really in for a real treat."

Nicholas kissed his fingertips. "He's *magnífico!*"

"I'm not saying we're going to let our cook go, but maybe he could use a little shakeup," Jeremy drawled. "After I sample what your man is cooking I just may offer to pay him twice what he's making to work for me." A series of gasps followed his statement.

The smile parting Nicholas's lips did not reach his eyes. "That's not going to happen."

Tricia placed her hand on her husband's arm. "What's wrong with you?" she whispered.

Jeremy gave Nicholas a long, penetrating stare. "If Nicholas can take our vet, then why can't I take his cook?"

Sheldon smothered a curse under his breath. "Come on, Jeremy."

Jeremy held up a hand. "Please stay out of this, Pop. This is between Nicholas and me."

"No, it's not," Peyton said. "This is between me and Jeremy." Sudden anger darkened her eyes. She didn't know what Jeremy was up to but she intended to end it before it escalated further and she would be forced to choose sides. "Nicholas never asked me to work for him. I approached him and every other horse-farm owner in the county to ask if they would hire me, because I don't want to rely on my name to advance my career. Nicholas was the only one who was receptive, but I had to wait a year because he had a contract with another vet."

"A Blackstone is a Blackstone and you can't change that," Jeremy argued, engaging in what could only be a stare down with Nicholas.

Nicholas ran a forefinger over his left eyebrow. "I can understand you being a little possessive when it comes to Peyton. I'm sure I'll be the same when she comes on-board. But this is not about me going behind your back to take your employees. I say that because I'm about to hire someone who grew up on your farm. I asked Jesse Baxter if he would take over as farm manager."

Everyone laughed when Jeremy let out a plaintive groan. "Who's next, Thomas? My firstborn?"

"Don't you mean your trifecta?" Nicholas taunted. "It takes a good man to make three babies at one time, and an incredible woman to carry them to term."

Jeremy threw up his hands when there was another round of laughter. "Please don't tell me you're trying to hit on my wife." He turned to Sheldon. "Hey, Pop. Where did you find this hustler?"

Pushing back his chair and rising to his feet, Nicholas touched his fingertips to his forehead, mouth and chest while bowing with a flourish. "Nicholas Francisco Cole-Thomas," he rattled off in an affected Spanish accent.

Dishes rattled when Ryan's and Sheldon's palms pounded the table, while Peyton and Kelly couldn't stop the tears rolling down their cheeks. Jeremy stood, circling the table and slapped Nicholas's back.

Nicholas put Jeremy in a headlock. "You're good."

Jeremy nodded. "So are you."

Caroline fixed her gaze on the two men giving each other rough hugs. "They were just joking with each other?"

Kelly blotted her face with her napkin. "Yes."

"What is this? A horse farm or comedy club?" the journalist asked.

Tricia waved at her. "Both. These guys take turns seeing who'll break character first. I'm sorry, Peyton, but the guys warned me not to let you in on their sick joke."

Twisting her mouth, Peyton pointed to Nicholas. "You're going to pay for this."

Nicholas wiggled his fingers. "Woo, I'm so scared."

Sheldon shook his head. "When did my family go off the deep end?"

"But you love us don't you, Pop?" Ryan asked, giving his father a warm smile.

Sheldon looked very much the patriarch. Although he was rapidly approaching sixty he still turned heads with his salt-and-pepper cropped hair, angular face, features verifying his mixed-race heritage, and attractive lines fanning out around large light gray eyes that missed nothing. "More than you could ever imagine."

Caroline leaned against Peyton. "I like your family," she said sotto voce.

Peyton shared a smile with her friend. "So do I," she admitted without a hint of guile.

They were loyal and supportive, and during the year she'd spent in Tuskegee she'd grown to love her extended family as much as she did her parents. She enjoyed teaching but not enough to accept a permanent position. Each day she stayed away from Blackstone Farms was akin to exile. Peyton hadn't formed any close relationships with her peers because she knew she wasn't going to stay.

There were times when she felt she'd been in over her head. The other lecturers and professors had had so much more teaching experience, while she spent hours writing and revising her lectures. The few times she was observed fortunately she'd been at the top of her game. She knew the material and was able to execute the lesson flawlessly, but whenever she returned to the apartment she would ask herself what was she doing? Why was she teaching when she should've been practicing veterinary medicine?

Emotionally she'd begun to spin out of control. She got up before dawn, reviewed her lessons, drove to class, taught and then returned her apartment to do it all over again. Although she called her parents, emailed Tricia and Caroline, Peyton felt something was missing. And she'd forced herself not to think about Nicholas and the last time they were together. The day that had begun with her looking forward to seeing him had ended with a passionate kiss in the moonlight and him questioning her sexual experience. Would it have made a difference to him if she was a virgin?

Whenever she dreamt of Nicholas the dreams were always erotic and she'd wake in a panic, her body shaking and throbbing from long forgotten passions that left her more exhausted than she'd been when she crawled into bed.

There were nights when she lay awake, staring into nothingness and willing herself to sleep. After a while she'd become an insomniac; the sleeplessness was compounded by her inability to eat more than a few forkfuls of food before feeling full. She lost weight she could ill afford to lose, her eyes were sunken and she operated on a nervous energy that made her heart beat a little too quickly. Under another set of circumstances Peyton knew she wouldn't have been able to drive fifteen hours, only stopping to refuel and drink enough water to keep her hydrated.

Nicholas had asked if she was sick and her reply was she was run-down, and if she had been forthcoming then she would've told him she'd been undergoing separation anxiety. She missed him, her cousins and her mother and father. The one time she broke down when talking to her father, he said he was coming to Alabama to get her. It took all of her powers of persuasion to change his mind.

When the semester ended, she didn't return to the farm, but to the little town in upstate New York. She needed to sleep in her childhood bedroom with the crush of tattered stuffed animals in bed with her.

And during the nearly twelve weeks she spent with her parents she had come to know her father better. Peyton recognized his drive to make certain his business survived the ups and downs in an unstable economy. She'd offered to give him the money her grandparents left her but when he let loose with an outburst of expletives she decided not to bring up the subject again. Peyton had been tempted to withdraw the monies from her account and deposit them into his business account but didn't want to start another row that would only end with her packing the rental and driving back to Virginia.

Dinner concluded with coffee and slices of homemade pound cake. Tricia begged off because it was time to feed her four-month-old son. "Watch it, Caroline," the nurse warned in a soft voice, "because Pop's going to offer you a substance that will take off your eyebrows and any hair you have on your upper lip without having to use hot wax."

Sheldon stood up and kissed his daughter-in-law's cheek. "Thanks for reminding me that we're celebrating a special occasion." Peyton met Nicholas's eyes across the table. Now he would get to sample the infamous aged bourbon.

Sheldon returned with a bottle of amber liquid, while Renee put out old-fashioned glasses. "The only thing I'm going to say is drink at your own risk," she said under her breath.

"Are you game?" Peyton asked Caroline.

Caroline flashed a wide smile. "Hit me." All of the Blackstones gave Caroline an incredulous stare. "We do drink more than Starbucks coffee in the Pacific Northwest."

Jeremy wagged his head back and forth. "I pity the fool," he said in his best Mr. T imitation.

Sheldon poured approximately an ounce of bourbon into Caroline's glass, then repeated it with Peyton, Kelly and then Jeremy, Ryan and Nicholas. He poured the same amount into his own glass, then extended it. "Dr. Peyton Blackstone." Everyone tossed back their drinks in one seemingly choreographed motion.

Nicholas covered his mouth, blowing through a fisted hand. "¡*Maldito!* Damn!" he repeated in English.

*"Boo-Yaw!"* Ryan rasped, blowing out his breath.

Caroline's face turned beet-red as she struggled to breathe. "Is this stuff moonshine?"

Throwing back his head, Sheldon laughed loudly. "Not all Southerners drink moonshine. We happen to make some of the world's best bourbon and whisky."

"My bad," Caroline apologized as the intense color in her face faded.

Sheldon held up the bottle. "Would anyone like another round?" His query was met with silence. "Well, this old girl will go back to bed until the next special occasion."

Peyton and Kelly helped Renee clear the table, stacking everything in the kitchen for Claire. Everyone claimed cushioned rockers, love seats and swings on the screened-in back porch. Peyton found herself sharing a love seat with Nicholas. Kicking off her shoes, she pulled her feet under her body and rested her head on his shoulder when Sheldon turned on the flat screen resting on a table, channel surfing until he found one featuring horse racing, muting the sound and turning on the close captions.

She glanced at Caroline who'd rested her bare feet on the rocker's footstool. Her friend had closed her eyes and with the gentle rise and fall of her chest it was obvious she'd fallen asleep.

"Your friend reminds me of you," Nicholas said in Peyton's ear.

"In what way?"

"You're both very outspoken."

Shifting slightly, she stared at him. "Is that a problem?"

"Not at all."

"I'm glad. Otherwise you might have a problem with your newest employee."

Nicholas pressed his mouth to her hair. "It doesn't matter what you say or do, I'm not going to let you go."

# Chapter 12

Clinton Patrick greeted Peyton warmly once she reached the gatehouse, waving her through. She followed the winding road until she reached Cole House, maneuvering around to the rear of the historic structure. Blackstone Farms was four times as large as Cole-Thom but the latter was a picturesque landscape of trees, flowers and gardens similar to grand British ancestral estates with flocks of grazing sheep. Peyton took her time walking from the back of the house and around to the entrance.

The front door opened before she could lift the knocker. A tall, thin, middle-aged woman with a dour expression stood in the doorway. She was the quintessential stereotypical librarian with her white blouse, black shirt and sensible rubber-soled shoes.

"Dr. Blackstone?"

Peyton smiled. "Yes."

"I'm Eugenia Jamison. The housekeeper for Cole

House." Stepping back, she opened the door wider. "Please come with me. I'll let Nicholas know you're here." Peyton followed her through the entryway and into an alcove that doubled as a drawing room.

Sinking down into a comfortable chaise, Peyton glanced around her. The furnishings were reminiscent of the blue-and-white porcelain that China is famous for; the pictorial fabric covered the chaise, throw pillows and a pure white sofa. A low white table positioned in front of the sofa held a silver tea set, silver candlesticks and a crystal vase overflowing with fresh lavender. Everything in the blue-and-white space had been selected with a discerning eye that invited one to come and stay awhile. Her gaze lingered on the pristine white rug, wondering how often it had to be cleaned. Either Nicholas or his housekeeper was obsessive compulsive, because she doubted whether she would ever install a white carpet in her home.

"Peyton."

She popped up from the chaise when she heard the soft drawling voice. Turning, she smiled at Nicholas. She hadn't heard him enter the room. Her eyes met his, and what she saw in his penetrating gaze made the breath catch in her lungs. It was a toss-up between desire and lust.

"Good morning."

He moved closer. "Good morning. How are you?"

Peyton always felt at a disadvantage whenever she stood next to Nicholas wearing flats. A bright smile parted her lips. "Wonderful."

Reaching for her hand, Nicholas held it in his larger one. "I'm going to give you a tour of the farm and introduce you to everyone before we come back to discuss salary and perks."

"Are you always this impulsive? You tell everyone I'm

hired. Now you want to introduce me to the other employees before you outline my responsibilities, salary and/
or perks. What if I'm not willing to accept what you're
offering?"

Nicholas gave her fingers a gentle squeeze. "Do you
really believe I wouldn't pay you what you're worth? I
know the average annual salary for a newly licensed vet
starts around forty-six thousand. A vet with experience
can go as high as ninety thousand. I'm willing to offer you
a salary commensurate with your experience. The perks
will include a bonus, profit sharing and commission. I've
told Dr. Richardson I'm not going to renew his contract,
so it's too late for you to back out now."

*It doesn't matter what you do or say, I'm not going to
let you go.* Nicholas had just paraphrased what he'd said
to her Sunday. Pulling back her shoulders, Peyton lifted
her chin in defiance. "You misunderstand me, Nicholas.
Money is the least of my concerns. You can't make de-
cisions that pertain to me without consulting me first.
And don't forget you made it quite clear that you're lord
and master of this farm, and if you're hiring me as one
of your employees, then as an employee I do have certain
rights. I'm good at what I do, very, very good, so let me
know now if we'll be able to work together without you
becoming a tyrant."

Nicholas looked at Peyton though half-lowered lids.
Under her cool exterior was a volatile fire that was at odds
with her fragile beauty. "I've been called many things, but
never a tyrant. I made it known I've hired you in order to
make your transition as smooth as possible. You told me
I wouldn't get any flack from Jeremy if I brought you on.
Well, I did get some resistance from him. His approach to
running Blackstone Farms is based on a military model,

which lends itself to inflexibility. He didn't want to lose you and he wasn't shy about letting me know it."

"I didn't know." Her voice was barely above a whisper.

"I didn't tell you before because I don't want to come between you and your family."

"That's not going to happen."

Nicholas smiled. "Good."

Peyton's cell phone rang and she chided herself for not turning it off or setting it to vibrate. "I'm ready to meet everyone."

"Aren't you going to answer your phone?"

Reaching into the back pocket of her jeans, she took out the phone and looked at the display. It was a number she didn't recognize. She prayed it wasn't Reginald again. For a reason Peyton wasn't able to fathom, her ex didn't want to accept or understand she wanted nothing to do with him. When, she thought, had he become so neurotic?

"I'll let it go to voice mail." She knew it wasn't her mother because of the ringtone.

Nicholas angled his head. "Do you usually ignore your calls?"

"It depends on who's calling."

Nicholas stared at Peyton as if she were a stranger as something clicked in his mind. Had his arrogance and sense of entitlement supplanted his common sense? He'd never given it a thought. Peyton could possibly be involved with someone. Because she was single and not seeing anyone at her family's farms he'd assumed she was fair game.

After all, she'd been away for a year and during that time she could've met someone. She claimed she was staying with her parents in New York for three months when she could've been living with her lover during that time. Had she not wanted to answer the call because she didn't want him to overhear her conversation? If she did have a boyfriend, then that would thwart his attempt to, as his father described it when he pursued his mother, court Peyton. "Are you ready?" he asked Peyton.

She nodded, smiling. "Yes."

Peyton sat next to Nicholas as he shifted gears in an old pickup. Each time the ancient vehicle lurched the springs under the seat stabbed her bottom. "Don't you think it's time you trade in this truck for a new one?" she said, grimacing when she felt another stabbing pain.

He didn't take his eyes off the road. "What's wrong with it? It runs."

She stared at his distinctive profile. "Right now my backside feels like a pincushion."

Nicholas gave her a quick glance. "I forgot about that. I meant to have that seat replaced."

"Wouldn't it be better if you replaced the truck?"

Pulling down the visor, he removed a pair of sunglasses and put them on when bright sunlight came through the windshield. "The truck was here when I bought this land. I don't know how long it hadn't been driven but the engine turned over the first time I put the key in the ignition. That told me there was still life in it, so I had a mechanic replace the transmission, clutch, the fans, belts and spark plugs. I know it needs some body work so when I have that done I'll also have them replace the seats."

She braced her hand against the glove box. "Please slow down."

Downshifting, Nicholas put the truck in Neutral and applied the emergency brake. "Come sit on me."

Peyton looked at him as if he'd lost his mind. "What?"

He adjusted his seat. "Slide over and straddle my lap."

"I will not!" There was no way she was going to sit on his lap and not be affected by the close, intimate contact.

Releasing the brake, Nicholas shifted into gear once again. "Suit yourself."

"Stop," she practically screamed when the vehicle lurched forward and another spring impaled her. "I'll sit on you."

Somehow she managed to get her right leg over the gearshift and sit facing Nicholas. Even when he'd kissed her she hadn't felt this close to him. Now it wasn't the exposed springs attacking her posterior but the muscles in Nicholas's thighs under hers and the hardness in his groin pressing against her mound.

"This is crazy," she whispered, burying her face between his neck and shoulder. He smelled of aftershave and fresh laundry.

"Are you in pain now?" He'd started up the truck again.

"No." Peyton held on to the seat back. The vehicle was so old it didn't have a headrest or seat belts. "How old is this truck?" Her voice was muffled against the strong column of Nicholas's neck.

"It's a 1964 model."

"If it's a classic, then you should have it fully restored."

Turning his head slightly, Nicholas's mouth brushed her ear. He wanted Peyton to stop talking so he could enjoy the soft press of her body against his. While he was drowning in the scent of her perfumed body, it took Herculean strength to turn off the switch in his head to keep from achieving an erection.

He was certain Peyton could hear his sigh of relief when he maneuvered up to the stable and shut off the engine. "I'll get a blanket to put over the seat before we go back." She slipped off his lap when he opened the driver's-side door. "Put your foot on the running board, then step down."

Peyton followed his instructions and managed to get out of the truck without falling on her face. She groaned under her breath when she realized she should've changed out of her flats and into the boots she always kept in her pickup.

Tilting her head, she looked up at the modern, state-of-the art stable. "How many horses do you have?" she asked when Nicholas cradled her hand, threading their fingers together.

"An even dozen: five Arabians, three Lipizzaners, and four quarter horses. I plan to buy a couple of Thoroughbreds, but I wanted to wait for you to come onboard before I go shopping."

Peyton walked into the stable, finding it spotless. There was no lingering smell of urine or manure. It was apparent once the horses were turned out to pasture the barn was cleaned. The floor was still damp and with the lingering scent of a sanitizer. The doors to the stalls stood open, but as she approached the opposite end of the stable she noticed one was closed.

Her pulse quickened as she came face-to-face with a magnificent gray colt. His ears pricked and he whinnied softly, tossing his magnificent head up and down when he spied Nicholas. The horse was easily recognizable as an Arabian by its very short head and the face's pronounced concavity. Peyton eased her hand from Nicholas's, walked over and touched the colt's muzzle. She smiled. The muzzle was very tapered and covered with exceptionally fine skin.

Turning she noticed Nicholas watching her. "Can I go into the stall?"

He nodded, then stepped forward and opened the door.

The bridle around the horse's neck was tethered to a ring in the stall, but that didn't restrict the colt when he pushed its head against her chest as Peyton continued to run her fingertips along its neck, shoulders and back. She counted seventeen pairs of ribs. Arabs differed from other breeds that have eighteen pair. Continuing with her examination, she checked the foal's teeth, eyes, shoulders, body and hindquarters.

"Has he weaned from his dam?"

Nicholas moved closer. "Yes."

"What's your name, handsome?" Peyton crooned as she continued to rub the neck.

"I named him Nublado. It's Spanish for cloudy."

"That's a wonderful name for a Thoroughbred. But you're not a Thoroughbred, Nublado. You're a beautiful purebred Arab."

Crossing his arms over the light blue chambray shirt, Nicholas stared at the golden shower of hair flowing midway down Peyton's back. He didn't know how she managed to appear so incredibly wanton and innocent at the same time in a pair of jeans, white T-shirt, flats and her hair pulled into a ponytail.

"Do you think Nublado would be an appropriate gift for Sheldon?"

Peyton stepped out of the stall, closing the door behind her. "Had you planned on selling Nublado?" She'd answered his question with one of her own.

"No. I wanted to breed him."

"I think Nublado would be an exceptional gift. I just remembered something."

"What?"

A dreamy expression swept over her features. "Giving a horse as a gift reminds me of a guy who went to veterinary school with me. He was part Kiowa and he said in his culture marriage was usually arranged by gifts of horses to the parents of the girl by the man or his family. A contract is made after the acceptance of gifts, and the husband usually goes to live with the wife's parents."

Nicholas was intrigued by the custom. "What if there is a divorce?"

"The wife would have to get her father's approval to divorce her husband. If daddy said yes, then the bride price is returned."

"What if the husband wanted to divorce his wife?"

"A man could divorce his wife for adultery."

Bracing a hand on the beam separating Nublado's stall from the next one, Nicholas leaned in close to Peyton. He was close, close enough to see the freckles across the bridge of her nose. "It sounds very cut-and-dry. No greedy lawyers draining bank accounts or ugly confrontations played out either in the media or cyberspace."

Peyton placed her hand over his chest. "Are you speaking from experience?"

"No. I've never been married."

"If it's not marriage, then you must not like lawyers."

"Only the unscrupulous ones," Nicholas admitted. "There are too many lawyers in my family for me to have an aversion to them."

"I noticed all the photographs in your office. You must have a very large family."

Nicholas nodded. "I do, and it gets larger every year. There's always a new baby and every couple of years there's a wedding."

"That's where the Blackstones differ. When I went online and did a search of the Blackstone name I came up with less than a dozen. Even though my father and Sheldon are third cousins they didn't know the other existed."

"One of these days I'll tell you about the Cole and Diaz families if you tell me about the Blackstones."

She smiled, nodding. "Okay."

Nicholas studied her face, making love to Peyton with his eyes. He wished he knew what it was about her that made him think of her when least expected. Even when he'd accompanied Rachel to dinner dances, fund-raisers and to her family cookout, in his mind he'd wanted her to be Peyton although their interaction had been minimal. However, that would change now that she would live on the farm.

"Come. I want you to meet the guys responsible for the stable."

He led her outside. Several grooms and stable hands were sitting on folding chairs at a card table playing dominoes. They came to their feet when seeing Nicholas. All of them respectfully removed their hats and caps.

"I would like all of you to meet our resident veterinarian, Dr. Blackstone. She will be living with us." He introduced each of the men who stepped forward and shook Peyton's hand, she telling each she was glad to meet them.

The men appeared to range in age from late teens to early thirties. Peyton found two staring at her a bit longer than was polite, and she assumed there probably weren't that many women on the farm.

After the introductions Nicholas asked one of the grooms for a blanket. "The other men are probably out cutting grass or repairing fencing."

"How many employees do you have?" she asked as they walked to the truck.

"If I count you, Jesse and the new cook, then it's fourteen. The two grooms and one trainer are married, but they don't have any children."

"So, Jesse agreed to manage the farm?"

"Yes," Nicholas replied. "When you and I leave to look for additional livestock I'll need someone here to make certain everything runs smoothly. Jesse went back to Florida with his folks, but he plans to return next week. The new cook is scheduled to report tomorrow."

"Who did the cooking after you let the other one go?"

"Eugenia."

"That poor woman! She has to cook and clean the house, too."

"I know it was a lot to ask of her but thankfully it ends tomorrow." The groom returned with the blanket. Nicholas shook it out and then folded it. "I hope this will do the trick." Opening the passenger-side door, he placed it over the ripped seat. Putting both hands around Peyton's narrow waist, he lifted her effortlessly and set her on the seat. "Is that better?"

Peyton smiled. Now there was a barrier between her bottom and the sharp springs. "It's much better. Thank you." She wanted to tell him buying a new truck would do the trick; it was obvious he had the resources to purchase a new one if he was adding three new employees to his payroll. "Let's see what happens when you shift gears. If it doesn't work, then I'll drive."

"Don't tell me you're like the princess in the Hans Christian Andersen fairy tale about the pea."

She gave him a puzzled look. "What do you know about fairy tales?"

"My mother used to read fairy tales to us every Sunday night before we went to bed. My brother and I wanted the scary ones, but Celia liked the stories about princesses."

"'The Princess and the Pea' is one of my favorite fairy tales along with 'Beauty and the Beast,'" Peyton admitted.

"You truly are a romantic," Nicholas drawled, turning the key in the ignition and shifting into gear.

Peyton stared out the windshield as the truck rattled loudly along the gravel road. "What's wrong with being a romantic?" She knew she sounded defensive, but it was too late to temper her tone.

"Probably nothing if you're into flowers and candle-light dinners."

Shifting on her seat, she gave Nicholas a long, penetrating stare. Peyton didn't know if he was being facetious. "Haven't you ever courted a woman with flowers and dinners by candlelight?"

Taking his gaze off the road in front of him, Nicholas gave Peyton a quick glance. "Of course I have."

"Then, you're a romantic, too."

"Not necessarily, Peyton. I've done it because I know that's what women want."

"You do and say all the right things with the hope you'll get into her panties."

Nicholas shifted into a higher gear without depressing the clutch and the truck stalled out. He gritted his teeth in frustration, a muscle in his jaw twitching uncontrollably when he started up the vehicle again. "I've gone out with a lot of women without ever sleeping with them."

"Why?"

"When I buy a woman dinner I don't expect her to become dessert."

Peyton applauded. "So, you're one of those rare guys every single woman is looking to marry?"

"Are you included in that equation?" he asked, grinning from ear to ear.

"Surely you jest," Peyton said quickly. "I'm not looking for marriage at this time in my life." She didn't want to tell Nicholas she was still dealing with an ex that didn't want to believe it was over. Perhaps if Reginald had decided to remain a part of her past she would be more receptive to having a relationship with a man. Just when she believed she'd achieved a modicum of emotional well-being, he'd call, reminding her why she shouldn't trust a man.

"What are you looking for, Peyton?"

"I want an uncomplicated relationship with a man without declarations of love or a commitment."

"I was under the impression many women your age are looking for a commitment and then marriage." Nicholas slowed, coming to a stop in front of a white vinyl-sided, one-story cottage with navy blue shuttered windows, screened-in front porch and an attached carport. He shut off the engine.

"I'm sorry to disappoint you, but I happen to be the exception."

Turning to his right, he rested his arm over her seat back. "I'm not at all disappointed."

"You're not?"

"No, Peyton. Like you, I'm not looking for a wife. What I'd like is a relationship with a woman who doesn't bore the hell out of me. I need someone who can talk about more than just themselves. I like challenges in life, as well as a woman who's not afraid to challenge me. I also wanted someone with whom I share similar interests."

Peyton felt the heat from his gaze on her face, but she refused to look at him. She wasn't so naive she didn't know who Nicholas was referring to. "When you speak of interests, are you referring to horses?"

"Yes."

"In other words, you want someone like me?"

"Yes."

She turned to face him. "Why me, Nicholas?"

"Why not you?"

"We've known each other for more than a year, yet

you never said more than hello or goodbye until Celia asked me to be her maid of honor. How many times have you sat at Sheldon's table and pretended I was invisible except when you'd ask me to pass the mash potatoes or string beans—"

"I never asked you to pass the string beans because I don't like them," Nicholas interrupted.

"Don't, Nicholas," she warned in a soft voice. "I'm really serious."

He managed to look contrite. "I'm sorry. Finish what you were saying."

Peyton closed her eyes for several seconds. Nicholas's jibe had shattered her concentration. "Forget it."

"I'm not going to forget it. Yes, I ignored you, because I didn't want to like you, Peyton."

She frowned. "That's so childish."

"Childish or not I wasn't ready to start up a relationship at that time."

Her eyebrows lifted a fraction. "A relationship? What made you think I was interested in a relationship?"

"You didn't have a boyfriend."

"Who told you that?"

"Sheldon."

Her jaw dropped with this revelation. "You had the audacity to ask my cousin about my personal life?" She prayed Sheldon hadn't told Nicholas about her short-lived marriage. Once she began divorce proceedings she'd asked everyone in her family never to broach the subject with anyone.

"How else was I going to know anything about you?"

"You could've asked me directly," Peyton countered. "Are you dating someone? Or are you sleeping with someone?"

Attractive lines appeared around Nicholas's coal-black eyes when he smiled. "Were you?"

"No."

"Are you seeing someone now?"

"No, Nicholas."

"Are you interested in dating?"

She paused, knowing he was referring to himself. The seconds ticked off becoming a full minute. "I am, but only if I don't have to share a man with another woman."

Nicholas traced the outline of her ear with his finger. "I don't think that will be a problem for you."

"Why not?"

He leaned closer, his mouth replacing his finger. "Because I don't believe in seeing more than one woman at the same time."

A shiver swept over her, bringing with it a chill despite the summer heat. "Are you asking me out?" Her query was barely a whisper.

# *Chapter 13*

Nicholas's eyes met Peyton's. "Do I have to walk around with a sandwich board handing out printed flyers publicizing I like Peyton Blackstone?"

She stared at him unblinking, then dissolved into uncontrollable laughter at the image of Nicholas standing on a corner with a board over his body. Covering her mouth with one hand and her belly with the other she laughed until tears rolled down her cheeks.

"I'm sorry," she apologized when she saw his closed expression. He could've been carved from stone. Peyton swiped at her face with the back of her hand, but Nicholas pulled it away when he shifted and took a handkerchief from his pocket.

"I didn't think you would be that insensitive," he said accusingly.

"It's not that I'm insensitive."

"Then what is it, Peyton?"

"I...I just can't wrap my head around you standing on a corner except to wait for the light to change so you can cross the street."

Cradling her jaw, Nicholas forced her to look at him. "Who or what do you think I am?"

If she hadn't grown up with an overbearing father Peyton knew she would've been thoroughly intimidated by Nicholas's glare. "You're the man who hired me to provide medical care for his horses."

"That's it?"

She gave him a sweet smile. "What else should there be?" Nicholas continued to stare intently at her, and then released her.

"This will be your place." His voice was shaded in neutral tones. "It's fully furnished, but you'll be responsible for decorating it." He caught her arm when she reached out to open the door. "I'll help you down."

She suffered Nicholas's closeness while he lifted her off the seat, her arms going around his neck. He held her aloft their noses inches apart. In what seemed minutes when in reality it was only seconds he lowered her to stand. Peyton wanted to scream that he was teasing her. He had to have known what he was doing to her when his gaze went to the rapid rise and fall of her breasts when her respiration quickened.

Her emotions had run the gamut with Nicholas: awe, fascination, infatuation and lust. The latter surfacing reminded Peyton of her premeditated celibacy. When first introduced to Nicholas she'd stared at him, mute, unable to form words until she realized he'd spoken to her. Then she watched from under lowered lids how he'd affected the European style of eating when he held his fork in his left hand, while holding the knife in his right. When he'd mentioned not liking string beans she remembered he never asked her to pass that particular dish. At first she thought he didn't like green vegetables, but even that impression was debunked when he ate greens, cabbage, broccoli and spinach. She knew he'd grown up in the South by his slow, drawling speech pattern, but it wasn't until she researched his name on the internet that she realized how little information was available on him and/or his family.

Nicholas handed her a set of keys. "One is for the front door and the other for the side door. If you lift the handle on the front door you'll find a keypad where you can program a code that will unlock the door if you lose or misplace your key. After you program it, I want you to give the number to Clinton. He'll enter it into his computer, so if he's on duty when you come in late he'll unlock the door remotely. You'll also be given a remote device that will activate the gate if the gatehouse isn't manned. I'll wait here while you go inside and check out your place."

"Who lives over there?" She pointed to a larger house off in the distance.

"The head trainer and his wife. All of the married employees live in two-bedroom cottages. The single men live in the dorms, and because you're the only single woman, you'll have your own cottage."

"What about Mrs. Jamison?"

"She lives with me."

Peyton stared at Nicholas, baffled. "You and your housekeeper are living together?"

Crossing his arms over his chest, Nicholas chuckled softly. "Shame on you," he taunted, shaking his finger at her. "She has an apartment off the kitchen, and besides Eugenia is old enough to be my mother."

"Now you're being naive. I really don't like the term, but you wouldn't be the first man to hook up with a *cougar*."

"True, but I have a preference for women closer to my own age."

"And I like my men to be at least five years older than me."

Nicholas cocked his head. "I believe I fit into that demographic."

Peyton bit her lower lip to stop the smile parting her lips. "You don't have to sell yourself, Nicholas."

*"Me?"* She did laugh when seeing his crestfallen expression.

"Yes, you."

Nicholas's deep laugh joined hers. "I don't think so, Doc. I knew I had you when you challenged Jeremy after he accused me of stealing you away from his farm."

"I was just telling the truth. And I could've choked you *and* Jeremy for that little farce."

"Hey, hey, Doc. I never thought you would be prone to violence."

"That's because you don't know me," Peyton retorted.

Nicholas sobered quickly. "This isn't the first time you said that I don't know you. Just what are you hiding?"

"Absolutely nothing," she said much too quickly. "I'm going inside to check out my new digs."

Peyton didn't have anything she wanted to conceal from Nicholas. The only thing she didn't want to acknowledge was an ex-husband with a penchant for hookers and a history of petty crimes dating back to his adolescence.

She walked up three stairs to the porch, smiling. It was the perfect place to sit to begin or end the day at any time of the year. Her father had enclosed their back porch with pocket doors and during the winter Peyton would sit there for hours reading and watching the falling snow. This winter would be the first one she would spend in Virginia.

She didn't know what to expect when she opened the door but it wasn't the organic minimalism giving the space the illusion of being larger than it was. The living room flowed into a dining area and beyond that the wall with a utility kitchen. The sofa, matching love seat with footstool, dining area table and chairs and kitchen was designed on a white palette. The kitchen's black granite countertop provided the only dramatic color in the pristine setting.

Peyton opened and closed overhead kitchen cabinets, the refrigerator/freezer and she checked out the eye-level microwave, oven, cooktop and dishwasher. There was a utility closet and another beside it with a stackable washer/dryer. Walking out of the kitchen, she stopped short when she stood in the doorway to the bathroom. It was a mini-spa. A black glazed tub with retractable nozzles was positioned in the middle of the space.

The black-and-white theme was repeated with large black-and-white checkerboard tiles. The shower enclosure, wall rack with hooks for hanging clothes and/or towels, the pine shelving unit and sink cabinets were stained a vivid brown/black. She walked over to the window that looked out onto a three-sided brick enclosure. Ideas were falling over themselves when she thought of how she could utilize the enclosure.

Nicholas had mentioned she had to decorate her home and Peyton looked forward to the project like a child waiting for Christmas morning. Turning on her heels, she walked across the hall to the bedroom. The brown/black color was repeated on a queen-size headboard, side tables and a storage shelf positioned against the foot of the bed. She opened a wall of louvered doors. There were drawers, shelves, rods and built-in cubbies, enough room for her clothes and shoes. A full-length, silver framed mirror was affixed to a wall near the closet. She flopped down on a club chair covered in a linen/cotton fabric in a soft blue/gray shade several feet from the window. Her gaze swept around the bedroom. She estimated the cottage to be no more than a thousand square feet, small enough for one person, and after she decorated it would be cozy enough for her to want to spend many hours in her new home.

She took one last glance around, mentally cataloging the layout of the entire house. It'd been a while since she'd gone shopping for home furnishings and Peyton planned to bring Caroline with her when they traveled to Waynesboro to buy everything she needed to make the house a home.

She locked up and walked off the porch. Nicholas was where she'd left him. He had his back to her as he leaned against the bumper of the truck talking on his cell phone. Peyton heard him laugh, and then he turned to catch her staring. She smiled, wiggled her fingers and waited for him to finish his conversation before she approached him.

"I really like it," she said, smiling.

"I know it's small—"

"It's perfect, Nicholas," Peyton said, interrupting him. "I don't need anything bigger, because I'd fill it up with things I'd want but are not practical for a small house. However, I need to know when you want me to begin working."

"Why?"

"I have to go shopping."

"How many days do you need?" Nicholas asked.

Peyton shrugged her shoulders. "Two or three."

A knowing smile lifted the corners of Nicholas's strong mouth. "Two or three probably means four or five. You can start on Monday."

Clasping her hands together Peyton blew him a kiss.

"Thank you. After I get settled in I'm going to get a kitten to replace the one I gave to Ryan."

Vertical lines appeared between Nicholas's eyes. "You had a cat?"

"Yes, Oreo. My mother shipped him to me before I knew I was leaving for Alabama. He's been living with Ryan because Sheldon's housekeeper is allergic to cats. Whenever I go to see him he completely ignores me. I think it's because the kids sneak him treats that I can't bear to take him back since they now think of him as their pet."

"Do you like dogs?"

Peyton rolled her eyes. "Of course."

"There are two puppies I want to find homes for."

She listened as Nicholas told her about finding the pregnant bitch with the broken hind leg. He'd decided to keep one puppy and give two away. "I'd love to have one of them."

"I'll take you to see them after you look over and sign the papers I need to hire you."

Peyton sat on the leather sofa in Nicholas's office going over the contract his attorney had drawn up. She'd believed she was going to become an employee when in reality she was, like her predecessor, a contract worker. He'd offered her a substantial monthly salary, bonus and profit sharing, room and board. Picking up a pen, she signed both copies. The contract was for one year with an option to renew at Nicholas's discretion sixty days before the expiration date. She handed them to Nicholas who scrawled his signature on the documents, then placed them in a large envelope.

"After my attorney countersigns them, I'll give you an executed copy." He smiled. "Welcome aboard."

"Thank you." She wondered how two words could convey gratitude yet sound so trivial. Nicholas had just made it possible for her to realize her dream. He owned a dozen prized horses needing optimal medical care in order to maintain good health, and that meant she had to monitor each one very closely.

"Is this when I ask you whether you'd like to go out to dinner so we can celebrate?"

Peyton moved closer to Nicholas and took his hand. She wanted to curse his timing. As much as she wanted to accept his proposal there was still the matter of her houseguest. "I'd love to but is it possible I can get a rain check?"

"Sure. When would it be best for you?"

She flashed a sexy moue, her gaze lingering on his mouth. She was close, close enough to see the emerging stubble, close enough to notice a nearly invisible scar on his right cheekbone, and close enough to feel the whisper of his breath across her face.

"Oh, so you're giving me a choice," she said teasingly, closing her eyes when Nicholas traced the curve of her eyebrows with his finger.

"With me you'll always have a choice."

Peyton opened her eyes, thoroughly amazed by the rush of feelings warming her from head to toe. "I guess that proves you're not a tyrant," she teased.

"I told you I wasn't. You're going to have to learn to trust me."

Her eyelids fluttered wildly. "I have a problem with trust when it comes to men."

Nicholas cradled her face. "All men?" She nodded. "What did he do?"

A beat passed before she said, "He deceived me."

"I want you to remember one thing."

"What's that?" she asked.

"Men do not have a monopoly when it comes to deceit."

Peyton couldn't pull her gaze away from the raven-black eyes that had the power to feel what she was feeling because perhaps he'd gone through the same experience. "Did she hurt you?"

"No, sweetheart. She deceived me."

"Do you want to tell me about it?"

Nicholas lowered his hands when he wanted to take Peyton in his arms and kiss her until she lost her breath. He didn't want to talk about his relationship with Arden. It was his past, and he'd made it a rule not to revisit the past. "I don't want to explain my ex tonight." *Not ever,* he added silently. "When we do celebrate your new beginning where would you like to go?"

Peyton scrunched up her nose. "Someplace funky that offers karaoke, sawdust or peanut shells on the floor and where dancing is optional."

Throwing back his head, Nicholas laughed freely. "You always impressed me as a woman who would only *dine* in the finest restaurants."

"Why are you making me out to be a snob?" she asked. Peyton wanted to tell him if anyone was a snob, then it was Rachel McGhee.

"When you asked me out last year you chose the best restaurant in Staunton."

Peyton had chosen the restaurant because she'd been there once and enjoyed the food, décor and impeccable service. "That's because they have the best steaks in this part of the state."

"That they do, baby. And one of these days we'll go back there. I know a place where we could go."

Peyton wondered if his calling her baby and sweetheart was deliberate or a slip of the tongue. She didn't want to make too much of it although he'd admitted he liked her, and for her there were different levels and degrees of liking.

She ignored her vow not to become involved with a man following her divorce when first introduced to Nicholas. She still didn't know why she felt drawn to him when it hadn't been that way with other men.

It had taken all of her resolve to sidestep the Tuskegee psychology professor who'd obtained her teaching schedule and would park outside her apartment to wait for her. Peyton finally had to tell him she was involved with a man in Virginia. Thankfully he believed the half-truth and retreated respectfully. She wished it had been the same with Reginald.

"Where, Nicholas?"

"There's a little honky-tonk-type restaurant only a few miles from the West Virginia state line. The food is good, the patrons are friendly and the DJ plays everything from country to club tunes. It's going to take at least an hour to get there, so we'll have to leave around six. Depending on the night the place fills up quickly and once you get a table it's yours for the night."

"That sounds like fun."

"So, it's the honky-tonk?"

"Yes."

Peyton checked her watch. It was close to one. "Can I see the puppy? I need to know what size crate I need to buy when I go shopping."

Nicholas stood up, then extended his hand to pull Peyton to her feet. "They are probably near the stables."

"This time we're taking my truck," she said, winking at him.

Peyton found Ginger and her puppies sleeping under a tree near the barn. She went to her knees and touched the head of one of the puppies when he looked at her. The cast on the bitch's leg was dirty and tattered. "How long has she had the cast?" she asked Nicholas.

"About a couple of weeks before she gave birth."

"How old are the pups?"

"Six weeks."

"Did Dr. Richardson x-ray her since he put on the cast?"

Nicholas hunkered down beside Peyton. "No. He said he'll be back next week to check on her."

Now she knew why Nicholas wanted a new vet. It was apparent Dr. Richardson wasn't as available as requested. "The cast needs to come off and the leg x-rayed. Please pick her up, Nicholas." She estimated the golden retriever/ collie mix weighed about forty pounds. He lifted the dog effortlessly while the puppies tumbled over his feet.

"Where are you taking her?"

"Back to the farm," Peyton said, picking up the squirming pups and cradling them to her chest. "I'll remove the cast and x-ray her leg. If we leave her babies it will probably stress her out and then I'll have to sedate her. Do you have a crate large enough to hold her?"

"Yes."

Nicholas got to see firsthand Peyton's skill when he stood off to the side in one of the state-of-the art examining rooms in the newly constructed Blackstone Farms Equine Center. The puppies were placed in a cage with paper shavings and a bottle of water attached to the door. The frisky puppies were scrambling over one another to investigate the bottle before they realized they could get water from the nozzle. Ryan assisted her when, using a handheld drill, they removed the plaster cast from

Ginger's leg. Her glove-covered fingers gently kneaded the limb.

She shared a look with Ryan. "I don't think I need to x-ray her. What do you think, Ryan?"

He repeated her manipulations, nodding. "I think you're right. Let's stand her up and see if she can support her weight." Together they got Ginger to stand up on her own before setting her down on the floor. The canine took one step, then another. She loped over to the cage where her puppies yelped excitedly.

Peyton stripped off her gown and gloves, leaving them in labeled bins. She smiled at Nicholas. "As you can see she's none the worse for wear. It may take a while before the muscles in that leg are as strong as the other three, but the more she moves around the better it will be for her. I'm going to take her for a walk."

Nicholas nodded, smiling. "How much do I owe you?"

Ryan exchanged a look with Peyton. "Give me one of the pups once they're weaned and we'll call it even. My boys have been nagging me for a dog because Vivienne has claimed Peyton's cat as her own. I don't know what's going to happen when she has to give it up."

Peyton walked over to a stainless-steel sink to wash her hands. "She can have Oreo. Nicholas has offered to give me one of Ginger's pups."

"And you can have one for your boys," Nicholas told Ryan.

Ryan blew out his breath. "Thanks, Nick. My sons believe Vivienne gets whatever she wants because she's a girl, so hopefully the dog will ease some of the sibling rivalry."

Nicholas shook his head. "I didn't realize it was like that."

Ryan removed his gloves. "Wait until you're married

with a couple of kids. They manage to disagree over the most asinine things."

Nicholas rubbed the back of his neck. "It'll probably be a while before I take that step."

"Don't wait too long, man. Before you know it you'll be forty and when your kids call you dad their friends will ask don't you mean granddad."

"Come on, Ryan, forty isn't ancient."

"No it isn't, but I'm willing to bet your father had all of his kids before he turned forty."

"It was different with them because my mother and father were college sweethearts and were committed to a future together."

Peyton deliberately blocked out the conversation between her cousin and Nicholas as she fastened a harness around Ginger's body, and then attached a leash. Walking the dog was the perfect excuse for not getting into the debate whether Nicholas should marry and father children before turning forty.

Her mother was twenty when she married her twenty-two-year-old husband, an age Peyton felt was much too young. She was twenty-three when she married Reginald and by the time she celebrated her twenty-sixth birthday she was a divorcée. Thankfully they hadn't had any children. Reginald wanted a child, but for Peyton that hadn't been an option at that time in her life. The few times they'd argued it was always about her becoming pregnant. The more pressure he put on her the more she balked.

Opening a door, she had to pull to get Ginger to follow her, and she suspected the dog had never been on a leash. "Come on, baby. Let's go for a walk."

Once Ginger became accustomed to being pulled along, she settled into a slow, measured gait. Peyton took the time to retrieve the voice-mail message from her cell phone. She activated the feature, then the blood seemingly congealed in her veins when she recognized a former high school friend's strident tone: "Peyton, please call me as soon as you get this message. I think I messed up when I ran into your ex a couple of days ago. We chatted for a bit, then when he asked where he could get in touch with you because his mother is terminally ill and she wanted to talk to you, I gave him your number and address."

"He knows my cell phone," she whispered. Reginald knew her cell-phone number and so did many others in her phone's contacts. She tapped the button for the most recent number. A man answered the call instead of Jaime. Peyton hesitated before finding her voice. "May I please speak to Jaime Rosen."

"I'm sorry, but this isn't Jaime's number. I'm one of her co-workers. She used my phone because she'd left hers home. If you want I can give her a message."

Peyton shook her head even though the man couldn't see her. "That's all right. I'll call her back later on tonight. I'm sorry I bothered you."

"No problem."

She hung up, the two words assaulting her like missiles. Her friend, in a moment of compassion, had revealed to Reginald what he needed to find her. Ginger pulling on the leash shattered the cocoon of dread that had enveloped her. Peyton realized Jaime's faux pas wasn't as grim as she originally thought. None of her friends, not even her parents, knew her address would change from Blackstone Farms to Cole-Thom Farms in less than a week.

Ginger quickened her pace to a trot, Peyton half jogging to keep up with the canine. Living on a horse farm definitely had its advantages. No one could enter or leave without being monitored. It was only when she left the property that she'd become vulnerable.

Peyton didn't want to believe her former mother-in-law was terminally ill. If that were true, then why hadn't Sylvia or even her husband called her? If not her, then her parents. Alphonso and Lena had gotten along well with Sylvia and Philip Matthews.

At that moment Peyton decided to rearrange her life-style one final time, because she refused to continue to be victimized by her ex-husband; she'd tired of his harassment, tired of him dictating how she should live her life every time her phone rang. Nicholas had mentioned she was about to embark on a new beginning and for her that meant getting rid of everything negative that had impacted her past.

Her plan to go shopping would be replaced with on-line shopping, and if Reginald was so inclined to come to Virginia to seek her out, then she would be more than ready for him.

## Chapter 14

It was their last night together and old habits were slow to fade as Caroline sat at the foot of Peyton's bed, her shoulders supported by a stack of pillows. When in college whenever they needed to talk either Peyton or Caroline would climb into the other's bed as if the physical contact made it easier to confide in each other.

Stretching her bare arms above her head, Caroline stared up at the diaphanous fabric draping the tester. "I know you've been waiting for me to tell you why I can't have children."

Peyton closed her eyes as she reclined on several pillows. "I figured you'd tell me when you were ready. If not, then it's no big deal."

"But it is a big deal—for me that is."

Peyton listened, without interrupting when her best friend revealed that she'd started babysitting twin boys of a widowed dentist the year she turned fifteen. What had begun with flirting and an occasional caress quickly became a full-blown affair where he took her virginity. Unfortunately Caroline found herself pregnant despite her lover using protection.

He'd convinced her to have an abortion to avoid his being charged with statutory rape. Then, he did the unspeakable. He wasn't licensed as an ob-gyn, yet he'd performed the procedure in his dental office.

"He put me under," Caroline whispered even though she and Peyton were the only two in the room. "But when I woke up I knew there would be some pain, but not the pain that made me feel as if someone was stabbing me."

"What happened, Caro?" Peyton asked in a quiet tone when her friend closed her eyes.

"The bleeding wouldn't stop and neither did the pain. I hemorrhaged and wound up in the E.R. and eventually surgery where I underwent a total hysterectomy. The attending doctor told my parents I'd contracted an infection from a botched abortion. By the time everything came out my lover had closed down his practice and fled the country to avoid prosecution and the loss of his license.

"When I met Eric I told him I couldn't have children, but he said he still wanted to marry me. It may have been okay with him but not his parents. They nagged and nagged him until he finally had to give in and end our marriage."

"Do you still love him?"

A sad smile flitted across Caroline's face. "A part of me will always love Eric because he was willing to accept me as I am. I just hope he's happy."

"Are you open to meeting someone new?" Peyton asked.

"Not really. I'm looking forward to moving into my condo, and then finding a permanent position with a magazine or paper. I have too much experience to scrounge around looking for something newsworthy to write about. I do thank you for giving me the information I need on doping and horse racing. Now, what's up with you and Nicholas?" Carolyn asked without taking a breath.

"Not much."

"How much is not much?" Caroline asked.

"I won't see him again until Sunday. And I'll begin working Monday morning."

Peyton had ordered bedding, dishes, flatware and glasses, throw pillows, lamps, kitchen gadgets and bathroom accessories online, opting for two-day express shipping. She'd had everything delivered to Cole-Thom Farms where Nicholas had arranged for the boxes to be stored at her cottage. Caroline helped her unpack, put up several loads of laundry and run the dishes, flatware and glasses through the dishwasher.

Caroline sat up, light brown eyes sparkling like copper pennies. "You know he has the hots for you."

Peyton cast her eyes downward, staring at her hands. "I wouldn't say that. He's admitted to liking me, but that's it."

Caroline scooted up to the head of the bed. "You didn't see the way he was looking at you, Peyton. A few times when he'd picked up a forkful of food I thought he was going to miss his mouth because he was staring so hard."

"Stop it!" There was a hint of laughter in the command.

"No, you stop it," Caroline countered angrily. "You meet a man who appears to have it all and you're acting like a junior high school girl with a crush on the cutest boy in the school."

Peyton frowned. "Why does it have to be junior high? Why not high school?"

"Because you probably were more mature in high school than you are now."

Her frown deepened. "Don't forget you said the same thing when I met Reginald. That he was the total package."

Caroline made a sucking sound with her tongue. "Well, I was wrong because I was blinded by his syrupy smile and gift for gab. Don't forget he had a lot of women falling for his line of bull."

"But I fell harder than the others because I married that jackass."

There came a beat. "Does he still call you?"

A pregnant silence ensued, and then Peyton revealed everything that had happened since she last mentioned Reginald to her friend, including the conversation she'd had with Jaime about letting it slip as to where she now lived.

Caroline's eyes were as large as silver dollars. "What's his obsession with you, Peyton? You'd think he would've moved on by now."

Peyton exhaled an audible sigh. "It wasn't until I'd left him that I remembered him telling me that he would never let me go."

"The warning bells didn't go off when he said it?"

She shook her head. "Not at the time. I was in love. Or I'd believed I was in love."

"Remember the night we sat up watching *Sleeping With the Enemy* and you said you didn't want anyone to love you that much?"

Peyton nodded. "Reginald's obsession with me didn't begin to manifest until after I left him."

"And now he's looking up your high-school friends to try and find you."

"He can look all he wants because I'm not going to be

here after tomorrow. And if he's ballsy enough to trespass then he'll be shot. The same goes for Nicholas's farm. You saw the posted sign about trespassers being shot on sight."

"I couldn't believe it when I read that."

"When you invest millions of dollars to set up a breeding and training horse farm you use every means necessary to protect your private property. You'll find more armed men at Cole-Thom than you will here because it's a stud farm. A horse put out to stud can earn fees that far exceed what it'll earn in racing purses."

Caroline shifted, facing Peyton. "You're safe as long as you're behind gates with armed security. What's going to happen when you have to leave the farm?"

Moving off the bed, Peyton walked to a chest of drawers, opening one. Returning, she placed a small-caliber silver automatic on the bed. "I'll carry this with me."

Caroline moved back as if it were a viper. "Oh, hell. What are you doing with a gun?"

"Don't worry, Caro. I have a license."

"When did you get it?"

"I got my license when I was a college freshman. I bought the gun a couple of years ago and Jeremy taught me how to shoot. I practiced over and over until I could hit a can dead center. I would never use it unless I found myself in imminent danger."

"And you would shoot your ex-husband?"

"If I had to shoot him, then I would aim for his knees, then run like hell."

Rising slightly, Caroline hugged Peyton. "Let's hope it won't come to that. But you have to tell someone that your ex has been harassing you."

"I don't want to involve anyone in this."

"Yeah, right. I'm willing to bet if you told Jeremy he

would go hunting for Mr. Crazy and make him rue the day he ever said hello to you."

Peyton slipped off the bed and replaced the gun under a stack of T-shirts. "That's why I won't say anything. And if Daddy found out about his calls I know he would break Reginald in two. He never liked Reginald and the feeling was mutual. It was obvious he saw something in his son-in-law I didn't get to see until it was too late."

"Speaking of late, Peyton. It's after two and I'd better go to bed. I don't want to fall asleep behind the wheel during my drive back. And now that we both live in Virginia there's no reason why we can't get together every other month."

"I'd love to visit D.C."

"All you have to do is call me and come," Caroline said. "I have a wonderful two-bedroom condo with incredible views of Rock Creek Park."

Peyton smiled. "I'm sold."

She hugged Caroline again, then watched as she walked out of her suite and into the one across the hall. Adjusting the pillows under her shoulders, she reached over and turned off the lamp on the bedside table. Peyton was still reeling from the revelation a man had seduced an innocent teenage girl and then fled the country after he'd rendered her sterile.

Her dilemma with Reginald paled in comparison to Caroline's inability to bear a child. Peyton could not understand how Eric could have agreed to marry her knowing the truth, then do a complete reversal when he said he wanted his own biological child. Deceit yet again had reared its evil head.

Turning over on her belly, she gripped the pillow. This would be the last night she would sleep under the roof of Sheldon's house. After breakfast and church services, she would leave for Cole-Thom Farms. It was a four-minute drive between the two farms but for Peyton it could be four hours. She would miss her young cousins most of all. They knew she was going away yet couldn't grasp the concept that she lived close enough to see them every day.

Peyton sat, reading from a prayer book while waiting for Reverend Merrill to begin the service. Her head popped up when the scent of a familiar masculine cologne wafted to her nostrils. Smiling, she watched as Nicholas slid closer to her. He smelled as good as he looked in a white linen shirt and black slacks in the same fabric.

"Good morning," she whispered.

Nicholas placed his hand over Peyton's. "Good morning. You look lovely this morning." He'd been truthful. She wore a deep rose-pink sundress with a scooped neckline. His dark gaze moved slowly over her face. Peyton's sun-bleached ash-blond hair was a shocking contrast to her deeply tanned face.

For a long moment she met his eyes. "Thank you. I didn't expect to see you here this morning."

"I only come here when I get up too late to attend mass at my regular parish."

"Late night?"

"The poker game ran later than usual," Nicholas whispered in her ear.

"Where was the game?"

"It was at the farm."

"How much did you lose?" Peyton asked.

Nicholas leaned against her shoulder. "What makes you think I lost?"

"You don't have the face for a good poker player."

"And you do, sweetheart?"

There. He'd called her sweetheart again. Peyton knew it was no longer a slip of the tongue. "Yes, I do."

"We'll have to see about that."

"Put up or shut up, Nicholas."

"Oh, it's on now, beautiful. We'll play tonight and I don't accept credit."

Peyton wasn't given an opportunity to reply when the pianist sat at the piano at the same time the guitarist and drummer took their places. The soloist stepped onto the stage waiting for the introduction to the opening hymn. The acoustic piano blended melodiously with the other instruments. The words to the song were projected on overhead screens that could be viewed from any angle in the modern minimalist church building as the sweet sound of voices swelled.

Jimmy Merrill's sermon was based on the human family: wives and husbands, children and parents. There were audible murmurs and groans from women when the minister read the verse about wives being subordinate to their husbands. Peyton refused to acknowledge Nicholas when he mumbled in agreement. The lingering feeling of fellowship continued after the service ended and everyone stood in the parking area hugging, kissing and greeting one another as if they'd been separated by weeks instead of hours.

Nicholas curved an arm around Peyton's waist. "What are you going to do now?"

She slipped on a pair of oversized sunglasses. "I still have a few things left to pack before I come over."

"Are you staying the night?"

"If you're asking if I'm going to sleep in my own bed at the cottage, then the answer is yes. After all, I don't want to be late for my first day of work."

Nicholas laughed, the sound coming from deep within his chest. "Don't worry, I won't fire you if you're late."

Rising on tiptoe, she kissed his clean-shaven cheek. "I'll see you at dinner."

He wanted to tell Peyton that he'd tried to stay away from her and had been successful until this morning. Even though he knew he would see her later it still wasn't enough. She'd accused him of not knowing her and Nicholas had to admit to himself she was telling the truth. He recognized her face, was familiar with the sound of her voice, but was clueless when it came to what she liked and more importantly what she needed.

"Do you want me to send someone to drive you over?"

"No, thank you. I'll catch a ride with Sheldon."

Nicholas walked to where he'd parked his car. It was as if he'd come full circle. Last year he hadn't been ready for a relationship. This year he looked forward to having one—with Peyton Blackstone.

"Auntie, pick me up."

Tugging on one of Lynette's braids, Peyton hunkered down to the child's height. "I can't, baby girl, because I'm holding your brother." Carter was fast asleep in the snuggly slung over her chest.

"Put him down, Auntie!" Lynette screamed, stomping her little foot.

Peyton was torn by mixed emotions she was totally unprepared to deal with. She'd told Tricia and Jeremy's daughters she was moving and they hadn't taken the news well. Elena and Lynette had begun acting out, while Michaela refused to talk to her, although she'd reassured the triplets they would still have their playdate and campouts.

*Why now?* she mused. They were in the dining hall at Cole-Thom Farms and from the looks directed at Peyton from her new farm family, Lynette's outburst had garnered everyone's attention.

Rising, she reached for Lynette's hand, and then she pointed to the small round table with a half-dozen chairs. "I'm going to give your brother back to your mother, then we're going to have a very special tea party. Okay, Lynn?" Lynette had insisted she wanted everyone to call her Lynn. Of the three sisters, Lynette was the most vocal and forceful in her demands.

"Okay, Auntie Peyton."

Nicholas stood off to the side watching Peyton's interaction with the fretful little girl. She'd remained calm and in control of the situation. A smile curved his mouth when she handed the sleeping infant boy to his mother, then took Lynette's hand, leading her back to the kiddie table with seating for six and sat down. The sight of her sitting at the table with the triplets and Ryan's young son and daughter would have been laughable if she'd been a lot taller. His gaze lingered on the braid tied with a black ribbon. Peyton had exchanged the sundress for a white tailored shirt, black stretch cuffed slacks and black strappy stilettos.

"Cookie wants to know if you're ready for us to begin serving."

Nicholas turned around. One of the stable hands who did double duty as a waiter for dinner waited for his reply. The young man's spiked coal-black hair still shimmered with moisture from his recent shower. It hadn't taken a week but everyone quickly learned that Jackson Hubbard aka Cookie ran his kitchen and dining hall like a drill sergeant. Those recruited to stand in as waiters were required to shave and shower each night before entering the dining hall. Nicholas had been so busy greeting his guests he hadn't taken the time to sit down and eat his salad or the appetizer of miniature empanadas filled with chicken and beef.

"Yes, Riccardo."

Nicholas told Jackson he was master and commander when it came to the dining hall. He was to set the rules and Nicholas would reinforce them if or when any of the employees refused to comply. The talented cook served a hot and cold breakfast, offered a buffet lunch of home-made soups, mixed salads and a variety of sandwiches using leftover meat from the prior night's dinner. The men had come to favor the paninis made with a variety of homemade breads. The grilled sandwiches were con-cocted with meat, cheese, sweet and hot peppers, mush-rooms and fruit and veggies.

Jackson had admitted preparing three meals for less than twenty was a cakewalk compared to the hundreds he'd served in his family-owned restaurant. Every night he put up loaves of homemade breads much to the de-light of everyone. Even Eugenia was impressed with the man's culinary skills because he eschewed store-bought sauces and salad dressings. Mayonnaises and pesto, oven-roasted tomatoes and caramelized onions were the most requested condiments.

Nicholas had hoped Peyton would join him at the table with Sheldon, Renee, Kelly, Ryan, Tricia and Jeremy but he'd lost her to the kiddie table. When he'd invited the Blackstones for dinner he'd asked one of the workers to drive into Waynesboro to purchase the round table and chairs. The few children living on the farm would sit with their parents during mealtimes.

Waiters, wearing pristine white bib aprons, wheeled serving carts into the dining hall. Cookie had prepared Puerto Rican roast pork shoulder, baked chicken, green plantain chips accompanied by a garlic dipping sauce, white rice and black beans, and corn bread with scallions and bacon. Another cart was wheeled in with carafes of chilled rum punch; sweet tea, water and natural fruit juice were set out on each table.

Eugenia walked in glancing around and Nicholas beckoned to his housekeeper. "You can sit with us."

The woman flashed a rare smile, the gesture lighting up her face. "Thank you."

Pulling out a chair, he seated Eugenia. Nicholas had grown up in a house with a live-in staff, and at no time had any of them crossed the invisible social delineation between employer and employee. He'd changed that when he insisted the people who worked for him call him Nicholas rather than Mr. Thomas. He'd also instituted an open-door policy where he welcomed and entertained suggestions and dealt with grievances. Many of the diners bowed their heads in silent prayer before filling their plates with the mouthwatering fare.

Peyton felt as if she were sitting in a restaurant rather than a common dining hall. There were cloth-covered tables with seating for two, four, six or eight. Hi-hats and wrought-iron ceiling light fixtures, pre-recorded music coming through hidden speakers and potted palms, cactus and framed black-and-white photos of champion Thoroughbreds positioned on the brick walls set the stage for casual, relaxed dining. She'd witnessed firsthand what Nicholas had bragged about. One bite of the moist, flavorful roast pork and she curbed the urge to moan in ecstasy. The infusion of spices made it indescribable.

Michaela chewed a mouthful of rice. "This is good, Auntie."

"Yes it is, baby."

Lynette stabbed a crisp plantain. "I like the bananas. Do you like the bananas, Auntie?"

Peyton smiled at the child. "I love bananas, Lynn." The flavor of the fried green bananas was intensified when she topped it with the sauce made of diced garlic, Spanish onion, salt, olive oil, white vinegar and citrus juice. "Use both hands when you pick up your milk," she reminded Elena.

For Peyton, moving to Cole-Thon was akin to downsizing. It was much smaller, a little more than one square mile when compared to Blackstone's fifteen. She would interact with less than twenty residents when Blackstone's was closer to fifty. She would be responsible for a dozen horses instead of three dozen. Securing a position as a resident vet, living in a house that afforded her ultimate privacy and Nicholas were a plus, and not necessarily in that order.

She met Nicholas's intent stare across the room. His fork was poised in midair, and now Peyton understood what Caroline had been talking about. Peyton blew him a kiss, and Nicholas froze, mouth gaping in shock. She was truly looking forward to their poker game later that evening.

Nicholas recovered quickly, running his tongue over his lower lip. It was her turn to be stunned by the unabashed erotic gesture. She lowered her gaze before someone noticed their silent sex play. Vivienne patted her arm, and Peyton shifted her attention to Ryan's seven-year-old daughter.

"What is it, Vivi?"

"May I have another piece of corn bread?"

She kissed the girl's neatly braided hair. "Of course."

Peyton focused on the children at the table, refilling their glasses and passing dishes when they asked for additional portions. She didn't meet Nicholas's eyes again until dessert and coffee were served.

She busied herself checking the faces of the children at the table, instructing them to use their napkins to wipe away any traces of food. Peyton hugged each of them before they ran to their parents. She stood there, feeling a sense of loss, and at that moment reality hit her full force. All that she wanted since she decided to become an equine veterinarian was real, too real.

It was only now that Peyton realized working for her family was a safety net. The responsibility of seeing to the medical and physical needs of the horses hadn't been hers but Ryan's, and she began to second-guess herself. Could she really do this?

"If you don't stop chewing your lip it's going to look like a piece of raw meat."

She closed her eyes when Nicholas's breath swept over her ear. "I was just thinking about something."

He chuckled. "A penny for your thoughts."

Shifting, she turned to face him. "I'm afraid a penny wouldn't begin to pay for it."

Nicholas came closer without moving. "How much then?"

"Too much."

"I'm hardly a pauper."

Peyton smiled, exhibiting straight, white teeth. "You will be after I take you for all you have in our poker game."

Nicholas laughed, the sound bubbling up from his throat until he doubled over, bringing the others in the room to look at him. "If you think I'm going to let a little slip of a woman wipe me out, then you need to be committed."

"Eight o'clock. My place." That said, Peyton turned on her heels and strutted over to Tricia.

"I should warn you that she's very outspoken, Nick."

He gave Ryan a sidelong glance. "Word," he drawled.

"My cousin is smart," Ryan said softly. "She's a lot smarter than she realizes. She sleeps, eats and breathes veterinary medicine. Kelly and Tricia have tried to get her interested in some of the men from the other farms but she acts like they don't exist. There are times when I don't blame her for being turned off. Any woman would if they found out their husband was a horse's ass."

A fist of fear squeezed Nicholas's heart. He didn't want to believe he was going after a married woman. "She's married?"

Ryan shook his head. "Nah. She got rid of him when he screwed up big-time. They weren't married a year when she filed for divorce."

Nicholas blew out an inaudible sigh of relief. Is that what Peyton meant when she said he didn't know her? He hadn't known she'd been married and divorced. "There's no use in hanging on to something doomed for failure." The moment the words rolled off his tongue Nicholas knew he was referring to his relationship with Arden. He'd known when he met her that they were complete opposites but he'd thought himself so much in love that he could change her mind. It ended when he was the one forced to accept what really couldn't be changed and move on.

"I promised your father that I was going to take good care of her, and I'm promising you the same."

Ryan's lids came down, hiding his innermost feelings. "You like my cousin, don't you?"

"Yes."

His hand came down on Nicholas's shoulder, his fingers tightening. "I like you, Nick, but please don't mess her over."

Nicholas flung off the vet's hand. How was he going to mess over a woman when what he was beginning to feel for her went a lot deeper than liking. "I don't take kindly to threats."

"It's not a threat. I just don't want to see her hurt again."

"I'm not going to hurt her, Ryan. You have my word on that."

Dark gray eyes met a pair so dark it was impossible to see their depths. "I'm glad we understand each other."

For a reason he couldn't fathom Nicholas didn't feel like being gracious, not when Ryan had implied he was going to hurt Peyton. "It's me that needs to be understood. Thank you for coming." He walked away before he said something he would come to regret, unaware Peyton had watched the interchange between him and her cousin.

One by one he thanked the Blackstones for coming. He patted Sheldon's back. "There's an open invitation for you to come back any time you wish."

Jeremy affected a Cheshire-cat grin. "We won't have to come back if we can lure your cook away."

"Forget it, Jeremy," Nicholas retorted, "you can't afford Cookie."

"I think if I juggle a few numbers I may be able to come up with enough to make a reasonable offer."

A sly smile parted Nicholas's lips. "Not if I call my brother and have him advance me a few million from the family's business account."

Jeremy twisted his mouth. "Damn, Thomas. You fight dirty."

"No, I don't. I'm only protecting what belongs to me."

A network of lines fanned out around Sheldon's eyes

when he smiled. "Come on, Jeremy. Stop busting Nicholas's hump. He's not giving up his cook, so let it rest. By the way, Nicholas, you picked a good one. Let Cookie know he's awesome."

"Thanks, Sheldon. I'll be certain to let him know."

The Blackstones left and within minutes all of the tables were cleared, wiped down and the floor vacuumed. Nicholas noticed Eugenia walking in the direction of the kitchen. She didn't drive and he wanted to know if she wanted him to take her back to the house.

He looked around for Peyton but it was apparent she'd left. It didn't matter. She wasn't going anywhere. He knew exactly where to find her.

# Chapter 15

Peyton lay on the cushioned wicker love seat, a blue-and-white throw pillow under her head and a matching one under her bare feet. She stared up at the slow-moving blades of the ceiling fan. The cooling air coming off the fan and the warm breeze filtering through the screen stirred the wind chime, creating bell-like sounds that carried easily in the hushed silence of the approaching dusk.

Sitting on the porch waiting for nightfall had become a magical moment for her. Lengthening shadows, the occasional thrill of a bird and gentle rustle of leaves made her feel as if she'd been transported to an enchanted forest with mythical creatures hiding behind trees, bushes and in flowerbeds surrounding the cottage.

She'd walked barefoot back to her cottage instead of accepting a ride because she'd overeaten. Peyton estimated the distance between her house and the dining hall to be about one-tenth of a mile. The walk not only served to help aid her digestion but gave her time alone to think about what she wanted from Nicholas other than employment.

Although they weren't officially a couple there was history between them. In fact she knew Nicholas longer than she had Reginald when she married him. If Caroline said Nicholas had the hots for her, then it was the same with her. There wasn't anything about Nicholas she didn't like or want, and she wondered if they would've become involved last year if she had not accepted the offer to teach in Alabama. Shifting in a more comfortable position, she closed her eyes, willing her mind blank.

Peyton lost track of time as she dozed off and on and then sat up, suddenly alert when she heard the sound of an approaching engine. Pushing off the love seat, she peered through the screen. The sweep of headlights lit up the landscape before the dark-colored sedan came to a stop under the carport.

She held the screen door open as Nicholas mounted the three steps to the porch. *"Bienvenida."*

*"Gracias."* Nicholas dipped his head and kissed her cheek. His gaze lingered on her face because he didn't trust himself to look below her neck. She should've been arrested for indecency. The tank top and shorts exposed more than it concealed. He didn't stare, but leered at her chest.

Peyton angled her head. "Are you ready to lose your shirt?"

"I didn't know we were playing strip poker."

"We're not," she said, locking the screen door. "I was using it as a metaphor. What did you bring?"

Nicholas held up a burl rosewood box and a decorative shopping bag. "Cards, chips, a bottle of red wine, two wineglasses and a corkscrew."

Peyton smiled. "Nice."

He waited for her to enter the house, then followed her inside. He stopped, glancing around the living/dining room, unable to believe how much it had been transformed. Table lamps, turned to the lowest setting, cast a soft golden glow against off-white walls.

"I can't believe what you've done here." He was unable to disguise the awe in his voice.

"You can look around if you want," Peyton suggested.

Nicholas set the box down on a glass-topped coffee table. Peyton had used a discerning eye when she decorated the cottage, playing off the black-and-white color scheme with accessories in splashes of gray and robin's-egg-blue. Small glass cubes filled with black marbles and rocks lined the countertop, breaking up the pristine white and stainless-steel kitchen.

He walked into the bedroom, stopping in the doorway. Nicholas had accused Peyton of being a romantic and his assessment was validated by the white eyelet dust ruffle, pillow shams, white and black duvet, pinstriped, hound's tooth and checkered-and-white lace-trimmed sheets, pillowcases and sheets. Lighted candles in decorative holders flickered in the semidark space.

A vivid picture of them in bed together, limbs entwined and writhing in ecstasy sent his libido into overdrive; the blood rushed to his groin and the flesh between his legs hardened so quickly he suddenly experienced light-headedness. Walking on shaky legs, Nicholas lay face-down on the bed, waiting for his hard-on to go down.

Suddenly it all made sense. For more than a year he'd ignored Peyton, pretending she did not fit the image of his ideal woman; she was too short, petite and too blonde for his personal tastes, but none of that mattered because somehow she'd managed to slip under the wall he'd erected to keep women from getting too close. There was no way he wanted to be that vulnerable again.

"What are you doing?"

Peyton's voice seemed disembodied, as if it came from a long way off. "I have a situation." Nicholas's words were muffled in the duvet.

"What kind of situation?" Peyton asked as she approached the bed.

"I was feeling light-headed."

The mattress dipped slightly when she sat beside him. "What's the matter?"

Nicholas had to decide whether to lie to her or tell her the truth. He didn't want to start whatever relationship he'd hoped to have with her based on lies. "I have a hard-on."

Peyton clapped a hand over her mouth. Shock had rendered her speechless. When Nicholas said he was light-headed she thought maybe there was something physically wrong with him. She lay on her back beside him. Reaching for his hand, she wound their fingers together.

"Does it happen often?"

Lifting his head slightly, he looked at her delicate profile. "Not usually."

Shifting slightly, Peyton turned to face him. "You have problems achieving an erection?"

Nicholas looked at her as if she'd lost her mind. "No! I have a problem controlling my erection because of you."

"You're blaming me for your loss of control?"

"Yes, I am. When I walked in here and saw the bed all I thought of was making love to you."

Peyton closed her eyes as a warming desire washed over her like an electric current. "I'm not going to pretend that I haven't fantasized about making love to you,

Nicholas. Why you? I don't know, because it hasn't been that way with other men."

"Not even your husband?"

An instant chill replaced the sudden warmth and she snatched her hand away. "Who told you I was married?"

Nicholas turned over, not caring whether she saw the bulge straining against the fly of his jeans. "Ryan happened to mention it." There was enough light coming from the candlelight to see her wildly fluttering eyelids.

"What did he say?"

"That your ex was a horse's ass."

"I wouldn't insult a horse like that. He's more like a slug."

Nicholas rested his hand on her jaw. "What did he do to you?"

Peyton told him everything, from when she'd returned to the States to enroll in Cornell for graduate courses to meeting Reginald at an after-work party at a club in Ithaca, New York. "I guess you could say I'd led a rather sheltered life, because even though Reggie was only two years older than me he seemed so erudite. We'd dated for a month when he asked me to marry him."

"How old were you, sweetheart?" Nicholas asked.

"Twenty-three."

"You were very young."

"I was old enough to know better than to hook up with a man I'd known exactly four weeks. I agreed and we eloped. When my father found out he was furious."

"How about his parents?"

"They were pleased that their only child had found someone. I must say my parents and his got along well."

Nicholas pressed a kiss to Peyton's forehead. His erection had finally gone down. "Why did you break up?"

"He called, asking me to wire him bail money. At first

I thought he may have been jailed for speeding or maybe even resisting arrest because he has a quick temper. He wouldn't tell me what he'd been charged with and I told him I wasn't sending him one copper penny until he told me the truth. He then claimed the vice unit had entrapped him but when I threatened to hang up he admitted he'd solicited a prostitute." Nicholas's exhalation of breath came out in a swooshing sound. "You have no idea how dirty I felt when he told me it wasn't the first time he'd paid for sex. I hung up on him, then packed my books and clothes and moved out."

"Where was he arrested?"

"Central Florida. He eventually got in touch with his parents who wired him the money. That's when I found out it wasn't the first time they'd bailed him out. He had an arrest record dating back to his adolescence, all of them misdemeanors. When I confronted my in-laws about his criminal history they said they'd hoped he would change once he was married. Apparently they were wrong because he didn't and couldn't change."

"What was he doing in Florida if you guys lived in New York?"

"He was there to recruit personnel for his father's PMC."

Nicholas's forehead furrowed. "Are you talking about private military companies?"

"Yes. My former father-in-law has contracts with the State Department and with several other national governments training soldiers and reorganizing militaries in several African countries, and unfortunately Reginald never lived up to his father's expectations. His parents were his built-in safety net and whenever he got into trouble they were there to clean up the mess."

"It sounds like he never grew up."

Peyton closed her eyes. "He didn't." And he still hasn't, she thought. She didn't want to talk about Reginald because it conjured up past hurt, but she had to unburden herself. "The first thing I did after moving out was to get tested. Thankfully it came back negative, but I didn't want to believe it so I took it several more times over the next year and they also came back negative. There are times when I still feel dirty—"

Nicholas pressed a kiss over one eye, then the other. "Shush, baby. You're not dirty."

"You know I want to make love to you, but I don't want to take advantage of your vulnerability. We *are* going to make love. Where? Either in this bed or in mine. Why? Because I *want* and *need* you that much. When? That will be up to you. But it can't happen until you learn to trust me. I've never been able to sleep with more than one woman at the same time, so that rules out me cheating on you."

Peyton was so overcome with emotion she felt like crying. Nicholas was offering her everything she wanted and needed since her marriage ended. He was giving her time to heal emotionally. Tricia and Kelly didn't understand why she'd been reluctant to date, even after she told them she wasn't ready for a relationship, especially not with men whose focus was getting her into bed.

If Nicholas hadn't been ready for a relationship the year before it had been the same with her. Now she was ready, ready to move forward with her professional and personal life. She didn't know what the future held for her and Nicholas yet that wasn't as important as where they'd come from. A year ago Peyton never could've imagined sharing a bed with Nicholas even if they weren't making love.

"Did she cheat on you?"

The seconds ticked. Nicholas knew he had to tell Peyton about his aborted engagement if he wanted an open and healthy relationship with her. That was something he hadn't had with Arden.

"No," Nicholas said after a pregnant pause. "It would've been more acceptable if she had."

"What did she do?"

He pulled Peyton closer, her head resting on his shoulder. "I grew up wanting to be like one of my uncles who'd gone to West Point. When it came time for me to select a military academy I applied to Annapolis and was accepted. I graduated and volunteered for the submarine fleet. A week later I met Arden at a buddy's birthday party. I definitely wasn't a novice when it came to dealing with women, but there was something about her that was so different from the other women I'd known, and that summer we dated exclusively. When she discovered I would be away for months at a time she said she was afraid of losing me, and to prove that wasn't going to happen I asked her to marry me."

"How long were you engaged?"

"A year and a half."

"Why so long, Nicholas?"

"We were separated more than we were together the first year. I was looking forward to an extended shore leave because I'd promised her I would become more involved in planning the wedding. I was also glad to be home because it would give me time to ride my bike. When you're closed up in a sub months at a time all you want when you dock is to have the wind in your face."

"Where was home?" Peyton asked.

"Palm Beach, Florida. One morning I went riding and everything changed when a car filled with teenagers who'd been drinking blew past a stop sign and hit me head-on. I was thrown about fifty feet and they spun out of control crashing into a utility pole. Two of the five kids died at the scene while the others were transported to local hospitals with minor injuries."

Peyton caught the front of Nicholas's T-shirt, holding it in a punishing grip. "Were you wearing a helmet?"

He nodded. "Yes. That's what saved my life even though I had serious head trauma, a spinal-cord injury and two broken legs. I was placed in a medically induced coma for more than a month. During this time doctors weren't certain if I'd ever walk again. Apparently Arden thought the same and she sent back my ring with a note saying she wasn't equipped to spend her life with a cripple.

"I knew something was wrong when I came out of the coma and Arden wasn't there. I was finally transferred to a rehab facility and that's when I realized she wasn't coming. The psychiatrist told my parents not to tell me about Arden's abandonment because it would negatively impact my physical and emotional recovery."

"When did you find out she wasn't coming back?"

"I was about seven months into my recovery when I stopped looking and waiting for her to walk through the door. Getting my legs to work was a lot easier than getting my brain to work because of cognitive impairment. There were times when I would have to grope for simple words. I'd remember faces but not names."

"How long did it take you to recover?"

"I don't know. It was as if I'd lost track of time. I remember the accident but I couldn't pinpoint exactly when I'd recovered my memory. One day everything was foggy, and then I remembered everything. My request for a medical discharge was approved and I found myself a civilian

for the first time in years. I moved back with my parents
and that's when I found Arden's note and the ring."

"I don't think it was as much about you as much as
it was about her not being strong enough to deal with a
partner with special needs."

"What ever happened to the promise to love in sick-
ness and in health?"

Peyton nearly recoiled when she heard the chill in the
query. "You weren't married, Nicholas, and that in and
of itself gave her an out."

"Wrong! I couldn't have been more committed to her.
The only thing that was missing was the marriage license
and vows. And if the tables were reversed I would've
stayed with her even if I had to physically carry her
around. I loved her just that much."

Peyton released his shirt, smoothing out the wrinkles.
"Some people love with their hearts and actions, others
with words. It was apparent your ex chose the latter."

"You're right about that. It took me a while to get over
her deception."

"Do you trust women?" Peyton asked him.

"I trust you."

"That's not what I asked, Nicholas."

"If you ask me the same question again I'll give you
the same answer."

"Why me?"

"I've had a lot of time to observe you and during that
time I realized you possess all the qualities I like in a
woman. I've never seen you lose your patience with your
demanding cousins who are definitely little divas in training. It's apparent you love animals and they appear very
calm when you're around. You're loyal. Sheldon, Ryan
and Jeremy adore you and I'm certain the feeling is mutual. Your ex probably recognized this when he asked you

to marry him, but he was either too stupid or arrogant to believe he could continue banging hookers and if caught, you would forgive him."

"Reginald didn't know me and he never took the time to get to know me."

Moving with the agility of a cat, Nicholas straddled Peyton while supporting his greater weight on his arms. "That's something I plan to do. I want to know what you want, like and don't like. And if there is anything you need and it's within my power to give it to you all you have to do is ask. Remember I'm your personal genie."

Peyton stared up at him through her lashes, wishing she could see all of his face in the diffused light. "There's nothing I want."

"Are you sure?"

She nodded. "Very sure."

"What about a second chance?"

"A second chance at what?" she asked.

"Love."

Peyton closed her eyes. Her heart was beating so fast it was her turn to feel light-headed. Nicholas was offering her what she'd wanted since ending her marriage but was too afraid to attempt again with another man. She'd blamed herself for marrying the first man who'd proposed marriage and in the end she had paid for her impulsiveness. It was so easy to fall in love with Nicholas. He was everything Reginald wasn't and couldn't hope to be. But once burned, twice shy.

She wondered why he was sending her mixed messages. He'd been forthcoming when he said *what I'd like is a relationship with a woman who doesn't bore the hell out of me.* He'd talked about a relationship so why was he now talking about love?

"Is that what you're looking for?" she asked.

Nicholas smiled. "I like being in love."

"We fall in love, and then what?"

His smile faded. "That would be up to you."

Peyton pushed against his chest, but she couldn't budge him. "You'd wait for me to fall madly in love with you, then ask you to marry me?"

"If it comes to that."

Forcing a brittle smile, she shook her head. "Do you really think I'm that desperate for a man, Nicholas? That I'd hook up with you, hoping you'll marry me?"

"No."

"Then what is it?"

"I just want you to keep an open mind that maybe what we have—"

"We have nothing right now," Peyton interrupted.

Nicholas sprang off the bed, pulling her up with him. "Wrong. We have friendship. And right now you and your friend are going to play poker and I'm not going to spare your cute little behind when I take everything you have."

She didn't want to believe Nicholas could talk about love in one breath, then playing poker as if he'd never brought up the dreaded four-letter word, wondering if he was still suffering from the effects of the accident. Giving up a military career and losing a disloyal fiancée paled in comparison to the possibility of his remaining in a vegetative state or possible death. He'd asked whether she wanted a second chance at love when Peyton suspected he was referring to himself. It was obvious he needed the second chance more than she did.

"I don't have anything to go with the wine," Peyton said as she walked out of the bedroom.

"Next time I'll bring cheese, fruit and a baguette."

"What do you know about baguettes?"

Nicholas caught Peyton around her waist, easing her

back against his body. "I remember being in Paris and getting up early to go to the bakery for baguettes fresh from the oven. I'd end up eating half before I'd make it back to my flat."

"You lived in Paris?"

Nicholas pulled out a chair in the dining area, seating Peyton. "My parents used to take us to different countries in Europe on holiday. One year it was Italy, the next Spain or France. Dad would rent a flat for two months and we would take day trips. The year we stayed in Paris we took the train to Rome and spent three days there. That could be the reason why I joined the navy because I loved traveling."

"My holidays were usually spent going up to Canada. We didn't live that far from Montreal and at least once a month we'd go up to shop. That was before you needed a passport. The year I turned sixteen I found out my father and Sheldon were cousins, and that's when I'd come down here for the summers."

Nicholas took the glasses, corkscrew and the bottle of merlot out of the bag. "You've never been to Europe?"

Resting her elbows on the table, Peyton supported her chin on her fisted hands. "No."

"Maybe one of these days we'll go together. Where would you like to go first?"

"Italy."

It was the first country that popped into her head. Peyton wondered if this was how he'd treated Arden. Had he been her personal genie, granting her every wish and when he needed her most she fled because she hadn't been emotionally equipped to care for someone who might never walk again?

"I'm glad you said that, because I got an email from my parents who are currently traveling throughout Eu-

rope. Dad says they found a villa in Venice they're thinking about buying."

"They see something and just like that," she said, snapping her fingers, "they decide to buy it?"

Nicholas uncorked the bottle and half filled the wineglass. "How much do you know about my family?"

"Not much," Peyton admitted. "Tell me about them
during the game."

Sitting down opposite her, Nicholas removed the cards
from the box, then stacks of chips. "How much in chips
do you want?"

"I'll start with a thousand."

He wiggled his eyebrows. "Remember the house
doesn't extend credit to first-time players."

Reaching for the deck, she shuffled the cards. "I don't
expect to owe the house."

"So my baby likes trash talking."

Peyton handed him the deck. "Shuffle."

Nicholas shuffled the deck several times, then dealt
the cards. He peered at his hand, clenching his teeth in
frustration. He'd started out with a bad hand. Placing his
cards facedown on the table he picked up the wineglass.
"To friendship."

Smiling, Peyton touched her glass to his. "Friendship,"
she repeated. The glasses were nothing like the ones she'd
ordered but fully leaded crystal. She took a sip of the
wine, savoring the sweetness. "I like the wine." She hadn't
sampled the rum punch at dinner because she was sitting
with the children.

"Thank you."

They played, Peyton winning the first two hands with a
straight flush and three of a kind: three queens, a five and
three, and Nicholas won the next with a full house. She
listened, intrigued, when he revealed that his gentleman

farmer great-grandfather went to Cuba after World War I to purchase a sugarcane plantation but failed because of anti-American sentiment. But the trip wasn't a total loss because he met the beautiful daughter of a man who produced some of the finest Cuban cigars on the island.

"Samuel Cole married Marguerite-Joséfina Diaz and brought her back to Florida where they went on to have four children together."

Peyton glanced up. "I noticed you said *together*."

"Samuel had an affair with his secretary and she had a son whom my father didn't recognize until Joshua was an adult. Samuel's accountant married Joshua's mother before he was born, so Josh became Kirkland instead of Cole. My great-grandfather was as astute a businessman as any you have today that head the Forbes list. He never lost his fortune during the 1929 crash because he'd withdrawn all but five thousand dollars from the banks and hid it in his mother's root cellar."

Peyton tossed a card on the table. "How did he make his money?"

"Coffee, bananas, Cuban cigars, soybeans and eventually vacation properties."

"He grew soybeans back then?"

Nicholas smiled. "Yep. Remember the Chinese had grown them for centuries even before it became popular in this country. He made it through the Depression unscathed and when the economy picked up again his wealth ballooned. There were rumors that he was a billionaire but that was something he never talked about. He'd set up five-million-dollar trust funds for each of his legitimate children and years later Joshua was given his share."

Peyton frowned at the five cards. She couldn't have been dealt a better hand. "What about the family owned company?"

"It's privately held. Only a direct descendant of Samuel Cole can become CEO. My father ran the company for thirty years and now my brother is CEO and my cousin Joseph is CFO. When Samuel passed away anyone with Cole blood inherited millions. I used the monies from my trust and my inheritance to set up the farm."

"So that's what you mean when you say you're not a pauper."

Nicholas nodded. "How many cards do you want?"

Peyton met his eyes. "What makes you think I want to change my hand?"

The light coming from an overhead fixture shimmered off her face and hair. "You're glaring at your hand."

"Because my children are being naughty—mama's going to put them in time-out."

Nicholas drained his glass, then refilled it. He glanced at Peyton's. She had barely touched hers. "My kids are behaving."

"Good for you." Picking up several chips, she dropped them on the mounting stack. "I raise you three hundred and call."

Nicholas placed his cards on the table. "Straight flush."

Peyton laid down her hand. "Straight flush." She had all hearts beginning with a seven, while Nicholas had all spades. His high card was a five. Reaching across the table she scooped up the chips. "Are you broke yet?" she taunted.

Nicholas stood up, reached across the table. One second she was sitting and in the next she found herself in his arms, with him striding in the direction of the bedroom. She opened her mouth in protest but he stole the breath from her lungs when his mouth covered hers in an explosive kiss.

"I never figured you for a poor loser," she gasped when he raised his head.

Nicholas shifted her body when he pulled back the duvet. "I told you before I don't like losing." He dropped her on the bed, his body following hers down after he'd kicked off his running shoes.

Eyes wide in fright, Peyton struggled to breathe. "What are you going to do?"

The smile on his face appeared macabre in the flickering candlelight. "I'm going to punish you for taking my money."

## Chapter 16

*What is he going to do to me? Please don't tell me I've hooked up with a psychopath. And who's going to hear me scream all the way out here? The nearest house is at least five hundred feet away.*

Peyton opened her mouth to scream, but it died on her lips when Nicholas kissed her again This time it was a long caress that left her wanting more. Her arms went around his neck, holding him fast while she parted her lips to his searching tongue. The press of his body, his heat and the taste of wine stirred her slumbering libido as she tried to get closer.

Nicholas kissed Peyton's mouth, the hollow of her scented throat, the curve of her shoulders. He pushed the straps to her tank off and down her arms, baring her breasts. The flesh between his legs grew heavy, but he didn't and couldn't stop until he tasted every inch of her satiny skin. His tongue swept over her breasts, smiling when the nipples hardened. He rolled one between his teeth, nipping it, and then gave the other equal attention until Peyton moaned, the sound coming from deep within her throat. He ignored the bite of her fingernails on his biceps when he increased the pressure. Her moans became a low keening that raised the hair on the back of his neck.

When he'd come to her house it wasn't his intention to make love to her. Not when he hadn't brought protection. His hands slid under the cotton top, covering her small firm breasts. After the accident he'd opted to remain celibate, while he'd resorted to other methods to assuage his own sexual needs, but it was the first time in a very long time he longed to be inside a woman.

Lowering his head he planted tiny kisses over her flat belly. He unbuttoned her shorts, pulling them down her hips and she went still. "It's all right, baby. I'm not going inside you because I didn't bring protection." Within seconds he felt her relax.

Nicholas relieved her of the scrap of fabric that barely covered her behind, tossing it on the floor. Her tank top followed, but he left on her bikini panties. His plan was to make love to her without having sex. Moving up the bed, he hovered over her. "Are you okay?"

Peyton swallowed to moisten her constricted throat. "Yes." She didn't know what Nicholas planned to do but she didn't want him to stop.

She expelled a breath when he reached down and took off his white T-shirt, then moved off the bed to remove his jeans, but not his pair of boxer briefs.

He returned to the bed and then erotic torture began. Nicholas's mouth was everywhere: her armpits, along her rib cage, inner thigh, the soles of her feet, before he flipped her over and fastened his mouth at the small of her back. The occasional nip of his teeth and butterfly kisses along her inner thigh had her close to climaxing.

He turned her over again, burying his face between her thighs, alternating blowing his breath against her mound. Peyton screamed for him to stop when she felt the beginnings of an orgasm but Nicholas was relentless. It was as if he knew she was about to come, yet he continued until she went still and cried out, her body bucking wildly when the first orgasm came, holding her captive. It was followed by another and yet another, and she collapsed exhausted by the sensations that had taken her to a place where she'd never been. The tears leaking from her eyes rolled into her hair spread out on the pillow.

Her limbs felt like lead and she couldn't move if her life depended upon it. The sensual fog cleared enough for her to ponder how could Nicholas give her so much pleasure without penetrating her? He lay beside her, pulling her moist body against his chest.

"Are you going to beat me again?" he whispered in her hair.

Peyton's mouth curved into the most beguiling smile. "Hell, yeah," she crooned, her mouth inches from his.

He also smiled. "It's obvious you like being punished."

"I like it a lot more than you like losing. Maybe you should've said the best of seven instead of five. That way you'd have better odds of winning."

"Yeah, right. I didn't realize I was being hustled by a card shark."

"It's math, Nicholas. Poker is based on probability. In five-card poker, there are fifty-one hundred forty-eight possible flushes of which forty are also straight flushes. If I had pencil and paper I would show you the equations."

He rose on an elbow, staring down at her. "You count cards?"

"Not really. But I had a friend in high school that did. Once he turned twenty-one he went to a casino and won nearly two hundred thousand before the croupier caught on to him. He was allowed to keep his winning but was banned from the premises."

"Did he ever do it again?"

Peyton smiled. "No. He needed the money for medical school and he didn't want to have to repay student loans once he graduated."

"That's quite a hustle."

"A hustle that could've gotten him beaten to within an inch of his life. I think the thing that saved him was that his father was in law enforcement. He dropped his father's name as soon as they put their hands on him."

Nicholas grunted. "Lucky kid."

"That's what I told him when he called me to tell me what had happened."

"How much do I owe you?"

"Nothing. I should've told you before that I don't believe in gambling for money."

Nicholas cupped her hip. "Now you tell me. I would've left the chips home."

"I couldn't resist jerking your chain."

"Please don't mention jerking, baby."

Heat rushed to Peyton's face as if she'd opened the door to a blast oven. "I'm sorry."

Nicholas kissed her forehead. "It's all right."

"I..." Whatever she was going to say died on her tongue when her cell phone rang.

"Let it go to voice mail," Nicholas said softly when she pulled out of his embrace.

"I can't. That's my mother's ringtone."

Pushing to sit, Nicholas watched the outline of Peyton's tiny body as she walked over the table beside the chaise.

Her unbound hair swayed with each step. Making love to her without taking his own pleasure was a new experience for him. Usually when he shared a woman's bed he shared her body.

But he knew when he first laid eyes on Peyton Blackstone that she was different. The way she'd looked at him made him slightly uncomfortable. It had been a mixture of curiosity and confusion. It was then that he'd noticed her slight squinting, wondering perhaps if she needed glasses. Reaching over, he turned on the bedside lamps when the candles began sputtering and going out.

Peyton answered the call. "Hi, Mama."

"Hi, baby. I've changed my mind."

Vertical lines settled between her eyes. "You changed your mind about what?"

"I decided to come down to see you."

Her face clouded in uneasiness. "What's wrong?"

"Nothing's wrong. Am I not entitled to change my mind?"

"Of course you are, but this is not like you. Tell me what's going on." Peyton felt her heart beating outside her chest when there came a prolonged pause. "Please, Mama."

"I'm leaving your father."

Peyton gripped the phone so tightly she was certain it would leave an impression on her palm. "Did he hit you?" she screamed.

"No. Al would never hit me."

"Don't you dare lie to me, Mama."

"I'm not lying. Please, baby. Don't make this harder on me than it is."

"Does Daddy know you're coming here?"

"Yes. I told him."

"What did he say?"

"There's nothing he can say. I'm a grown woman and I can come and go as I please. I need some alone time. I'll be fifty in a couple of weeks and I've never been anywhere by myself."

Smiling, Peyton closed her eyes. Her mother had to wait until she was fifty to come into her own. "Good for you. Come on down."

"I'll call the airlines tomorrow and make a reservation. As soon as I get a flight I'll let you know."

"Mama?"

"What is it?"

"If Daddy gets funky I want you to call and let me know."

Lena's laugh came through the earpiece. "I don't think that's going to happen because he's too shocked to say anything for at least a couple of days."

"What did you say to him?"

"I told him if he didn't stop trying to run my life I was going to divorce him."

Peyton knew the threat must have brought Alphonso Blackstone to his senses. Never had his wife ever raised her voice or talked back to him. "Call me when you finalize everything. If I don't answer my phone, then be certain to leave a voice-mail message."

"Thank you, Peyton."

"For what?"

"For being you. I love you."

She felt hot tears prick the backs of her eyelids. "I love you, too."

Peyton set the phone on the table, combed her hair with her fingers until it covered her naked breasts and walked back to the bed. She sank into Nicholas's embrace when he extended his arms.

"My mother's coming down." She didn't know how much of the conversation he'd overheard but she repeated what her mother had told her.

"If she needs time alone, then she can stay here and you can move in with me."

Peyton shook her head. "I can't do that."

"Why not?" Nicholas questioned. "You know this place is too small for two people. When your mother says she needs alone time that means without you hovering over her. She needs to get up when she wants, eat whenever she wants and go to bed whenever she wants."

"You're right."

Nicholas ruffled her hair. "I know I'm right. Now, when is she coming down?"

"I don't know yet." Peyton squinted. "I need to stock the refrigerator just in case she prefers cooking for herself. She likes to watch television, so that's also on the shopping list. And of course a radio. Can you think of anything else, Nicholas?"

Nicholas massaged her scalp with his fingertips. "You can stock the fridge from Cookie's pantry. We buy everything in bulk or restaurant size and that means you'll have to buy containers for the condiments, flour, sugar and dairy. We'll have to go into town for the electronics equipment and I'll have someone set up the cable connection."

"How long can she stay?"

He gave her a steely stare. "Why on earth would you ask me something like that?"

"I don't want to take advantage of your hospitality."

Nicholas shook his head in exasperation. "Did I not tell you that if there is anything you need all you have to do is ask? You asked me whether your mother could stay here and I said yes. Shouldn't that be enough or do you want me to repeat it in Spanish?"

Peyton refused to look at him. "Facetiousness isn't a very endearing quality."

"Neither is distrust."

This remark garnered a withering glare from her. "Erasing distrust isn't like pulling down a shade to shut something you don't want to see." Nicholas buried his face in her hair, pressing kisses to her scalp. He lay on his back, bringing her to lie atop him, her legs sandwiched between his. "I hope I'm not too heavy."

"I probably can bench press you with one arm."

Peyton counted the strong beats of his heart under her cheek. "I don't think so."

"Do you want me to prove it?"

"No, because I'm too relaxed to move."

Nicholas cradled the back of her head with one hand and her hip with the other. "You don't have to move."

"I'm falling asleep on you," she slurred.

He kissed her hair. "Go to sleep, sweetheart."

Minutes later, Nicholas closed his eyes and he, too, fell asleep.

Peyton glanced at the monitor in the airport, her gaze scanning arrivals. She smiled. Her mother's flight was on time. Minutes later her cell phone chimed the familiar ringtone. "Yes, Mama."

"We're on the ground. I just have to pick up my luggage at baggage claim."

"I'll meet you there."

The past three days had become a whirlwind of activity for Peyton. She'd moved her clothes from the cottage and into a closet in a bedroom at Nicholas's house. He'd accompanied her when they traveled to pick up miscellaneous housewares and to an electronic store for a flat screen, satellite radio and DVD player. Jackson filled containers with flour, sugar, mayo, mustard and an assortment of spices, loaded up cartons with eggs, butter, pasta, coffee and tea. Peyton knew her mother preferred canning her own fruit and vegetables, and she informed the cook not to put any canned goods in the carton.

She'd awakened the first day in her new home disoriented. Nicholas had left a little after midnight with a promise he would see her the following morning. It took most of the day to process what had happened between them. At first she'd believed it was another erotic dream but when she saw the impression on the pillow beside hers and could still detect the lingering scent of his cologne she knew it had been real. And when she saw the wineglasses in the sink, the chest with the cards and chips, the corked bottle of wine on the countertop she knew it had been very, very real. The most obvious sign of their lovemaking was the dark red splotches on her breasts and along her inner thighs. Each time she caught a glimpse of the love bites it excited her all over again. Although most of her clothes were stored at Nicholas's house, Peyton decided not to move in until after her mother's arrival.

It was apparent Nicholas had informed his housekeeper that she would be moving in when Eugenia greeted her at breakfast with the news she'd readied her bedroom for her. Peyton also wondered how the other employees would react when they discovered their vet had moved in with the boss, and when she'd voiced her concern to Nicholas he countered that it was none of their business.

Checking on the horses had become her sole focus. She'd continued her practice of rising early, going to the stable and checking each of the horses before they were washed, groomed, fed and turned out to pasture or exercised. Peyton checked their vaccination records, examined their teeth and hooves, and constantly checked their skin for parasites, cysts and warts.

Most of the men had become accustomed to seeing her in the stables or sitting on the rails watching the trainers exercise the horses. Jesse had returned from Florida and he and Nicholas spent hours together either in the office or touring the farm. Peyton knew Nicholas wanted Jesse to familiarize himself with the farm as quickly as possible because he wanted to attend a horse auction to buy several fillies.

She walked into the baggage claim area at the same time her mother neared the carousel. Smiling, she waved to get her attention. Lena Blackstone returned the wave. Peyton closed the distance between them, hugging and kissing her mother.

Lena looked the same as when she saw her earlier that summer. Her graying blond hair parted off-center was cut in layers, the back barely grazing the nape of her neck, the sides falling softly around her jawline. There were no new lines around her large expressive dark blue eyes, but her face appeared thinner, cheekbones more pronounced. Barely five-one, Lena was only five pounds heavier than she'd been in high school. Vain to a fault, Lena monitored everything she ate or drank, and Peyton suspected it was because her father was quick to comment on his wife's weight if she put on a few pounds.

"How was the flight?"

Lena gazed lovingly at her daughter. "It was good. It was chilly and raining when I left New York, but the weather is beautiful here. It's warm even at night." She angled her head. "I don't know what it is, but you look as if you're glowing. Are you in love?"

Peyton couldn't stop the blush suffusing her face.

"No." She wasn't in love with Nicholas, but her feelings for him were growing deeper with each passing day. They hadn't shared a bed again, and for that she was grateful because it gave her the chance to become objective about their relationship. Resting an arm over Lena's shoulder, she led her over to the carousel. "I wanted to tell you you're not going to stay at Sheldon's farm."

"Where are we staying?"

"I'm the resident vet at a neighboring horse farm."

"When did this happen?"

"Monday was my first day. You'll be staying in my cottage."

Lena frowned. "Where will you live?"

"I'll stay in the main house. It's only temporary. Which bag is yours?" Peyton asked when the bags started coming out.

"I have two hard cases with zebra stripes."

They quickly retrieved the bags, rolling them out of the terminal as Nicholas maneuvered up to the curbside. He popped the trunk, then got out of the Lincoln to pick up the luggage. Peyton waited until he'd stored the luggage to make the introductions.

"Mama, this is my boss, Nicholas Cole-Thomas. Nicholas, my mother, Lena Blackstone."

Nicholas extended his hand, smiling. "It's my pleasure, Mrs. Blackstone."

Lena took his hand, smiling. "The pleasure is mine, Mr. Thomas."

"It's Nicholas."

Lena's bright smile was still in place. "It's Lena. I'm so glad you hired my Peyton. She told me she wanted to make it on her own as a veterinarian."

Cupping Lena's elbow, Nicholas opened the passenger-side door. "I can assure you she's quite knowledgeable."

Peyton averted her head so her mother wouldn't see her roll her eyes. Lena had always been her personal cheering section. She opened the rear door, got into the sedan and settled back to listen to her mother charm the pants off Nicholas. She'd always suspected her father's need to dominate his wife was based on jealousy. Lena was attractive, friendly and an interesting conversationalist.

The smooth rolling motion of the car lulled her into a state of total relaxation as she stared out the side window. Lena hadn't been able to get a morning, direct flight and it was late when, after two layovers, her plane landed at Shenandoah Valley Regional Airport at ten-forty. Peyton was sound asleep before Nicholas reached Mt. Sidney.

Nicholas parked under the carport at Peyton's cottage. Both of his passengers had fallen asleep. He didn't need a key because he'd memorized the programmed key code. He unloaded the trunk and carried the luggage inside. By the time he'd returned to the car, both Lena and Peyton were awake.

"I'll wait out on the porch while you show your mother around."

Peyton, nodded, covering her mouth to conceal a yawn. "I won't take long."

Nicholas flopped down to the love seat, stretching out his legs. Aside from shopping he and Peyton hadn't spent much time together. He'd missed eating with her because he was spending so much time with Jesse. But all of that would end tonight. She would sleep under his roof for as long as Lena remained at the farm.

When Eugenia asked which bedroom she should prepare for Peyton he'd recommended the one at the opposite end of the hall from his. The woman gave him a long, penetrating stare, then walked away. The farm was like a small town wherein gossip was rampant, and he knew it was just a matter of time before everyone would know he and Peyton were living together—albeit temporarily.

The bell-like sound of the wind chimes punctuated the silence of the warm late-summer night. Lacing his fingers together at the back of his head, Nicholas felt a gentle peace sweep over him like a warm comforting blanket on a cold night. Schools were open and summer activities were winding down, while fall festivities were gearing up. Blackstone Farms would celebrate Sheldon's sixtieth birthday this coming weekend, and Labor Day was the following weekend. He looked forward to the fall for pumpkin picking, hayrides and bonfires.

Nicholas came to his feet when the door opened and Peyton joined him on the porch. He took her hand. "Are you ready to go home, sleepyhead?"

She nodded. "Yes. Mama loves the cottage."

He curved an arm around her waist. "I told you she would like it."

Peyton yawned again. "I think I'm going to sleep in a little late tomorrow morning."

Nicholas looked at his watch. "It's already tomorrow morning."

"Let's go before I fall on my face."

Bending slightly, he picked her up. "I can't have that happen."

Peyton rested her head on his shoulder when he carried her to the car. She didn't remember Nicholas carrying her up the staircase or when he placed her on the bed in her bedroom. She did remember him undressing her and then getting into bed beside her. Then her whole world went dark.

# Chapter 17

Peyton felt as if something was holding her down, not permitting her to move. When she opened her eyes she realized it was Nicholas's arm resting on her lower back. It was impossible for her to turn over. "Nicholas," she whispered. She called his name again, this time louder.

"Go back to sleep."

"I have to get up."

Nicholas opened one eye. "I thought we were sleeping in."

Muted light came through the lacy panels at the tall, narrow windows. It was raining. "We are but I still need to get up."

He raised his arm and she sat up. Peyton stared at a nightgown she hadn't worn in months. She smiled. Nicholas must have found it in her lingerie drawer. It was a lacy black garment, with narrow straps and a revealing décolletage, that ended midcalf. He'd left her a modicum of modesty when not removing her panties. She walked out of the bedroom feeling the heat of his gaze on her back and into the connecting bathroom.

Nicholas covered his face with his arm; it was the second time he'd slept with Peyton and hadn't had sex with her. He'd never taken advantage of any woman but Peyton had ceased to be any woman when she'd become his sister's maid of honor. It was then he recognized her inner strength as well as her outward beauty. When she'd challenged Celia with the threat of sleeping with Gavin it was enough to shake Celia from the paralyzing premarital jitters.

He'd counted every month she'd been away, hoping *and* praying she would return for the college holidays and recess. He'd delayed traveling to Florida for the weeklong family reunion between Christmas and New Year's Eve because he'd expected her to celebrate the holiday season with her relatives. His moods vacillated from euphoria when seeing the newest members of his family spanning four generations to a blue funk when many of the adolescents invited their romantic interests, reminding him of how sterile his life had become.

Nicholas was more than aware he'd changed following his near-death experience. The most profound transformation was his stance toward women. During his sessions with the psychiatrist he'd admitted he feared loving and losing. That to become emotionally involved with a woman would make him vulnerable and that was something he never wanted to experience again.

As much as he attempted to deny it Nicholas was emotionally involved and invested with Peyton. He'd admitted to liking her but if he were honest with her *and* himself he would've said he was in love with her. If he'd acted on his feelings instead of exhibiting indifference, Peyton would not only be the farm's resident vet but also his wife and possibly the mother of their children.

Lowering his arm, he sat up, supporting his back against the headboard. Nicholas didn't need his shrink to tell him if he didn't act on his feelings he would derail his life again. His mother had accused him of being in denial when he told her Arden needed time to adjust to the possibility that he would spend the rest of his life in a wheelchair. Nichola would probably tell him he was not only in denial but also a liar if he denied being in love with Peyton. Throwing off the sheet, he slipped out of bed and made his way down the hallway to his bedroom. It was time to stop lying to himself and begin planning his future.

Peyton returned to the bedroom, a large bath sheet wrapped around her body toga-style. Nicholas was gone. He probably had changed his mind about sleeping in. She walked over to the double dresser, opening the drawer with her underwear. She took out a bra and matching panties.

"It's a waste of time to put them on because I'm just going to take them off."

She spun around. Nicholas stood in the doorway, a towel wrapped around his slim hips. Peyton gave him a sexy moue. "What do you plan to do?"

Nicholas hadn't moved. "That all depends on what you want me to do."

"Let's go back to bed and talk."

He entered the bedroom, closing the door behind him. "What do you want to talk about?"

"The weather."

Nicholas laughed. Just when he thought he figured her out, Peyton figuratively pulled the rug out from under him. "What about the weather, princess?" he asked, dropping the towel on the floor. "What's the matter?" He saw the direction of her gaze then realized it was the first time she had seen him naked. He was semi-erect. Opening one hand, Nicholas showed her the condoms on his palm. "Only if you want to."

Peyton approached him and dropped her towel. "I want to."

He stared down at her under lowered lids. "You want what?"

Resting her palms on his smooth chest, she went on tiptoe, her mint-scented breath mingling with his. "I want you to make love to me."

Placing the condoms on the table beside the bed, Nicholas picked her up as if she were a child, placing her in the middle of the bed. He pressed a kiss to her forehead, smiling. "You are so incredibly perfect," he whispered reverently. "In and out of bed."

He took possession of her mouth in a slow, drugging kiss that elicited a rush of moisture between Peyton's thighs. She squeezed them together to stop the pulsing, but to no avail. Nicholas's rapacious mouth moved lower to her breasts and back to her mouth, and she was lost, lost in a maelstrom of desire which set her aflame with a surge of desire so intense she feared passing out.

The heat from his mouth swept from her own mouth to her core. Waves of passion shook her until she could not stop her legs from shaking. He suckled her breasts, worshipping them, and the moans she sought to suppress escaped her parted lips.

His tongue circled her nipples, leaving them hard, erect and throbbing. His teeth tightened on the turgid tips, and Peyton felt a violent spasm grip her womb.

Her fingers were entwined in the cotton sheets, tightening and ripping them from their fastenings at the same time she arched off the mattress.

"Nicholas!" His name exploded from her as he inched down her body, holding her hips to still their thrashing. He buried his face between her legs and this time there wasn't the barrier of silk to stop his sensual assault. His hot breath seared the tangled curls between her thighs and she went limp, unable to protest or think of anything except the pleasure her lover offered her.

She registered a series of breathless sighs, not realizing they were her own moans of physical satisfaction. Eyes closed, head thrown back, lips parted, back arched, Peyton reveled in the sensations that took her beyond herself. Then it began, rippling little tremors increasing and shaking her uncontrollably and becoming more volatile when it sought an escape route.

Nicholas heard Peyton's breath coming in long, surrendering moans, and he moved quickly. He opened the packet and rolled the length of latex down his erection. He moved up her trembling limbs and eased his sex into her body. He was met with a resistance he hadn't expected. Gritting his teeth, he feared spilling his passion inside the latex sheath without penetrating her. He drew back, and with a strong, sure thrust of his hips buried his hardness in the hot, moist, tight flesh pulsing around his own.

Peyton bit down on her lower lip, feeling as if she'd been impaled on a red-hot piece of steel when Nicholas penetrated her celibate flesh, but the burning subsided the moment he began moving in a slow, measured rhythm, quickly renewing her passion.

Her arms curved around his waist as rivulets of moisture bathed his back and dotted her hands. She could not think of anything or anyone except the hard body atop hers as their bodies found and set a rhythm where they were in perfect harmony with each other. Reaching down, Nicholas cupped her hips in his hands, lifting her higher and permitting deeper penetration; he quickened his movements.

Peyton assisted him, increasing her own pleasure as she wound her legs around his waist. Nicholas's heat, hardness and carnal sensuality had awakened the dormant sexuality of her body, and she responded to the seduction of his passion as hers rose higher and higher until it exploded in an awesome, vibrating liquid fire that scorched her mind, leaving her convulsing in ecstasy.

She hadn't returned from her own free-fall flight when she heard Nicholas's groan of satisfaction in her ear as he quickened his movements and then collapsed heavily on her sated body. There was only the sound of their labored breathing in the stillness of the bedroom as they lay motionless, while savoring the aftermath of a shared, sweet fulfillment.

Nicholas reversed their positions, bringing her with him until she lay sprawled over his body, her hair flowing over his face and shoulders. "Did I hurt you, baby?"

"No," she drawled, placing tiny kisses on his throat and shoulder. There had been a momentary discomfort but it was offset by the pleasure he had offered her.

"I hadn't expected you to be so small," Nicholas murmured through the curtain of heavy hair masking his face. "I—"

She stopped his words when she placed her fingertips over his lips. "I'm all right, Nicky."

His right hand moved over her bare hip, caressing the silken flesh. She had no idea how sensuous her voice sounded. He drew in a deep breath, luxuriating in the intoxicating fragrance of her bath gel mingling with the lingering scent of their lovemaking.

He could not believe the passion she had aroused in him; if possible Nicholas had wanted to make love to her all day long. Inhaling her scent, tasting her flesh, caressing her silken body, had tested the limits of his control. And he'd discovered something he'd denied for far too long.

He was in love with Peyton.

"When are you going to return Daddy's phone calls?" Peyton asked her mother.

Lena ran her thumb over the tips of the nails on her left hand. She spread out her fingers, studying her handiwork. She didn't know why she hadn't become a nail technician because she manicured her nails better than her regular manicurist. "You're in love with him, aren't you?"

Peyton gritted her teeth. Whenever Lena didn't want to answer a question she usually posed one of her own. "I don't know what you're talking about."

"Don't you?" Lena looked directly at her daughter. She thought she may have been mistaken when she saw her in the airport terminal, but now she knew for certain there was something more than an employer and employee connection between Peyton and Nicholas.

"If you answer my question, Mama, then I'll answer yours."

"No, I haven't returned his calls."

"Why not, Mama? Because he keeps blowing up my phone claiming he's worried sick about you."

"Did you say anything to him about me?"

"No. I keep telling him I'll give you the message."

Lena crossed her feet at the ankles. "I'm going to let him stew a little bit more before I call him." She exhaled an audible sigh. "I never knew what it meant to truly be my own woman until now. I went from my father's house to my husband's house, unlike most women my age who either went away to college or left home and set up their own apartments." She closed her eyes. "My fire-and-brimstone-preaching daddy never let me go to or have a sleepover with my girlfriends. His way of thinking was so archaic that he didn't even want me to go to college."

"Why not, Mama?"

"Because he knew I would leave and never come back." She opened her eyes, meeting Peyton's shocked gaze. "I never told you this, but I hated the way he treated my mother as if she were his property. But anytime I mentioned it to her she quoted the bible about how a woman is supposed to submit to her husband. My father wouldn't allow me to date, because he knew of the temptations of the flesh. Then I found out he'd picked out a husband for me. A widower with four little children. That's when I snuck out of the house one night and slept with the first man that smiled at me. I know how dangerous that is nowadays, but I wanted to punish my father because he'd bragged to my prospective husband that I was a virgin."

Peyton put her arm around Lena's shoulders. "But you didn't count on getting pregnant."

The older woman nodded. "When I told my father he flew into a rage, damning my soul to hell. Your father was our nearest neighbor and he'd overheard my father's tirade. He always liked me but I was too afraid to say anything to him. He approached my father with a request for my hand in marriage. Three weeks later I became Mrs. Alphonso Blackstone. I'd become my mother all over again when I thanked him every day for saving me."

"He didn't save you. He saved your father's reputation. How was he going to preach about adultery and fornicating when his own daughter was doing the same. You've been a wonderful wife and a selfless mother. What you've done is surrender your will to a man who uses it to boost his own ego. Please don't get me wrong, Mama. I love my father. What I don't like is how he thinks of you. You're not his chattel, but his partner and the mother of his child. You're a queen and he should treat you like one. You've honored your marriage vows because you've been with him in the good and the not so good times. I've never interfered with you and Daddy when you had your squabbles, but if you plan to leave him, then I'll help you any way I can."

Lena shifted slightly on the love seat. She stared at her daughter, seeing things Peyton refused to see. She had enough strength for the both of them. "I noticed you said leave and not divorce."

Peyton's mouth twisted in a wry smile. "Divorces rarely go smoothly, so that's something you really must be prepared for if you believe your marriage isn't worth saving."

"Like yours wasn't, Peyton?"

A pregnant silence followed the query. "Yes, Mama. Like mine. There was no way I could stay with Reginald when he has a weakness for hookers."

"You say has. Do you keep in touch with him?"

"No, but he keeps in touch with me." Peyton told Lena about Reginald's harassing phone calls and his recent contact with one of her high-school friends.

Lena's hands were trembling. "Why didn't you say something before?"

It was Peyton's turn to panic. "What are you talking about?"

"I thought it was my imagination, but now that you tell me he was talking to Jaime, I thought I saw him a couple of weeks ago when I went into town to do my banking. Peyton, you have to be careful."

"Jaime told him I lived at Blackstone Farms. She didn't know I'd moved here."

"You better let Sheldon know that your crazy-ass ex just might turn up unexpectedly. And what about this afternoon's surprise party?"

Peyton's smile did not reach her eyes. They were cold, a frosty gray. "Everyone must have an official invitation. No invite, no entry."

Lena rested a hand over her chest. "That's a relief. Now, about you and your boss. What's going on between the two of you?"

Peyton learned as a child never to lie to her mother because somehow she always knew when she wasn't telling the truth. "I'm in love with him."

"How long have you known him?"

"Too long."

Lena settled back against the cushioned love seat. "We have at least an hour before we have to leave, so tell me about this incredible man that has my baby all lit up like the Rockefeller Center Christmas tree."

Peyton told her everything about Nicholas from their initial introduction to their current living arrangement. When her mother asked if she was happy, her response was one word: *very.*

Lena's cell phone rang and she answered it. "Yes, darling. I didn't return your calls because I've been very busy. Of course I miss you. No, I don't know when I'm coming back. Why don't you take off a couple of days and come down and visit with your cousins. Really!" She winked at Peyton. "Are you certain you want to drive? It's true we never had a real honeymoon, so spending a week in Virginia Beach sounds divine. Yes, darling. Don't forget to call me before you leave. And Al, please stop and check into a hotel or motel if you get too tired. Yes, and I love you, too. Bye."

Peyton gave her mother an incredulous stare. "When did you become a femme fatale?"

Lena's eyes sparkled like Ceylon sapphires. "I was always one. It's just that it's been a while since I've allowed her to come out."

Peyton and Lena were still on the porch when Nicholas drove up with a horse trailer hitched to his car. His aunt had shipped the decanter and when Peyton opened the box it was even more spectacular than the photograph. Eugenia had offered to gift wrap it and when she returned the box with red wrapping paper and a black velvet bow she said she couldn't resist using the colors of Blackstone Farms' silks.

"Let's go, Mama. We have a milestone birthday to celebrate."

To say Sheldon was surprised to see the crowd that had gathered to celebrate his sixth decade of life was an understatement when he truly was at a loss for words. The committee had arranged for caterers to serve the sixty guests rather than have the farm chef and his assistants cook and miss out on the fun. They'd also arranged for a DJ to play nonstop music. Peyton and Kelly had gone over the playlist because they wanted music spanning genres. Buffet-style dining created a less formal atmosphere where guests and family members were able to mix and mingle under the large white tent.

Peyton had prepared herself for an assault when the triplets and Vivienne launched themselves at her, and soon she was falling to the ground under a tangle of arms and legs. She felt like Gulliver when the Lilliputians bound him, not permitting an escape.

"You're going to have to let Auntie Peyton up so she can give each of you a kiss." One by one they got up, stood in line like soldiers and she hugged and kissed each.

Nicholas stood motionless, stunned when he saw Peyton rolling on the grass in a white silk blouse and taupe linen slacks. Wisps had escaped what had been a wealth of neatly coiled hair on the nape of her neck. She kicked her legs like the children who smothered her face with kisses.

He was in love with her and he wanted her in his life and in his future.

Jeremy approached him, smiling. He offered his hand. "Thank you for coming."

Nicholas shook the proffered hand. "I wouldn't have missed this."

"Pop is truly beside himself. He can't believe you gave him an Arabian."

Crossing his arms over his chest, Nicholas angled his head. "I can't take credit for it. Peyton suggested I give him the colt."

Jeremy studied his cousin. "She's something else, isn't she?" He gave Nicholas a sidelong glance. "I guess you know that now."

"I'm in love with her."

Jeremy's hand slapped Nicholas's back. "Hey, man. Everyone knows that. What took you so long to finally admit it?"

"I don't know."

"So, when's the big day?"

Lowering his arms, Nicholas shook his head. "There's no big day. Not yet. I have to tell Peyton that I love her."

"And if she tells you that she loves you?"

"Then I'll ask her to marry me."

"Long or short engagement?" Jeremy asked.

Nicholas chuckled. "Very short. I suppose she'd want

to marry here, but then we'll just have to do it again in West Palm Beach on New Year's Eve. Of course all of the Blackstones are invited. I'll make arrangements to fly everyone down and back and also put you guys up in hotels."

"Sweet!"

"You guys do all right, but you haven't partied until you attend a Cole function."

Jeremy snorted. "Bragging, Lieutenant Commander Thomas?"

"You betcha, Sergeant Blackstone." Inky-black orbs met and held a stormy gray pair. "Would you do me the honor of standing in as my best man if she does say yes?"

Whistling softly, Jeremy rocked back on his heels. "Hell, yeah! Now you better ratchet up the mojo if you want to tie the knot by the end of the year."

Nicholas didn't want to interrupt Peyton's time with her little cousins so he headed for the tent to get some water. There was a nip of fall in the air during the morning hours but by afternoon the temperatures were in the upper 70s. The weather had cooperated for Sheldon's birthday and he hoped it would hold off for the walk he intended to take later on that night when he revealed to Peyton what lay in his heart.

# *Chapter 18*

"Do you know how long it took for me to track you down?"

Peyton's blood ran ice-cold in her veins when she recognized the voice at her ear. How was he able to evade security? How long had he been there? She'd gone into the smaller tent to get some lemonade and she had no way of knowing Reginald was waiting for her.

"How did you get in here?"

"Turn around and you'll see."

When she did turn it was to see her ex-husband in the same uniform worn by the waitstaff. If she was shocked that he'd located her, Peyton was more shocked by his appearance. His hair was sparse, face gaunt, pitted, eyes shrunken in his skull-like head, and the rich color in what had been a smooth milk-chocolate complexion was now ashy.

"What the hell happened to you?" He smiled and in

what had been a mouth filled with straight, white teeth more than half were missing. "You're a flippin' meth head."

"So," he sneered, "you recognize the ravages of the drug, Dr. Blackstone." He'd spat out her name. "You see what you turned me into?"

"Get away from me. Better yet. Get outta here."

Reginald grabbed her upper arm. "If I'm getting, then you're coming with me."

He held on to her left arm, which gave her full use of her right. Her fingers curled into a fist and she swung, connecting with his left eye. He groaned and before she could swing again she felt something sharp pressing into her ribs.

"What do you think you're going to do with that?" she shouted, garnering the attention of those in the tent. "Let me go!"

It was as if the world stood still. She saw Nicholas and Jeremy out of the corner of her eye. Then Billy Ritchie and her mother. The pressure against her ribs increased, and she knew Reginald intended to hurt or kill her.

"Jeremy! Get the kids inside." Peyton didn't want the children traumatized when they saw their auntie with a crazy man holding a sharp object against her side.

"What the hell is going on?" Nicholas shouted.

Tears were streaming down Lena's face. "That's Reginald. Her ex."

Reginald put his free arm around Peyton's throat. "No one come any closer or I'll gut her right here."

Peyton felt something warm trickle down her side, and she knew it was her blood. Reginald was mad and only half-alive. She knew he didn't care about his own life because he was killing himself with methamphetamine.

"Nicky, no! Please don't come any closer."

Nicholas didn't want to believe the scene playing out in front of his eyes. He had no intention of standing by and watching some lunatic hurt the woman he loved. A feral grin touched the corners of his mouth. "If you think I'm going to stand here and watch you hurt my wife, then you're real crazy. We can do this two ways: twelve jurors or six pallbearers. The choice is yours."

"She can't be your wife." Reginald's chin quivered as he tried not to break down and cry.

"Why can't she, Reggie?"

He bared his rotten teeth. "Don't call me that! I'm not a little boy!"

Peyton's gaze shifted from Sheldon, to Jeremy and back to Nicholas. "Let me go, Reginald, and everything will be all right."

"It's not going to be all right. It was all right before you left me. Now everything is mixed up. Crazy."

She moaned, stiffening in pain as the blade dug farther into her side. The pain had become excruciating, and she feared if he stabbed her again he was going to puncture her kidney. Peyton was also losing blood and when she glanced down the entire side of her blouse was red. First she was standing, then she felt the ground come up at her at the same time she heard a sharp crack. Someone broke her fall, and when she opened her eyes she looked into the eyes of the man she would love forever.

"I love you," she whispered as blackness descended, swallowing her whole.

Peyton opened her eyes to the sound of machines monitoring her vitals. Turning her head slowly, she saw the IV taped to the back of her hand, giving her sore body the nutrients it needed for survival. "Nicky." Why did her voice sound as if she were in a tunnel?

Nicholas moved off the chair where he'd spent the past two days waiting for Peyton to regain consciousness. He'd left the chair long enough to shower and change clothes in the small private hospital with a wing named for Sheldon's first wife who'd died from breast cancer. Hospital administrators had provided him with a suite where he could sleep, shower and take his meals but he preferred sleeping in the chair next to Peyton's bed. He wanted to be there when she woke up.

He smiled. "Welcome back."

She tried smiling but her lips were dry and cracked. "How long have I been away?"

"Two days." Leaning over, he kissed her lips.

Her eyelids fluttered. "That long?" Reaching up with her free hand, she combed her fingers through her hair. It was oily. "I need to wash my hair."

Nicholas sat down on the side of the bed. "That will have to wait until you're able to stand up on your own."

"What happened?"

He knew she wanted to know about her ex. "He didn't make it. He was shot by one of Sheldon's security team. The man was a former army sniper and he just grazed Reggie's scalp. It wasn't the bullet that killed him but his heart."

She tried to sit up, but Nicholas gently pushed her back to the pillows. "What about the children?"

"They didn't see anything. Thankfully they were in the other tent, and Tricia's grandfather got them far enough away so they didn't even hear the gunshot. Your father's here."

"Daddy?"

"I arranged for the ColeDiz jet to bring him down. We sat up all night talking about you."

She sighed. "What about me?"

"I told him how much I loved you and that I wanted his permission to ask for your hand in marriage."

Peyton had closed her eyes again. "Did he give it?"

"Of course he did. And as soon as you're out of that hospital bed I'm going to take you shopping so I can pick out a ring for you."

"We can't go shopping yet."

His brow furrowed. "Why not?"

She reached up and touched his bearded jaw. "You need a shave."

"I'll shave when I get you back home. Now, why can't we pick out rings?"

"You didn't ask me whether I wanted to marry you. You don't even know if I love you."

"I know you love me because you said it just before you passed out."

Peyton sighed again. "Who heard me?"

"Everyone close enough to hear you."

She hit the mattress with a fist. "That's not how I wanted you to know."

"It doesn't matter. If you hadn't told me I was ready to tell you. If you don't believe me then ask Jeremy."

"When did you and Jeremy become best buds?"

Nicholas wound several strands of her hair around his finger. "When I asked him to be my best man just before the crazy clown grabbed you."

"How much damage did he do?"

"He nicked your kidney, but the doctors were able to repair it. However, you did lose a couple of units of blood. Fortunately we're the same blood type so I was able to give you one unit and your mother the other."

Peyton sat up again. "Where's Mama?"

"She's sleeping. The first day she was here 24/7, so

when your dad came he took her back to the cottage. They'll be here later."

"When can I get out of here?"

"What's the rush?"

"I have to plan a wedding." Healthy color flooded her face for the first time in days. "I forgot to ask. When do you want to be married?"

"I'll leave that up to you. Tell me when and where and I'll be there."

Peyton beckoned him closer. "We can have a church wedding on Blackstone Farms and then repeat our vows in West Palm on New Year's Eve. I want Tricia's daughters to be my flower girls, Ryan's youngest son as the ring bearer. Caroline will be my maid of honor and Celia, Kelly, Renee and Tricia my matrons of honor. It will be your responsibility to come up with three groomsmen, because you already know who's going to be your best man. The farm wedding will be a black-and-red color scheme and black and silver for New Year's Eve."

"Did you just think of all of this?"

"Hum-m-m."

"How about babies?" Nicholas teased. "Do they also fit into your grand scheme?"

"Of course. But I'd like to wait until the beginning of the year before we start trying for a baby."

"That'll work. How many babies do you want?" Nicholas placed feathery kisses across her forehead.

"As many as you'll give me."

"I'd like two girls and two boys."

"That's a nice even number." He sat up straight, reaching for his cell phone.

"Who are you calling?"

"My parents. They just got back from Europe. I want

to tell them they're going to get the second daughter they always wanted."

Peyton smiled as she watched the man she loved tap keys, then speak Spanish to someone she assumed was his father, then hand her the phone. "Hello...Dad."

"Hey, I like you already. Nicholas says you're a little under the weather."

"He's right, and I plan to blow this nightclub in another day or two."

"I told Nicholas that his mother and I are coming to see him. My wife is afraid of horses, but she's just going to have to endure the magnificent beasts if she wants to see her son married."

"I'll tell Nicky to keep the horses far enough away so she won't have to see them."

"Peyton?"

"Yes, Dad."

"Welcome to the family."

"Thank you."

She gave Nicholas his phone at the same time a nurse came in to check on her. She shooed him out of the room while she changed the dressing on Peyton's incision, injected a syringe with a painkiller into the IV, adjusted the sheet and blanket and left as quietly and efficiently as she'd come.

Peyton was drifting off to sleep when her father walked in with a bouquet of flowers. "Hi, Daddy."

Leaning down, he kissed her cheek. "Hey, baby girl. Welcome back."

When she smiled it came out lopsided. "Thank you. I'm getting married."

Alphonso Blackstone nodded. "Nicholas is a good man, and I know he'll be a better husband to you than

I've been to your mother. But I told her I'm working on it." His eyes flooded with tears. "I don't want to lose her."

Peyton patted his hand. "You won't if you can remember that she's your queen, which means you must respect her and treat her with tender care."

"How did you get so smart?"

"Upbringing. You and Mama raised me right."

"That's more than that crazy boy's parents did. They gave him everything except boundaries, and in the end he self-destructed."

"I don't want to talk about him." Peyton was slurring her words. The painkiller had kicked in. "Can you please tell Nick…Nicholas to go home and sleep. Let him…know I'll be here when…"

Her words trailed off as the saying about good things come to those who wait flooded her consciousness before she surrendered to the welcoming arms of Morpheus. A smile curved her mouth as she slept. Images of white wedding gowns, flowers, champagne toasts and wedding bands crowded her dreams. Nicholas had asked if she wanted a second chance at love and she did. She knew he would be the last man with whom she would exchange vows.

Eternal vows.

* * * * *